Hawk Mountain

Hawk Mountain

CONNER HABIB

doubleday

TRANSWORLD PUBLISHERS
Penguin Random House, One Embassy Gardens,
8 Viaduct Gardens, London SW11 7BW
www.penguin.co.uk

Transworld is part of the Penguin Random House group of companies
whose addresses can be found at global.penguinrandomhouse.com

First published in Great Britain in 2022 by Doubleday
an imprint of Transworld Publishers

A CIP catalogue record for this book
is available from the British Library.

ISBN
9781781620601

Printed and bound in Great Britain by Clays Ltd, Elcograf S.p.A.

The authorized representative in the EEA is Penguin Random House Ireland,
Morrison Chambers, 32 Nassau Street, Dublin D02 YH68.

Penguin Random House is committed to a sustainable future
for our business, our readers and our planet. This book is made
from Forest Stewardship Council® certified paper.

To Jeb.

To Greg. To Jason. To Chad. To Mike.

To Harry.

Prophecy

AFTER SANDOR CSOORI

the last winter will arrive
with the sound of bells

and wheels covering cobblestones
horses too will neigh and whinny

from their tar-black nostrils
eternity will pour its lullaby

men and women will declaim
of their innocence

and sink into the shadows
children will take to the streets

fire will arrive
light the lakes and water

no god will condemn
no god will forgive

but people will burn
all day and all night

and there will be
no resurrection

—PAUL PERRY

The road I took
Kept turning back
Finding darker ways to go.

—JOHN MORIARTY, FROM *TURTLE WAS GONE A LONG TIME*, VOL. 1, *CROSSING THE KEDRON*

PART ONE

ONE

Before Todd sees Jack for the first time, his eyes are closed. He's in class.

Around him are the sounds of other people who don't want to be there: students, the teachers in other rooms, cafeteria workers, custodians in the halls. They're all held together by this school at the top of a hill in Lanchester, New Hampshire, where nothing happens. Outside, the world is living out its rhythms; wrens dart past the window, and a cloud dissolves in front of the sun.

Todd is seventeen. It's the start of senior year. Just nine months between now and graduation, but still, it feels there's no end in sight.

He opens his eyes and Mrs. Call is at the front of the room with another boy.

Everything is about to start.

The boy is blond with a swipe of freckles across the middle of his face, which Todd can see even though the boy is looking at the floor. He's wearing the uniform they all wear: a white shirt with a red tie. The boys wear dark blue pants and the girls wear blue skirts; they don't like it. He's holding two pieces of paper. Mrs. Call has her hand on his back.

"Jack Gates is our second Community Hope Scholarship Student," she says, though no one knows what that means or who the other Community Hope Scholarship Student might be. "He wrote an essay on wild-life in Maine, and we're going to read it later this week."

The boy looks up: green eyes, Todd sees. Like cracked sea glass.

"*Jack. Gates,*" Mrs. Call says again. "Not an easy name to forget. If you say it, you'll remember it." She gestures to the class and they say his name in unison, except for Todd, who is caught off guard by these two syllables. *Jack. Gates.*

"Jack, where are you from?" she asks him.

"Me and my dad moved here from Alhashee, Maine," Jack says in a Maine accent, thick like a slur, looking up at her. Jack isn't short, but she is taller than him.

"*My Dad and I,*" she corrects him, but Jack just stands there. He doesn't know that he's supposed to parrot her, so there's a moment of nonsense, of quiet that isn't supposed to be quiet.

"*My Dad and I,* Jack," Mrs. Call says again, and some of the students shift in their seats, since the repetition of a moment is unbearable, because their lives are full of repetitions.

"Oh," Jack says. And at that moment Todd giggles a little and looks over at Hannah Grace, who has black hair, and black lipstick on her polite smile. Then Todd hears Jack repeat after Mrs. Call, finally, "*My Dad and I.*"

Todd turns back to the front of the room, and Jack is looking right at him. Into him, with his sea-glass eyes. He sees that Jack has spotted him laughing. *But no, no, he's misread,* Todd thinks, *I wasn't laughing at him, just the moment.*

But Jack's face is taut. It's trembling with anger.

ONE

The beach had gone still, except for the waves. Todd was on a towel, his son, Anthony, at the edge of the miles and miles of ocean, and the sound of water pulling away, like a dream ending.

There was nobody else. The few other beachgoers were hundreds of feet from him as the afternoon ended. Their voices and stereos were covered up by the wash of the surf. Anthony was six, wading up to his knees in the water, which must have been cold, too cold to swim in. Todd was thirty-three, the season was almost over, the whirring of the cicadas was dead, and the gulls were still circling.

Not much had happened for almost four years, after an uneventful divorce from Livia, who had let go of their marriage and custody the way an enemy might let go of your hand if you were drowning. At the end, Livia said she'd never really wanted either of them. The last time he checked, she was in Rome. But that was more than a year ago. Anthony was too young to know much about her, except that his mom had gone away somewhere, and Todd had hoped that would be that. Four months ago, Todd had gotten his job in New Granard, bought a house, and now there was just over a week before Anthony started school.

Todd rubbed sand on the bottoms of his feet to scrub away the dead skin. The beach was pocked with bits of wrappers and cigarette butts and every once in a while a can. Why couldn't people keep after themselves? Down the coast, away from Todd and everyone else, there was a little flesh-colored knuckle of movement; someone walking up the shore.

Todd had spotted Anthony's first-grade teacher down the beach on the way here. She, Ms. Paige, would be his first teacher ever, since Todd had kept Anthony out of kindergarten. She was by herself, which seemed unlikely. He'd thought about asking her on a date. He hadn't been on a date with anyone since Livia and hadn't really had a desire. The whole district would have a meeting soon, he could talk to her then. Maybe it was time to ask someone out and see how it went. That was what he was supposed to do, wasn't it? Fall in love, or act like it?

"Fall in love," he whispered, but was unconvinced.

He loved his son. He loved being alone.

A colony of gulls split open from the beach into the air as the stranger walked closer. Maybe he—Todd could see the stranger's bare chest now—was on his way to see Ms. Paige and she wasn't single after all. Well, if she wasn't, maybe there would be a conflict, or he'd have to convince Ms. Paige to be with him. That was something that could happen, wasn't it? Maybe it would be exciting to feel what that was like. He'd forgotten what it was like to date anyone, but here was a vague idea: You ask someone to go out with you. But when? Do you have to talk first for a bit, or do you just come right out with it? Then you sit there at dinner or wherever, which would mean he'd need a babysitter for Anthony, something he hadn't found since moving here. Then, if it goes well, you're supposed to have sex, something that Todd and Livia had barely done in the nearly two years they were together, and which he hadn't done since.

He closed his eyes and thought of the books he'd teach this semester, when he was allowed to actually teach between standardized testing. *Lord of the Flies*, which they had to read over the summer. *The Catcher in the Rye, A Separate Peace.* Books about white kids that he read growing up. He liked them, but needed to add something else. Maybe not *A Separate Peace* this year, but then what? Other English teachers loved *The House on Mango Street.* Maybe that. Maybe *The Woman Warrior.* He taught a story by ZZ Packer at his last school, and got an angry letter from a parent about the swearing. The administration told him not to introduce contemporary works because their tone was too close to the students' lives. Maybe he'd have the kids read *Crime and Punishment* or *Moby-Dick.* Those older books weren't in most curriculums now, but he'd read them in high school and loved them for their struggle and sweat and tension.

He opened his eyes. Squinting through his sun-blindness, then shielding his eyes with a saluting hand on his brow, he saw that the man walking along the water was standing, now, by Anthony.

Todd felt a lurch in his stomach. He didn't want to cry out yet—didn't want to display panic and make Anthony afraid of everyone who approached—but that was the way Todd felt when he saw this figure, tan, golden-haired, tall, talking to his son. Menace. He watched and tried to slow his heart. *Go out to him*, but he didn't. It wasn't like the man would just carry him away, not like he would—what?—drown his son? Hold him under for the pleasure of it? He had to remind himself that those things didn't happen. Mostly they didn't happen.

The man looked over his shoulder up toward Todd. He looked for a long time, as if trying to settle something. Then he started walking up the sand. The sun was behind him. The light was like a crown, so bright that it obscured his visage.

Closer. Todd sat up.

Closer.

Anthony was standing in the distance, now, looking at them both.

Closer.

Closer. Until here he was, standing above Todd, and it was only in the absence of the sun, when the stranger's head had blocked it out completely and forced Todd into shadow, that Todd could see who it was.

He was different, of course, fifteen years later, but unmistakable. His body had been pulled taller with time and into light muscles. The same swipe of freckles on his face was darkened by the summer, and his hair had leaned away from blond toward light brown. His chest was smooth, and his legs were sparsely covered with a rush of golden hairs. His eyes were still that same color green. Clear but opaque, like cracked sea glass.

Jack opened his mouth to say something but stopped. The waves rolled in once more, and then he laughed.

"No fucking *way*, I *knew* it!" he said. His voice was delighted.

"I . . ." Todd couldn't speak.

Jack sat down on the sand next to his towel. His bare feet were covered in coagulated sand that followed him up from the shoreline. "Don't pretend you don't know," he said. He was smiling in a happy, challenging way. There was the gap between his two front teeth.

They said his name at the same time.

"Jack?" Todd said in a vulnerable tone.

"*Jack!*" Jack exclaimed.

Then he leaned and knelt into Todd, hugging him. Their bare chests were touching, and Todd wondered if Jack could feel his heart racing. Or maybe that was Jack's heart, or maybe it was both of them, filling in each other's beats. Maybe it was both of them at once.

"I saw that kid—that's your *son*, isn't it? I guess I was all wrong about you," Jack began, laughing.

"Yes, that's . . . Wrong? About me?"

"A kid! I saw that kid and I knew—"

"Anthony . . ."

"*He looks just like Todd Nasca*, is the first thing I thought. Like a mini–Todd Nasca, and then I saw you . . . Hey, are you married too? Do you live here?"

Everything had been so quiet a moment before, and now the ocean, it seemed, had caught up with him. Memory was alive in him again, and he felt the impulse to leave, to get in the car, to drive, to not come back to New Granard. To go get Anthony first. Of course, of course, to get his son. Then to flee. He would answer Jack's questions one by one, he guessed. One at a time. But Jack was hugging him again, and Todd could feel the light and warmth in his skin.

"It's so weird when you see someone out of place, you know?" Jack said. "Like you could see your worst enemy where you live and hate them, but if you saw them, say, in Florida, you'd want to go up and say hi!"

Are we enemies, then? Todd thought. *Still?*

"Sorry, I'm talking too much," Jack said. "Okay, so, do you live here?"

Todd took a breath.

"We do."

"You and . . ."

"Anthony!" Todd yelled at the water, and Anthony, obedient, started to make his way back up to them slowly, swinging his arms dramatically along the way.

"Are you married?"

"No, and . . ." Todd added hurriedly, "can you not talk about that when he gets up here? He doesn't really know his mother."

"Accident?" Jack asked.

"No, we wanted . . . Well. I wanted . . ." But then Anthony was there, and he stood behind his father like a fawn behind a doe.

"Jack, this is Anthony," Todd said.

"Pleased to meet you," Jack said. "Again." He put his hand out, but Anthony didn't take it.

"Are you my dad's friend?" Anthony asked.

For a moment, there was no answer.

TWO

He's trying not to think about it, but then he'll close his eyes and see it: Jack Gates's face, trembling.

Todd's at his new locker, at the end of the day, turning the dial back and forth, but it won't catch.

"I'm hopeless," he says to Hannah Grace, who is waiting for him to get gum for her.

"Everything is hopeless," she says. She loves gloomy pronouncements. Once she showed Todd how she'd drawn a skull on the inside of her uniform skirt with black Magic Marker. She said it was because we should all remind ourselves that death was always with us. Then she asked him not to tell anyone she'd done that.

"I can never open them the first day either," she says.

"You'll get it next year," Todd says.

"We're seniors," Hannah responds.

"You're right," he says, "we are fucking seniors." The locker opens. Todd has friends, a few good friends, at this school. So strange that he's known almost everyone in his class, all 150 of them, most of his life now. They all went through it together. They were kids, and they were friends, then some became strangers to each other, some moved away, some moved in, some were enemies, some became friends again. Senior year is the feeling of an extended family rushing to an end; they will never all be together like this again. Everyone is more relaxed. Friendlier. But he still slams his locker.

Everyone slams their lockers.

He hands Hannah a cube of gum, and then she smells like fake strawberry. Down the hall, which is filled with people, she holds his hand a little; they haven't *done* anything. Last year he had a girlfriend from a different school, and after she left him for another boy, she felt bad and sent him a letter apologizing and saying she wanted him back. He called her and read it to her on the phone in a mocking tone and made her cry. It was the meanest thing he'd ever done, but some of his friends, Justin Geiger and some of the other boys, thought it was funny. He's nice to everyone else, though. He's nice to Hannah. So they're holding hands, even though no one is really supposed to hold hands in the hallways. But it doesn't feel like a violation of that rule, because Todd, and maybe Hannah too, can sense that nothing will ever arise from this small gesture.

They pass Jack Gates. He closes his locker and looks at both of them. Todd tries not to look, but Hannah stares at Jack over her shoulder, and her hand and Todd's let go of each other. It's just for a second, but it's like slow motion: the space between their unclasped hands, the space between her face and Jack's, it all lingers. Then she squeezes Todd's hand again, and time goes back to normal, and she starts talking about class.

"Hey, do you know anything about that guy?" Todd asks.

"Just what you know," she says. Then adds, with a laugh, "Are you jealous?"

"No, I just. He . . . I feel like I know him."

"Oh," she says. "So should *I* be jealous?"

"You should go get your stuff," he says. "I'll meet you outside." And Hannah goes to her locker, one floor up, and Todd goes to the back doors of the school where already the kids are doing what they do every year: they loosen their ties and spit on the blacktop, they make jokes and light cigarettes as they amble away; they huddle in groups, finding each other against each other. It's the second week of September, and the air has gone cold, but the girls' legs are still bare, and the boys are allowed to wear shorts for as long as they want, as long as they're the uniform shorts. For the seniors, it's the first day of the last year. An end to everything they've known; it's a mini-apocalypse, and most of them are ready for it.

Todd is passing through the doorway of the school out into the world, when he sees Justin and heads over to him. Then he feels a little jolt under his left foot. He stumbles forward and turns around.

"What the fuck?" he says, and then sees Jack behind him.

"You think my voice is funny? You can't even walk," Jack says. Todd backs up into the parking lot.

"No, I wasn't laughing at your—"

"You know where I grew up?" Jack says, cutting him off, and takes a step closer. And in this step, it dawns on the other kids that something is about to happen. Gradually, Todd and Jack become the center of gravity. Justin backs up, everyone crowds in and somehow makes room at once, a space is created.

"We don't let people come into the country," Jack says. "We hold down the border. You think my voice is funny?"

Todd is angry but afraid. Then he sees Justin lingering and Hannah standing nearby. "Oh sure," he says, and laughs, "you *hold down the border.*"

And now Jack is even closer.

"With guns," Jack says. "And knives. And bear traps we set to snare people's legs."

When Todd looks over for Hannah again, she's gone.

"I wasn't . . . I wasn't laughing at you. I just . . ."

"And when we find some *faggot* stuck in one of those," Jack continues, and the word *faggot* makes Todd feel like the blood is running the wrong way in his veins, "we just beat the shit out of him there. While he's standing there, snared. Till he falls down. And then we come back the next day, after a long night, when he was all alone in the dark and he's pissed his pants and shit himself and he's had some time to think, *Why did I try to sneak into the country?* And then? We do it all over again."

There's a pause. There's going to be a fight. Someone is going to get pushed. Todd is going to get pushed. And then maybe he'll push back and then Jack will swing. Todd has never gotten in a fight before, but he knows his friends won't help him, that's not the way of these things. But then a teacher, Mr. Appel, comes out. He's the Cultures teacher and wrestling coach. He reaches into the scene and pulls Jack by the arm. "Get inside," he shouts. Instantly everyone goes about their business, like a hex has been broken. Todd doesn't even think about turning away, he knows he's supposed to go to the principal's office too.

He follows Mr. Appel and Jack and waits as Mr. Appel knocks on the principal's door. He tells them to sit down and then beckons the principal out of his office to tell him what he saw, which was not much.

While Mr. Appel and the principal are in the other room, Todd and Jack sit next to each other in metal chairs with cushioned seats. Their knees are touching. Jack is looking ahead, and Todd whispers, "What are we going to say?" But Jack only stares forward.

Todd has only been to the principal's office once before in high school, for taking his necktie off in class. It was the day of a civics test he hadn't studied for, and after the teacher put the sheets of paper on his desk, he felt his throat constricting. He shifted in his seat and tried to calm himself down like his father told him: *Breathe deeply. It's difficult to feel anxious if you're breathing slowly and deeply.* But he didn't think he could.

The tie felt like a garrote. He took it off in a panicked, noisy way. The sudden gesture broke the focus in the room. Kids looked up from their tests, they looked at each other, they looked at each other's answers. In exasperation, the teacher sent him to the office to be punished. Since then, he had a fear of being caught, even when he'd done nothing wrong.

Like today. First when Jack saw him laughing. Then by Mr. Appel, by everyone in the parking lot.

"I'll cover for you," Todd says. So when the principal comes in and interrogates them, Todd says it's nothing, they were only joking. And Jack nods his head.

"Hannah just worries about me," Todd says.

"Is she your girlfriend?" the principal asks.

Todd's face stumbles around an expression. "I . . . don't know?"

Jack looks up at the ceiling. The principal laughs. He's relieved that this is going the way it's going. "You've got to get her under *control*, Todd," he says. "So, okay, you're sure?"

The two of them nod.

"Well, good to know that our second scholarship kid isn't a trouble-maker on his first day."

Jack looks down at their knees, which are still touching. Then he stands up before anyone else. The principal stands and shakes Jack's hand like it's the end of a business meeting. Todd stands and then moves to the hallway, which is empty now, hollowed out. It feels like, with the halls empty this way, the students are all in classrooms. But they're not. The lights are off, the only illumination is sunlight, coming through short windows near the ceiling. Jack is gone already, Todd is alone, everything is quiet, and Hannah isn't waiting for him when he leaves.

TWO

In a parking lot, two teenage boys, short and tall, chased each other around a car. A girl sat on the hood, smoking a black cigarette. The short boy was fast, but the tall boy's legs were longer, so there was no hope of catching him. Around and around, while she blew what must be clove-flavored smoke out of her lungs. The boys looked angry, but they were only playing. And when the tall one finally gave it a rest, the short one smacked his ass, and then the chasing began again.

Todd looked out the Pizza Palace window at them, sitting in the booth with Anthony on his side, and Jack across from him.

Jack filled his hard plastic cup with beer from the plastic pitcher, and Anthony watched, mesmerized, as Jack took a straw from the straw holder, tore a piece off the wrapper, and then blew the entire wrapper off, right at him.

Anthony laughed and leaned over the table to get a straw of his own.

"I was thinking the army," Jack said, "but fuck, I'm glad I dodged that. No serving my country. No . . . well, not much of anything now."

Todd looked back over. "Weren't you going to be a writer? Wasn't that how you—"

"You *remember* that?" Jack asked. "No. I mean, I guess I thought I would be. For a minute."

"So where's your wife?" Todd asked, eyeing Jack's ring.

The waiter came over and put a full pitcher of beer on the table, not taking anything away but instead shoving the empty pitcher and the pizza stand to the back of the table.

"I thought I'd be all sorts of things when I was a kid," Jack said. "At some point, you figure out what you are and what you want. Or . . . what you don't want, at least."

"Jack, where's your wife, though?"

"You know how it goes," Jack said. "What about yours?"

Todd gestured to Anthony with his eyes and shook his head tersely, *Not around him.*

Jack reached for his hoodie and searched through the pocket. He'd laid it across his backpack, which was the only thing he'd had with him.

He held up his phone, which had thirty missed calls on it. All from a caller named Linda.

"Ten times a day," Jack said. "She doesn't know where I am."

"What happened?" Todd asked.

Then Anthony, frustrated with his straw, asked for help. "Daddy, can you do this?"

"I'll do it," Jack said, and showed Anthony how.

Todd looked back outside. The headlights of the car the kids were leaning on blinked, and a man with glasses walked toward them, waving them away. The girl hopped off, the man got in the car, gesturing angrily. As he drove away, one of the boys grabbed his crotch at him and the other held up his middle finger. They were shouting, "Fuck you," Todd could tell, but it was muffled, so he could only see the words. The girl looked at the boys, then grabbed one of her tits at the car in solidarity, and the boys cracked up.

A straw wrapper hit Todd's face. He flinched, and Anthony was laughing his head off.

"Now you shoot me!" Anthony said.

"Hold on," Todd said. Then, to Jack, "Don't you think you should let her know where you are?"

Jack tore the end of another straw off and handed it to Todd. "Well, go ahead, shoot him," Jack said, and drank the rest of his beer.

"Jack," Todd said. "Did something . . . happen? Did you do something?"

"*Do* something? I left," he said. "That was the best thing I ever did."

Todd thought about his last days with Livia, just after Anthony was born. "You're going one way," she'd said to him, "and I'm going another. And we just happened to meet here for a while." He didn't hate her anymore, but, for a time, he had. People could hate and leave and forget each other for lots of reasons or for no reason at all.

"You know what, Todd?" Jack said. "Fuck her. Let her think I'm dead." His hands went under the table.

"Sorry," Todd said quickly, "there's a six-year-old here."

"It's okay, Daddy, sometimes grown-ups use those words," Anthony said. Jack laughed and Todd smiled in spite of himself. He'd said that exact phrase to Anthony before.

"Anyway," Todd said, "you seem like you're past your limit."

"Drunk on Pizza Palace beer," Jack said. "Like the King of Pizza Palace." He leaned his head against the window.

Then there was a *bang bang bang* sound. Todd jumped, and Jack sat up and looked lazily over. One of the kids outside had smacked his hand on the window, and now the three of them were laughing, running toward the edge of the parking lot.

"Just kids," Jack said, and laughed.

Todd froze. The sun was almost tucked out of sight.

"You okay?" Jack asked finally. He must have seen Todd flinch.

"Yes, yes," Todd said, and shook his head. He closed his eyes, he lifted his eyebrows.

"Daddy got scared."

Jack stood up and left the booth without another word. Todd figured he'd gone to the bathroom. A minute passed, and then Jack appeared in the window himself, outside, walking toward the three kids, who were all smoking. He was taller than all of them.

"What the fuck?" Todd mumbled under his breath.

One of the boys leaned toward Jack, but Jack didn't move. The girl tugged on the other boy's arm, pulling to say, *Come on, let's go.* Finally the boy challenging Jack slinked back, and they all walked away slowly.

Jack reemerged, drunk and laughing.

"What did you say?" Todd asked.

"I told them they scared my friend—"

"I wasn't scared, though, I was just—"

"I said Anthony. They scared Anthony." At this, Anthony looked up. "And I said is that what they're into? Scaring little kids?"

"You didn't have to," Todd said. "Anthony is fine now."

"I wasn't scared, though," Anthony said honestly.

"And then the one kid said, 'What are you going to do about it?' like he was going to fight me," Jack said. He laughed. "So I said, 'I'll break your neck,' and I just looked right at him, and that . . . that didn't go well. For him, I mean."

"You said what?" Todd noticed the ring wasn't on Jack's finger anymore.

Jack's face was slack. And then, "Kidding! I'm kidding. I told them I'd tell their parents. Todd, the look on your face, you must think I'm crazy! I didn't like that they scared you, that's all."

I wasn't scared, Todd thought. But he was.

THREE

Todd sits in English with Hannah next to him. Jack sits three rows ahead. Now he's a source of anxiety. Todd tries to get to English early, so he doesn't have to walk past Jack's face. Mrs. Call is talking about *Grapes of Wrath*, which Todd tried to read over the summer and found boring. Why are they always reading novels about history? Even the Agatha Christie novels, which Mrs. Call is obsessed with, are old-fashioned. There are no current novels. No horror or science fiction. Everything has to be *about* something, as if the novels don't matter unless they teach a lesson. There were parts of *Walden* that seemed just to be about themselves. They'd read that last year. Among the political stuff and the money and accounting bits, which Mr. Fairing told them they could skip, there were passages describing the world. Todd liked those. He thought, as he read them, that maybe the world didn't always have a point beyond just loving some things. That was what mattered, if only people could see it: what you loved and what you hated. He tried to focus on this. If he focused on the normal problems, the everyday, then the thing with Jack would disappear.

A folded-up piece of paper lands on his desk. He holds it underneath his desk and opens it as quietly as he can, trying to look forward the whole time. Eyes forward, all day, every day at school, eyes forward; if your eyes aren't forward, if they're down or up or closed or to the side, you must be doing something wrong. There is only one way your eyes should be. Eyes forward, hands moving under the desk, quietly unfolding. He looks down as quickly as he can.

It reads: *I'm sorry. Please forgive me.*

He looks over at Hannah, whom he's ignored since she got Mr. Appel to break up the fight. There's a flicker of understanding that she didn't do anything wrong, but it's overwhelmed by the feeling that she did.

She betrayed him, and it didn't even help. It made things worse. The day after Jack came at Todd in the parking lot, Rick Barnes said to Todd that it was a good thing his girlfriend had saved him. And Justin asked when the real fight was going to happen, and if it did, would he ask Hannah to fight for him. Justin and Rick had been joking, but he could see they were getting carried away by the possibility of tension and violence. The almost-fight meant that something was *happening* in the school. Right at the beginning of the year. Could he blame them for being excited? He grew up with these boys, and he understands. An event means people have to take sides.

He tosses Hannah's note by her feet in rejection. Mrs. Call stops. Hannah's eyes widen. Mrs. Call had heard the paper hitting the floor. Teachers are as vigilant as cats. The slightest movement, the slightest sound, could get their attention.

She looks to the floor and strides back to the space between Todd and Hannah. She picks up the note. Then, back to the front of the class, she unfolds the paper and holds it up.

" 'I'm sorry. Please forgive me,' " she reads. The whole class laughs. She turns the note around so that everyone can see the purple ink and what must be a girl's handwriting.

"So, who would like to be forgiven in this class?" Mrs. Call asks. "Or from the back of the class, I should say."

The front three rows turn around to the back three.

Jack stares right at Hannah. He smiles, and Todd sees it. Hannah looks down. Is she blushing? Probably because of the note, Todd thinks.

"Well," Mrs. Call says. "Apology accepted. I forgive you."

The rest of the class slowly turns back, still giggling a little. But Jack keeps looking. His eyes go to Todd, and his smile fades. He looks at Todd with—what?—determination? Todd covered for Jack, he chose his side. Not with Hannah, who saved him, but with Jack, whom he saved.

When class ends, he walks up to Jack, who is ahead of him, and thinks about putting his hand on Jack's shoulder. Instead, he says, "Hey, Jack!"

Jack stops and Todd starts, "I just wanted to say—"

Jack crashes Todd up against the lockers. A combination lock jams into Todd's back. He's been pushed hard; he can feel the place where a bruise will form.

"I covered for you! I covered for you!" Todd shouts. He keeps his back to the locker, leaning into it, away from Jack. He sees some of the other students have stopped to look. Logan and Justin and Hannah and Rick Barnes.

"Yeah?" Jack says. "And who the fuck asked you to do that?"

"I'll tell—"

"What? That you lied? Sure, go ahead. 'I'm in love with Jack, so I lied to protect him.' You won't say anything."

"You should tell your *Mom*, Todd," Logan says, and the boys laugh. Hannah walks away. Todd regains his footing. *What's happening?* Todd thinks frantically. Things have turned too quickly. The pain runs fast up and down his back.

As Jack walks away, Todd can sense disappointment in the rest of the kids; they wanted to see more. They wanted someone to really get hurt.

Down the hall, Jack says something and laughs, and everyone with him laughs, and then they're around the corner.

Around a corner, but not gone. They're in the same building. Every day, they will be in the same building. Maybe down the next hallway. Maybe around the next corner.

THREE

Jack was looking at the statuette with the dark light hovering around it: Heracles wrestling the Nemean lion, small and heavy on the side table. Todd had taken Anthony up to bed and was now in the living room, tucking a sheet behind the couch cushions.

"What . . . the fuck," Jack said, fumbling through his words.

"It's a statuette," Todd said, and Jack laughed.

"Oh, is it? I *know* it's a statue, but why is there a statue of a naked guy and a lion?"

"Here," Todd said, and handed Jack a comforter cover. Todd's right hand bore two small scars from high school. Did Jack look at it as he pushed the comforter into the opening? "It's Heracles wrestling the Nemean lion," Todd said.

"Hercules?" Jack said.

"Heracles is the Greek, Hercules is the Roman name, after the Romans stole everything."

"But why do you *have* it—" Jack said, and then his phone buzzed and he absentmindedly dropped his edge of the comforter and cover to pull it from his pocket. "No, no, no," he said as he looked at it. He declined the call hurriedly.

"Why don't you turn it off?" Todd suggested, clicking the snaps of the cover into place as Jack started to open his belt and push one shoe off with the other.

"Here," Jack said, "I'll be Herc . . . *Heracles*, and you'll be the Nemean lion." He pulled his pants down to his ankles, but they got bunched up at his remaining shoe, still on his right foot. He sat on the couch and pulled his shirt off. In a moment of calm, he looked up at Todd.

"*You of all people, can you believe this?*" Jack said.

He stood and hugged Todd, his arms around him, his skin against Todd's shirt. He laid his head on Todd's shoulder, half asleep now. Todd patted him on the back, quickly, with one hand. "Jack," he said. "Jack, your shoe is still on."

Jack stumbled back a step, looked down, and slumped onto the couch. He pulled his shoe off. Then his pants. Todd folded his arms, and Jack pulled the comforter over his body and closed his eyes.

As Todd walked away, Jack called his name.

"Yes?"

"After all these years, you know?"

"Yes," Todd said. It was almost too much to be a coincidence, but what else could it be?

"It's *early*," Jack said, suddenly realizing. "What . . . what time is it?"

"It's early, but you're drunk," Todd said. "We'll get you on the road and on your way tomorrow. Just go to bed," he said.

"Your kid goes to bed too early," Jack said, and laughed a little. "Tight ship around here."

"He's six," Todd said.

"Aye aye, Captain," Jack said, and laughed.

"Okay, Jack."

"Todd," Jack said, and rolled over and opened his eyes.

"Yeah."

"After all these years, and I found you," Jack said.

"Were you . . . looking? For me?"

Jack had closed his eyes again and responded only with a sigh.

Todd walked through the kitchen. He picked up Anthony's favorite book, *Wolf Story*, from the kitchen table, then went up the stairs, but Anthony was already fast asleep, his body was cut in half by the blanket, his head turned to the left, his mouth open. He was dreaming. When Anthony was younger, he looked so still in his sleep that Todd would creep to the bed and put his hand to Anthony's mouth to feel for his breath. He was, obviously, always alive. Soon he'd start school, though, and his life would change.

The thought of Anthony going to school, *becoming* a *kid in school*, filled Todd with dread. It was unnatural. Livia had been almost wealthy and just handed money over to Todd in the divorce. No fuss, really; no conflict. But no child support after that either, that was the agreement. So Todd took a year off before he started teaching again. He spent every day with Anthony. It was a good year, and when he went back to work and hired a series of nannies, he still felt connected to Anthony. But what now? It wouldn't be him and Anthony and whomever he hired to help. It would be the first-grade teacher, the art teacher, the principal, the music teacher, and all the other kids. Kids who would, Todd knew from teaching them, be cruel and petty and stupid. They'd share their illnesses and have bad judgment and fight and hurt each other. He felt like he was pushing Anthony off a precipice. He considered sending him to a private school, but since he was a public school teacher, it seemed like a slap in the face to the district, at least this early in the game. Besides, when Anthony got to high school, Todd would be there in the school with him and could help him navigate his troubles.

Todd closed the door to Anthony's room and walked down the hall.

Todd sometimes put on music, light classical music, Brahms or Steve Reich, before he went to bed; it helped him sleep. Anthony slept deeply and never woke in the evening, but Todd wondered if Jack would be able to hear the music downstairs as a hum through the floor, if that would rouse him. He undressed and turned the music on, then turned it down, then turned it off entirely.

There was never real quiet till the winter came, though. Outside, the insects in the evening did what the birds did in the day. A katydid sounded off each moment of its life, a cricket gave a serrated hum. The first frost, the killing frost, would come, but not now, not for a little longer.

FOUR

"Jack," Mrs. Call says. "Are you ready?"

"N . . . now?" Jack says.

"When else?" Mrs. Call says. And a few people giggle, but not Todd.

Jack stands and goes to the front of the room, and Mrs. Call hands him a sheet of paper.

" 'In Alhashee—' " Jack begins, but Mrs. Call cuts him off.

"Hold on, hold on. I want everyone to close their eyes. Go ahead." The rest of them close their eyes. Todd puts his hand over his eyes too. "Okay, and I want you all to *imagine* what Jack is reading. To *envision* it. And, Jack? Make sure you read *slowly*, okay? This is your award-winning essay, show it respect." Todd imagines Jack nodding to this.

Then Jack's voice, calm. Calming.

" 'In Alhashee there's wind from the coast that never stops. It just keeps coming at you. It hits the houses and the cars and your hair. It knocks branches off the trees and when it rains it makes the rain fall hard against the roofs. Seabirds live in the wind. They get picked up by it like my mom . . .'"

He takes a breath.

"'. . . like my mom used to pick me up before sleep and carry me up the stairs. Higher and higher until they disappear, since they're white birds and the sky is white. My dog Badger is white, too, and he likes to run into the high grass, and I have to go find him. It's quiet, but I always know where he is. When you walk through the high grass, frogs jump away from your steps. No one knows me in the high grass.'"

Todd raises his head slowly and looks. Everyone else has their eyes closed now, even Mrs. Call. Everyone but him, and Jack, who is looking at his essay.

"'Like how no one will know me when I leave Alhashee and move to a new town. Dad decided on it for a job now that Mom's not around. We're migrating like the seabirds do when it gets cold. That's the time when they don't just disappear into the sky, they leave.'"

And here Jack pauses. Just for a minute. He looks and sees Todd's eyes are open, that Todd is holding the expression of someone who is moved, trying to wrestle with a new feeling. He looks into Todd's eyes.

Without looking down at his paper, he says the rest by heart.

"'Whatever tracks you leave in the mud or the sand, the wind smooths them over. Bit by bit. Soon, no one knows where you've been or even that you were alive at all. That's what Maine is like. It carries you so you can sleep.'"

There's a second when everyone opens their eyes again and no one knows what to do, and then that second is over and everybody starts clapping. The kids who would never clap at anything like this all clap. They recognize something in it. Mrs. Call claps and Jack looks at her, and Hannah Grace claps and looks at Jack, and Todd claps too, but looks away, down to the floor, so that no one will see his face.

FOUR

The predawn light was on the statuette now, making the first Labor glow, and the seagulls were crying out in the New England air; they always woke up first. The comforter was twisted and the sheets had come untucked. The pillow was on the floor and at the edge of the couch Jack's foot was uncovered, and his white briefs hung off his toes, pushed down in the night. Jack's skin was smooth and tan. His back, uncovered to halfway down his ass, was blemishless.

Todd stood looking at him. There was a Mendelssohn concerto playing. Todd had reaffirmed his right to play the music as loudly as he wanted. This was his house, after all, wasn't it?

"Hey, Jack," he said finally.

Jack rolled over and looked at the mess he'd made in his sleep.

"Fuck," Jack said. "Nightmares."

"What about?" Todd asked.

Jack looked up at his face and opened his eyes wide. "I don't remember anymore."

Todd knelt to pick up the pillow and handed it Jack. Then Jack leaned forward to pull his underwear off his foot and maneuvered the briefs onto himself under the blanket. Then he started to untangle the comforter and put it back over his body.

"Do you have fresh clothes?" Todd asked. "You only have that backpack with you. What were you expecting to do?"

"I know it's crazy, but I left my suitcase at the bus station parking lot."

"Why would you do that?"

Jack sat up and sounded surprised, even pleased with himself. "You know? I'm not sure? I just . . . Nothing from *that* life. I should've said yesterday, the fact that I packed a bunch of my stuff is one of the reasons Linda probably *doesn't* think I'm dead. So I got to the bus station and it all felt like, I can't do this. I can't bring this fucking *weight*. So I got into the parking lot, I pulled out some stuff and put it in my backpack, and I let it sit there. Maybe some homeless person found it."

"Or they thought it was a bomb," Todd said.

Jack laughed, and Todd smiled lightly.

"I'm fine with what I have," Jack said. "I'll figure out the rest."

Todd reached over to the nightstand and picked up Jack's cell and offered it to him.

"No fucking thank you." He sneered at it.

Then there was the sound of feet running down the stairs and into the room and Anthony was there, jumping onto the couch.

"You stayed here!" Anthony shouted.

"I did," Jack said, and gave him a hug.

"Want to give your dad a hug?" Todd said, and Anthony reached over. "Good morning!" Todd said.

"Good morning, Daddy," Anthony said, hugging him.

Todd stood, holding on to him. "What do you want for breakfast?"

"French toast!" Anthony declared.

"I don't think we have any eggs," Todd said. "Do you want . . . cereal?"

"There aren't eggs in French toast," Anthony said.

"Ha, well, yes, there are, you have to make a batter from eggs. So we have cereal and—"

"Do you want me to go get some?" Jack said.

"Yeah!" Anthony said.

"No, that's okay, we have plenty of food here," Todd said. The thought occurred to him that there might be some eggs in the fridge, actually. Hadn't he gotten some two days ago?

"No, no, let me do something for you," Jack said.

"My car is a stick shift," Todd protested.

"So is mine. Well, was mine."

"Daddy, yes yes yes yes," Anthony said, leaning all the way back, arms around Todd's neck, jolting and tugging with every yes.

"No," Todd said. "You're having cereal." He maneuvered Anthony away from him and onto the floor. "Go into the kitchen," he said, then walked over and got Jack's backpack and brought it closer to the couch. Jack stood and straightened his briefs while Todd looked away.

In the kitchen, Todd reached for the cereal and bowls and spoons, and Jack came in, with shorts on now. "Hey, I just want to say thank you," he said. "Seriously. For letting me in, for letting me stay here."

"Sure," Todd said casually. "Anthony, what kind of cereal do you want?"

"French-toast cereal," Anthony said. He was sullen at the table.

"You know, they used to make that," Jack said, and opened the fridge, looking through.

"Daddy, can we get that?"

"I don't think they make that anymore. We have Cheetah Puffs and Crispy Penguins."

"I hate those," Anthony said.

"You don't hate them, you picked them out!"

Todd was getting exasperated. But he was getting exasperated too quickly, he thought.

"Anthony," Jack said then. "I've got good new-oos." Then he turned around with a half carton of eggs in his hand. "These were right here on the second shelf, Todd. I think Daddy is still a little tired."

Todd set the bowls down on the counter. "Okay, okay," he said.

Jack knelt in front of Anthony and touched the tip of Anthony's nose with each word: "French. Toast. It. Is!" and Anthony squealed, laughing.

FIVE

Time could be a line that moves straight forward, leaving permanent scars. Or it could jump, from past to present to future, with a sweep of anxiety or regrets. Time could never settle, even in death. Todd is trying to figure all of this out. His bedroom is the usual: upstairs, down the hall from his parents', posters on the wall, a little bit of a mess. More books than the other kids in his school. Mystery novels and horror novels, comic books fanned out carelessly. He's on the bed reading *A Separate Peace*. He's in his underwear and a T-shirt, on his belly, with his legs bent and swaying behind him. The book feels boring because it's slow and ponderous, but it's also compelling: it moves downward into him as he reads. It stirs something in him he doesn't understand and will not ever understand.

Nothing endures. Not a tree. Not love. Not even death by violence.

It's a weird thing to see on the page, because isn't this the same book that tells Todd, *The world, through his unleashed emotions, imprinted itself upon him, and he carries the stamp of that passing moment forever?*

Which is it? Do moments last forever or do imprinted moments disappear? Maybe both? There's a knock at the front door.

Nothing happens, but Todd gets a bad feeling.

Then the doorbell rings, and rings again, and he hears his mom or dad go to it.

"Ta-odd!" his mom yells up the stairs. He walks to the bedroom door, realizes he doesn't have pants on, and replaces his underwear with gym shorts. He wonders why he didn't just pull the shorts over his underwear. And he realizes as he comes to the stairs that he brought the book with him. Sometimes he doesn't know who he is, can't track his own actions. They just happen. *How does that work?* he thinks, and then, on the first step down, he can see the bottom of the doorway. Three sets of legs. He descends slowly.

It's Jack and Justin Geiger and Logan Krevanchy, whom Todd barely knows. Jack is standing right in the middle of the doorway, the other two boys behind him and on each side. Todd's mom is back in the house now, somewhere in some other room, as if living a parallel life.

"What are you guys doing here?" Todd asks, noticing the smell of beer. He doesn't drink, almost not at all, but the other kids all started a couple years ago. It's something that he supposes he has complete control over, but that still makes him feel left out.

"Are you going to invite us in?" Jack says.

Todd looks at Logan and Justin. "Hi, Justin," he says, but Justin looks at Logan instead, and smiles. Todd doesn't see why they'd want to hurt him. He doesn't understand what's happening.

Todd says, "What's up?" again.

Jack holds on to either side of the doorframe and steps over the threshold with half his foot, leaning in. Todd takes a step back.

"See what I mean?" Jack looks over his shoulders at the other guys. "I don't want to bite your neck, Nasca. I don't want to suck your blood."

"Or suck anything," Logan says, and they laugh again.

"I saw how you were looking at me today," Jack says.

"So?" Todd responds.

"*Thhoo?*" Jacks says back in a mocking lisp.

"I'm not the one writing about *birds* and *wildlife* and *nature*," Todd lashes back. It's not fair that he has to pretend he hated the essay, or that kind of writing, or Jack's reading. It's not fair that he has to be a bully like Jack to defend himself. But the statement does something.

Justin and Logan let out a noise that is both shocked and impressed. Jack leans forward, angry, and knocks the book out of Todd's hand. It flies up and falls through time, landing on the floor with its cover up, an image of a boy standing by a tree.

"You gonna call your mom?" Justin says.

"Yeah, call her, I bet she'll invite us in. *All* the way in," Logan says.

"Maybe from the back door, though," Justin says.

When did Justin become like this? Todd wonders. It was like a tide had pulled Justin out and away. How did this happen so quickly? There's nothing for him to do but stand there. He tries to turn everything off inside himself, but his heart is pounding. Where are his parents, anyway?

"Listen," Jack says, and leans in again. "I just wanted to stop by to let you know that I'm going to beat the shit out of you after school tomorrow."

And then the three of them turn and walk off the porch back to the car, Jack spinning around once, walking backward and shouting, "Faggot!" Then they walk down the street and Logan is singing the word all the way back to the car, "Faaaaaaagahhhhht!" Justin is quiet, but he hurries away with the others.

There is no recourse. There is nowhere to go. There is no one to talk to. Todd closes the front door, and only then does his mother come in and ask who it was. Todd kneels down and picks up his book. It's just the new kid, he tells her. He moved here a few weeks ago.

FIVE

Todd and Livia had met at a fundraiser for the local bookstore in Mary-
mount, which was in danger of closing because the big bookstores had
moved nearby. The store was called Cavalier's, and though it had been
there since the 1960s, everyone was always mispronouncing the name.
An old man ran the place, perched at the counter among the new and
used books. The huddled stacks, the disorder, the warm glow of a lamp
on the counter, people felt, were how a bookstore *should* be. Not fluorescent lights and neat, open space. But the truth was, no one was shopping
there anymore. It was a place of interest, but not of commitment.

"It closed the next year," Todd told Jack in the kitchen. He washed
the dishes while Anthony played outside. "Not too long after, the two
corporate bookstores closed too. So that was the landscape then, in just
a few years. No more bookstores, I had a son, and Livia had left." It was
true that Anthony was an "accident," conceived before Todd and Livia
got married, one of the few times they'd had sex, but Todd wasn't about
to share that with Jack.

"That's the story? That's it?" Jack said, looking through the cupboards to figure out where to put the dishes. "Sorry, I should have probably washed the dishes, and you should've dried them, since I have no idea where you put stuff yet."

"Don't worry about it," Todd said, noticing but ignoring the *yet* at the end of Jack's sentence.

"Don't worry about what, the story or the dishes?" Jack asked, continuing to look through.

Todd thought about the first thing Livia had said to him, bold and unignorable. She'd approached him, beautiful, with a book in her hand. She'd said, "Oh, you don't have any idea how you look to other people, do you?" And Todd had fumbled around for a minute, his eyes landing on her book of Greek myths. "And neither does anyone else at first," she continued. "Someone could just glance past you at first but then, suddenly, you're just . . . there, and someone realizes they can't stop looking at you." Todd still remembered this as a compliment. Then, as if she hadn't said any of that, she moved on to talking about the store. Even when she smiled, she looked like she was up to something. She loved the bookstore, she told him, even if (and she whispered) she never really shopped there. He asked her about the book in her hand and she said she liked myths because they were cycles, they just happen again and again; you could keep reading the same story and never be totally satisfied or unsatisfied. Maybe that was a comfort to her, but Todd said, if they're cycles, how do you break free from them?

But he didn't relay any of this to Jack.

"You said she'd given you a bunch of money after the divorce, right?" Jack asked.

"So?"

"So, if she had a ton of money, why didn't she just save the bookstore?"

Todd had never thought about it before. "She's the sort of person that wants the credit without doing anything, I suppose," he said. "Saving the store would have been a long process. Listen, don't worry about the dishes. Just sit down."

Jack stopped trying and sat down at the table.

He looked out the backdoor window and saw Anthony in the backyard, playing with action figures. Anthony was making explosion noises and having the plastic people talk to each other.

"Action figures always seem sort of lonely. Playing with fake little people instead of real people."

"I play with him and his action figures sometimes," Todd said, putting the last plate away.

"Does he have friends here?" Jack asked.

"No one really knows us here yet."

"He seems like a great kid."

Todd didn't respond.

"It's not that I didn't want kids, really. If I gave that impression. I just didn't know who I would ever have them with."

Jack looked out the window. "I can't believe she would leave you. And him? Look at him." He smiled.

"So, what are you trying to say?"

Jack leaned back in his seat. "What's this door?" he asked.

"The backyard," Todd said, puzzled.

"No, I mean the one behind me." He gestured to the old-looking door with the slide lock on it.

"Oh, the basement," Todd said. "Just the laundry and a workbench. Nothing you'll need, anyway."

"A workbench for . . . your construction projects?" Jack smirked.

Todd dried the bowl he had mixed the batter in and put it on the top shelf in a cupboard. "So, tell me more about Linda."

"Here we go," Jack said. "There's nothing to tell."

"How did you meet? Why did you separate? Why aren't you contacting her?" Todd took a breath. Yes, he thought he'd push a little more. "I mean, if you're staying here, I'd like to—"

"Does that mean it's okay to stay another night?" Jack asked.

Todd was caught off guard. "Well, I was saying, you're in my house, so I want to know what's up."

"Fine. I met Linda when I was twenty-six, we got married a few months later. She . . . *hates* me. I left."

"But you've been together for . . ."—Todd did the math in his head— "six years? Seven years? Something must have happened."

"It's more like nothing happened. Linda is the same person I married, which she thinks is fine. I'm different now. And she thinks it's fine to yell at me the way she yelled at me our first year together, to get into it. And I won't. I just don't want to fight anymore."

Todd wanted to ask if Jack hit her. If he intimidated her. If he insulted her. If he pushed her. If he ridiculed her. If he made her feel afraid and anxious and threatened. If Jack remembered what kind of a person Jack was. If he remembered—

"I think you want a story of some sort," Jack said. "But this is it. This is the story. I became less interested, which made her angrier, which made me less interested, and so on. Until she slapped me in the face . . . right in the middle of a nothing argument. About what TV we should buy. Out of nowhere, and I decided then that I'd leave."

"You were in an abusive relationship," Todd said, prying. Trying to get him to admit to something.

"I don't know. I mean, yes, she hit me. That's abuse, right? She hit me a few times. I was never anything but, well, maybe an asshole sometimes. But mostly just kind and sometimes withdrawn. I get that's frustrating. Would you say it's abuse if a woman slaps you in the face?"

Todd didn't respond.

"Anyway. Relationship problems. They're all like that."

"Abusive?" Todd asked.

"No, I mean . . . one person feels abandoned, and the other person feels overwhelmed. So the abandoned person clings tighter and tighter, which makes the overwhelmed person pull away more and more, which makes the abandoned person feel more abandoned, and so on."

"I think it's more complicated than that," Todd said. "Sometimes it's worse than that."

"I don't know," Jack said. "But that's why I left. She hit me in a Best AV store while we were talking about TVs. I'd had enough. I waited a week and then left."

"But why did you lose interest? In the first place?" Todd asked, and stopped and leaned back against the counter and looked right at Jack's sea-glass eyes. He realized he must have sounded like he was blaming the victim. But Jack Gates was not a victim. He couldn't be, could he?

Everything was quiet for a moment. Todd wasn't moving, Jack wasn't moving, and then Anthony came in, crying. He'd fallen and scraped his knee, and there were bits of gravel in the wound.

Jack stood up, anxious to help. "It's okay," Todd said quickly.

He picked Anthony up and took him upstairs and washed his wound out and put on a Band-Aid.

"It's nothing," Todd said to him, smoothing Anthony's hair and looking at his flushed face. "Don't worry, it's nothing."

SIX

Time is all messed up for Todd, waiting to leave school to get beaten up. He didn't sleep well last night, he was in bed thinking about Jack, about what had happened, wondering if Jack was asleep. Could Jack sleep after that. Wherever he lived. And how he found out where Todd lived, how Justin probably told him. Although everyone sort of knew everyone here. All the kids walked home from high school, and middle school before that. They'd all walked together. Could Jack just threaten that violence was coming tomorrow and go to bed tonight? *Beat the shit* out of some-one—and that was an image too, since Todd knew that when people are afraid for their lives or when they are killed, they shit themselves and piss themselves. He made a mental note to go to the bathroom at the end of the school day, in his last period of classes.

Was Jack in bed, exhilarated, thinking about Todd? Planning his moves, planning what to do while everyone was watching, planning what to say? There was something about him that was *rehearsed*, but Todd wasn't sure what. Todd tried to think of comebacks. He tried to think about how to be sick tomorrow or convince his parents to let him stay home or to leave school early. Or he could tell. But who? It was a non-thought, almost. Telling was just something you *could not* do.

Todd finally fell asleep, but suddenly, so that it was like not sleeping at all. When his father woke him in the morning, he was up and getting ready before it waved through him. Today was the day.

Soon, too soon, it's the last hour of the school day, the hour reserved for electives, and Todd has chosen Classic Movies, so there's a movie on called *Rope*, based on a play, based, sort of, on a true story, about two men murdering someone together. Comrades. Strangling. Todd thinks through multiple scenarios, the multiple ways it can play out. Maybe, for instance, Jack isn't all that strong or quick, and Todd can win. (But Jack *is* strong, Todd felt it the day Jack pushed him, and Jack *is* quick, the way he smacked the book out of Todd's hands.) Maybe Todd is a better fighter than he knows. (But he doesn't know, how can he rely on that?) Maybe others will join in, like Logan and who knows who else, to kick Todd when Jack knocks him down. (And would Justin join in now?) Because mostly in Todd's imagination he loses: Jack punches him in the face or the head, and Todd falls backward, and then Jack gets on top of him, straddles him so he can't move, and then, from above, begins to hit him again and again. He could run, he thinks. He could run.

"Being weak is a mistake," says a man in the movie on the big TV screen in the room. It's timed too perfectly to Todd's thoughts. Things are lining up. Even though the movies are broken up into different periods, so that you never get to see the whole thing at once, and Mrs. Freeman has to talk about the movie for ten minutes in the beginning of class, still, the words are lined up perfectly. A sign. Todd is not prepared. Maybe he can talk to Jack, find him and talk to him. He realizes that he's forgotten to go to the bathroom, so he motions to Mrs. Freeman, who looks at the clock and sees there's still thirty minutes left, so yes, he can go. He gets up and goes to the hallway. He thinks he should have brought his bag and left. He'd get in trouble, or maybe Mrs. Freeman wouldn't notice. He could say he wasn't feeling well and there were only thirty minutes of school left anyway. Too late, though.

The halls are empty, like the day when he and Jack left the principal's office. He walks down the hall to the bathroom and turns the corner around a dividing wall. No one at the urinals, the stalls are open. The thing he keeps coming back to is that no matter what happens today, he will probably be hit. Jack will probably get at least one punch in, and Todd has never been punched. He stands in front of a urinal and balls up his right hand. He brings it to his face slowly and softly knocks the side of his face with it, right in the center, against his right cheekbone. There's a dull inner *thunk* in his skull. Even a blow sent to his skull this slowly and timidly is a little jarring. He imagines that it would hurt Jack's hand too. He moves down below his cheekbone to his jaw; this time there's cushioning. If he's hit here, it wouldn't hurt Jack's hand, and it could probably knock his jawbone out of place. He wishes he knew anatomy better, what violence can do to the body. In the front of the face, if Jack's fist came at him, there would be a broken nose, broken teeth. He has to punch himself harder in the side of the head, he thinks. Otherwise he would have no idea what's going to happen. He tightens his fist and breathes in, deep and fast.

Then he hears the door swing open and he quickly loosens his hand and pulls himself out of his pants and pretends to be pissing. Another boy, a sophomore, he thinks, stands one urinal away and starts to piss for real. Todd feels too self-conscious to go, and it's not the fight, he always feels this way with another boy next to him. He stands holding his dick in his hand, knowing that the sophomore boy, if he's paying attention, won't hear Todd pissing. So Todd shakes himself and zips up and walks to the sink and washes his hands and walks out, and he's almost back to the classroom before he realizes he forgot to go to the bathroom in case Jack is going to actually, truly beat the shit out of him. He should've gone to his locker too, to get his sweatshirt so he could walk out as quickly as possible, with all his stuff in tow; but his locker is one floor up. Too late now.

He walks back in and sits down. The movie is off, and Mrs. Freeman is talking about it, talking about murder. Could he die? If Jack hit him in the side of the head, near his temple, he supposes. Or if the fist hits him in the nose the right way. He's heard about this with some movie star, who was it? The bones of the nose go up and into the brain.

"So we'll watch the end," Mrs. Freeman says. "It's a shame that you couldn't watch the whole way through, because Hitchcock wanted to give the feeling of one *continuous* shot. But it wasn't one continuous shot, it was actually broken up a few times. So . . ."

Todd writes in his notebook, *everything is broken up, even when it's supposed to be continuous.* But maybe, he thinks, it's the other way around, and everything is continuous even if it seems broken up. He doesn't know what he's even thinking about, trying to distract himself. But then the end of the class arrives, and his thoughts snap off.

He walks to his locker as quickly as he can. He fumbles with the lock twice, then gets it, grabs his sweatshirt and his bag, and heads to the back door of the school. The halls are already full; everyone wants to get out of here as fast as they can. They're all dealing with their own urgent troubles.

He walks out into the parking lot, eyes darting around, but trying to keep from swiveling his head. Then he sees him. Jack, with a group of boys. But they haven't seen him yet. And . . . Hannah? Hannah Grace is with them, talking and smiling and rolling her eyes in play. Todd freezes, not sure when this happened or what to do.

Just then, Jack looks away from the group, over his shoulder, and sees Todd standing a small distance from his huddle. There's nothing on his face. Not anger, not hatred. A sort of passive calm. He's looking directly at Todd. And Todd is looking at him, still frozen. Then Jack turns back to the group and starts talking. Todd moves hesitantly at first, the way a rabbit gets back to its life after being chased by a dog. Slowly, slowly, until he realizes no one is coming for him. Behind him, he hears Hannah Grace laughing at something, and he decides to start running away, toward home, as fast as he can.

SIX

Anthony was running ahead of them on the mostly empty boardwalk, which was barely a boardwalk. A wooden walkway along the ocean with a stand selling beach-plum jam, a bicycle rental shop, an ice-cream stand, and a general store. Only the general store and ice-cream stand were still open. In other beach towns, maybe this wouldn't be off-season. It was still warm in the day; but the nights were cold, breathing chill into the edges.

"It's not a prison sentence," Jack said. "Think about what comes *after*. That's more like prison. Bills, work, health insurance, figuring out what a 401K is, which I still don't know. Something to do with retirement, right?"

Jack had been out for hours the night before; he said he was taking a walk, but the light got dimmer and dimmer till dark came and he hadn't returned. Before bed, Anthony had asked Todd where Jack went. He didn't know. Todd wasn't worried, exactly. But what to do? He thought that maybe Jack would disappear from this place like he'd disappeared from his old life. And Todd thought he wouldn't tell anyone Jack had been there. It'd be like a dream, forgetting itself bit by bit until only a feeling remained. At ten p.m. there was a quiet knock at the door, and Jack was apologizing; he'd just taken a walk to the movie theater and watched a movie and forgot to text. And then he asked if he could stay another night.

"Falling in love," Jack went on. "Trying to, at least. Feeling like a failure when you can't figure that out." Anthony ran past a man and a woman in their seventies who looked at Jack and Todd as they walked by. Todd worried that they thought the two of them were a couple. "You're a teacher," Jack said. "Doesn't this sort of . . . not make sense?"

"I'm a teacher because I want to make things better for them," Todd said. "Maybe I can be the teacher that's, like, stability. Like an anchor. Or maybe when things get difficult a lighthouse, or—"

"Or something related to you and the ocean," Jack quipped.

"But twelve years is a long time," Todd finished.

"Things change from year to year. If you fucked up off and on for twelve years as a kid, you can get still the next twelve years right." Jack mused on this for a second and smiled. "And then fuck it up again."

Anthony ran off the wooden walkway onto the sand to chase a seagull. Every time he approached it, it hopped up into the air and re-landed a few feet away. The bird wanted neither to be bothered nor left alone.

Todd stopped and Jack stopped too. "Jack. I think we should . . ." he took a breath. How to start? "Why did you come?"

"Ouch, well, we already went over this?" Jack said, scrunching up his left eye in confusion. "Maybe not my proudest moment, but it's not a crime to run away. My wife and I—"

"No, no. I mean, to Lanchester. Back when you moved. In high school."

"Oh," Jack said. "The short version is that my mom was a drug addict. That's pretty much it. She made the money for us, and she started . . .

I don't know. I think she was drinking first, obviously. I take after her there—"

"Do you think you have a problem?" Todd said.

"I'm telling you a story about my mom now," Jack said.

Todd realized he was being rude, though he felt he was looking out for his son. "Sorry," Todd said. "I'm just . . . thinking about Anthony."

"I'm trying to answer your question," Jack said.

"Okay."

"Okay. So. She drank. And then she started taking pills, I think. And then she was tired all the time, so she took other pills to stay up. I don't know, she was probably doing other stuff too. And one day, I was in my room upstairs, it was at night, and I heard my dad's truck in the driveway. And then I heard him come in. Who knows where the fuck he'd been that night? Then there's this shouting downstairs. First some weird sound, then my name. I thought he was calling me down to give me shit, so I stayed in my room, but then he really starts going at it and I hear him coming up the stairs. Losing his shit. So I get downstairs and mom is . . . well, I guess she shit herself and her . . . she lost a lot of blood, too. So I get downstairs and she's lying on the floor and her pants are soaked black, just, black! And she's not moving, her face is perfectly still, her eyes were open, and there's this awful, Jesus Christ, awful smell. My dad was screaming, Call the hospital! But I knew. Way too late."

Anthony shouted at the bird and made his way closer to a valley in the sand where shallow water had gathered.

"I'm sorry, I didn't know," Todd said to Jack. Then he turned toward Anthony and shouted, "Don't go in the water!"

Anthony lingered by the pool, though.

"Did you hear me?" Todd said, till Anthony nodded.

They watched him for a minute.

"Sorry, Jack. And I—I'm sorry for . . . You have to watch your kids all the time. I'm sorry for interrupting."

"I took off school most of that year," Jack went on. "My dad didn't give a shit. He was pretty much checked out before that too. But he really turned into a complete asshole after. My English teacher and the guidance counselor actually came to the house. And they both told him I should apply for this private school essay-writing scholarship. I think they thought I was a good writer . . ."

"You were," Todd said. "Maybe you still are."

"I'm not sure how they knew we were moving before I did. I guess my dad must have filled out some paperwork. He got a job near Lanchester, but you know, we lived a good half hour away from the school. He took me there most days."

Todd hadn't known. He started getting a feeling that this was too much for him to hear. Was it an excuse? An explanation? Either way, it was too different from the story he knew and carried.

"And then we got this letter from our school saying I was in. My guidance counselor had sent in an essay I wrote."

" 'Soon, no one knows where you've been or even that you were alive at all,' " Todd said, pulling the line from memory.

"What's that?"

"That's from your essay," Todd said. "Never mind."

"Jesus fucking Christ." Jack laughed. "How did you remember?"

"I remember a lot," Todd said.

"Yeah, but—"

"Anthony, I said *don't*," Todd called toward the water.

"Anthony!" Jack surprised Todd by shouting. "Come here!"

"It's okay, I just don't want him to go in the water," Todd said. *Why are you calling my son?*

"No, I . . . Hold on. *Anthony!*" Jack shouted again, and Anthony made his way to the pair.

"Jack . . ."

And then Anthony was with them, and Jack knelt down and whispered something in his ear and Anthony's eyes widened and he got happily agitated. "Yes!" he shouted. Then Jack picked him up in his arms and held him. Close to his father's face.

"Daddy," Anthony said, in an affected voice, "can Jack stay with us?"

"A little longer," Jack coached.

"A little longer," Anthony parroted.

Todd, not sure what to say, stood in place, not moving, maybe not breathing at all.

"I have to figure my life out. You know what that's like? Just for a few days. A week, maybe. You know what that's like, right? Starting over? And, I know, I know, you'd figure, don't I have friends? Can't I stay with friends? But Todd, I know if I go back . . . I can't, I can't. I'll slip right back into my life. It'll overwhelm me." He said this all urgently, but then calmed a bit. "I can't talk to them anyway. I mean, they know Linda, but also, it's not like . . . They're just not the same."

"As what?" Todd asked.

"Pleeeeeeeease, Daddy," Anthony whined.

Todd shook his head vigorously, once. It looked like a no at first, but then it became clear that he was trying to dislodge something. A memory. A suspicion. A lost feeling.

"Okay," he said meekly.

"Yeah?" Jack said.

"Yeah," Todd said.

"You can stay!" Anthony shouted.

"Yes, I can!" Jack said back, then hoisted Anthony onto his shoulders.

"Daddy, look, I'm on his shoulders," Anthony said.

"I told him he could ride on my shoulders," Jack added. "If I could stay at our house."

"Our . . . house?" Todd said, genuinely trying to parse the meaning for a moment. Dizzy, almost.

"Your house," Jack said.

"*My* house," Anthony said, laughing.

"Okay, yes, *your* house," Jack said to him.

"Daddy, Jack made it my house," Anthony said.

They got into the car and drove back, the beach at their side seeming to follow them, then turning to sparse woods.

When they got out, Jack said, "So, show me around."

"What?" Todd asked.

"Our house," Jack said, then laughed. "*Your* house."

"Can I watch TV?" Anthony asked, and Todd turned it on. There was an animated show about three animals on a skiing trip. Every episode, the three animals did something different but the same. The people who made the show animated the same facial expressions and nearly the same dialogue each time. Only the backgrounds were significantly different. Once, the penguin, the bear, and the giraffe went to a rain forest. Once, they went to a cave. Once, they went hiking up a mountain. Anthony loved this show.

"There's nothing to see, really. There's the living room." Todd gestured around himself. You've seen the kitchen. There's the backyard. The basement."

"So show me the basement, show me the backyard, show me upstairs, don't you give tours of your house?"

"I . . . yes. There hasn't been anyone over yet."

"I'm your first guest?"

"My only guest," Todd said.

When they were halfway up the stairs, a phone chimed, and Jack said, "I need to turn this the fuck off or throw it away." But then he checked, and it wasn't his.

"Oh," Todd said, both embarrassed and a little annoyed; he hadn't gotten a text or a call in days, even though his new job was about to start. Jack's presence illuminated the absence of everyone else.

At the top of the stairs, Todd pulled out his phone and looked at the message. He wandered into his room wordlessly. Jack followed him, stopped at the doorway, holding on to the frame, and leaned in a bit.

"What's up?" he asked.

"N . . . nothing," Todd said, distracted.

"Uh-huh," Jack said, and crossed the threshold. Todd's room had a bookshelf, two nightstands with lamps. A comforter with one mismatched pillowcase. He crossed to the window on the other side of the bed. A hawk sitting in the maple tree at the yard's far edge.

"Hey, check this out," he told Todd.

Todd looked over his shoulder.

"Come on," Jack said, and Todd climbed over the bed and stood next to him.

"A hawk," he said.

"Probably looking for something to kill," Jack said.

Todd didn't say anything. He thought of the field trip they took to Hawk Mountain as seniors. The long bus ride, when he sat in the back by himself as they crossed the state line. How, during the hike, he fell forward, tripping on an exposed tree root. How the other boys and girls were up ahead with the teacher. How, when he fell, Jack was standing there above him.

"You ever think it's good luck to see one?" Jack said. "I think about that stuff all the time. Like, is every animal you see a symbol of something."

"I think they're animals," Todd said.

"Seems like an English teacher wouldn't say that?"

"What do you mean," Todd said. The hawk leaned and tilted its head.

"Metaphors, foreshadowing, symbolism. That kind of stuff."

"That's in books," Todd said. "In life, I don't think it's the same."

"So nothing means anything?" Jack said. "Don't you believe in . . . well, that things happen for a reason?"

Todd remained still.

"What happened?" Jack asked finally. "Who texted?"

"Livia," Todd said. He held up his phone.

I know it's been a long time so I didn't want to call out of the blue but have been thinking so much about our son and I'd like to see him. I hope you agree he should know his mother. I'll call you soon if OK. In Rome now and US shortly.

"When's the last time you talked to her?"

"Spoke to her? Three years? She's sent a few messages, but. Spoken to her? More than three years? Anthony doesn't know her at all."

"See, this is why you have to disappear. Then no one can find you and do this shit to you."

I tried, Todd thought. *I tried, but here we are.*

And when they looked back out the window, the hawk was gone.

SEVEN

Todd is in Cultures class, staring at the back of the chair in front of him, where the name HANNAH GRACE is written in black marker. Next to it, in red marker, a disembodied cock and balls shoots raindrops of cum onto the name. There are dots on the balls meant to represent hair. This wasn't here yesterday.

Hannah is relatively popular and happy. Why this now? The picture arouses Todd. Would it always be like this, he wonders, so that even something this ugly and crude could stir him?

When the class ends, he walks into the hall. Justin Geiger and Rick Barnes are standing just outside the door, and when he passes by them, they burst out laughing.

Rick starts making high-pitched moaning noises.

"What?" Todd says.

"Didn't you get the note we left about your girlfriend?" Justin says.

"She's not my girlfriend," Todd says.

"Hope not," Justin says.

"I don't get it," Todd says.

Justin makes the jerk-off motion with his hand. Rick kneels under it and opens his mouth, making a moaning sound again, and they keep laughing and laughing.

"Hey, why are you doing this?" Todd says to Justin.

"Oh, are you guys in a lover's quarrel?" Rick teases, and Justin pushes him and laughs and tells him to fuck off.

There was a moment, Todd's not sure when, when all the guys started making jokes like this, jokes where they pretend to be gay.

"So am I gay or is Hannah my girlfriend?" Todd says out loud, angrily. "Fucking pick one."

"Which one do you think?" Rick says to Justin. Todd turns and walks away. He's filled with frustration, but English class is almost starting, with Jack and Hannah.

He wants to tell Hannah about the chair in the other classroom, but he also knows she'll get upset and he doesn't know how to handle that. He thought, in class, about blocking out the image somehow, but he didn't have a marker, and even if he did, it would have been hard to do it without getting caught. And the Cultures teacher was Mr. Appel, who was already wary of him. He's not sure how Justin and Rick were able to draw it. And he definitely wasn't going to tell Mr. Appel about it. Hopefully the custodian would see it tonight and try to clean it off, somehow. But it would be there the rest of the day at least. Maybe forever.

He has his nature-writing essay in his backpack. They've spent two weeks reading nature writing but they've never gone outside. It would be easy enough to go out, take a walk, and write what they see. He told his mom about that, and she said, "But that's not nature, Todd, that's just Lanchester." Anyway, in the spring they'll do it. They'll go to Hawk Mountain, the wildlife preserve an hour away, a mountain that rushes up in thin peaks, like a hand reaching out to the sky. They went there when they were kids too, in first grade. He remembers climbing up the hill to the Wildlife Center where the ranger introduced them to an eagle he was rehabilitating. The ranger had a thick glove on so the talons wouldn't tear into his skin. The eagle was awkward and breathed out of its mouth so you could see its tongue. It was supposed to inspire wonder, but Todd was afraid.

Is he an adult yet? He wonders what it'll be like to go back.

Each morning there are robins, his essay starts. *Tilting their heads to the ground. They seem innocent, but they're hunting.*

It's not as good as Jack's essay was, but it's not bad. He decided to defy his mother and, instead of writing about where he went on vacation or a camping trip or whatever, to write about his backyard. So much could happen close to home.

When he gets to the classroom, things haven't started; not the formal procedures yet, when the signal is given to sit and the teacher tells everyone to quiet down. Everyone is still standing or sitting on the desks instead of chairs, and Mrs. Call is looking through her desk drawers for something, and then Todd sees Hannah. She's talking to Jack. Jack spots Todd and lifts his eyebrows, then goes back to talking to Hannah, then class begins and they all sit down. Todd glares at Hannah, but she's staring ahead, obviously trying to ignore him. It dawns on Todd then what the joke was about. Hannah had sex with Jack. After she *saw* that Jack was going to fight Todd, after she *saw* that, how could she? And now Justin and Rick knew. *Jack did it just to get to me*, Todd thought.

"You fucking whore," Todd whispers at Hannah. How could she do this to him? If Hannah hears it, she makes no move, but the girl in front of them both hears and turns around and smiles with wide eyes, scandalized and excited. He starts writing in his notebook. Maybe it's a note he'll give to her or maybe it's just to himself; he's working through that. *I thought you were my FRIEND, and you KNOW what he's trying to do. Don't you SEE that he USED you to get to ME, how could you BE so stupid.*

"Todd," Mrs. Call says. "Would you like to read what you've written?"

Todd immediately closes the notebook, heart pounding, fragments of excuses and evasions filling his head, but none will save him. "It's nothing," he says hastily, and Mrs. Call's face crinkles. "Can you read your essay to us?" and a few people laugh.

He can still feel his heartbeat. He still doesn't want to do it. "Do I have to?" he says.

"No," Mrs. Call says. "But you're a good writer. Come on."

"Come on, Todd." Jack's voice emerges from the front of the room. "You love wildlife." And people laugh again, including Hannah this time.

Todd shakes his head no. He feels like he's trying to control himself from running out of here.

"Okay, okay," Mrs. Call says. "Does anyone want to go? I want five volunteers, or else I'll pick people." A long moment passes. Then a hand goes up. She asks for more. Two more go up. No one wants to do anything, or they're afraid to. Every action has to be dragged out. This is how they have learned how to relate to the world. Finally she selects two more students, but not Todd.

They read their essays. The readers are popular kids; their essays are clumsy. One is about hunting and the boy reads about how his dad drank deer blood once, how he said it was hot and salty, and everyone laughs or groans at this part. One by one they stand and read until the class is done.

And that's when Hannah turns to Todd and says, "I'm not a whore," and the girl in front is electrified with attention.

"You fucked Jack," Todd says, and then checks to see if Jack is still there. He's not. Todd has never fucked anybody, he feels so behind everyone else, but no one's ever questioned him about it.

"I did *not*," Hannah says, and gathers her things and stands. "God, *fuck off*, Todd."

"Don't *lie* to me." They walk toward the hall together. This is how conversations have to happen here, quickly, between one class and the next.

Before they walk out, she says, "Okay, I kissed him. It's none of your business. It's not like you and I are doing anything. You've had plenty of time to—"

"Oh, that's not what everyone is saying," Todd says. "Did you fuck him or not?"

And they walk into the hall and down it, and coming the other way, toward them, are Justin and Rick, and Justin and Rick laugh, and Rick says, "Me next, Hannah!"

Hannah says, "You know that didn't happen. Who told you that? Jack? Who told you?"

"I wanna Hannah-job-a!" Justin says in a mock Italian accent.

"Hannah, there's a drawing in Mr. Appel's room," Todd starts to say. "On the back of one of the chairs . . ." She's welling up, and as Jack approaches, she hurries past them toward the bathroom, so no one can see her face.

"What the fuck is your problem?" Todd says to Jack, and the other boys make a sound like they're shocked, thrilled.

Jack turns to his friends. "Guys, what did I actually say?"

"That you made out after school," Rick says.

"Then why are they telling everyone you fucked?" Todd says.

Jack shrugs. "I can't control what *they* tell everyone." Then he starts walking away. "Don't be late for class, faggot," he says.

SEVEN

Todd stood in the doorway of Anthony's bedroom in the late morning. The bed was made. The pajamas were folded. Everything was still, the house was quiet too; and Todd was lulled by the ordered emptiness, only for a moment, before he realized his son was missing.

"Anthony!" he shouted, and ran down the stairs. Into the front room, where his son was not, through the kitchen, into the backyard. His heart was racing because, *he knew, he knew! He knew something was coming, that Jack would do something, from the moment on the beach, standing by his son in the water, oh God . . .*

There was no one in the backyard. Just one more place to look, and that was the basement. He rushed back into the kitchen.

He knew!

As he crossed toward the basement door, he saw a small slip of yellow paper on the table. Red, unfamiliar writing.

NICE DAY. AT BEACH. SPOT WHERE WE MET.

Next to the writing, a little scribble of a drawing that Anthony made. Clumsy lines forming a sun and its rays. Then a tall figure holding the hand of a smaller figure. A man. A boy.

Todd went to his car, cursing. They must have walked there, but when? It was a half-hour walk, and he was sure he'd see them on the road. Except it was almost eleven now, he'd slept in so late, exhaustion had overtaken him the past few days.

"You can't just take someone's fucking *kid*," he said out loud, to no one, as he drove. He was trying to work out what he'd say. He thought he'd say he'd call the police. He'd kick Jack out. He'd kill him. "I will fucking kill you if you touch my kid again," he said in the car. It didn't feel quite right, but what else did he have? But then he was at the beach, in the parking lot.

He got out and walked toward where he and Jack had met just the other day, which felt like weeks ago now. It felt like Jack had been back in his life for a long time already. Like he had moved in. Like he was taking over.

Not quite at the spot, he saw a towel and the cooler from his house in the sand. There was nothing else, and no one on the beach. Did they drown together?

He looked up the beach toward the bathroom and shower area and headed toward them. Around the corner of the open door, in the roofless section of the changing enclosure, Anthony was standing by a low spigot jutting from the wall that was spraying water onto his feet. He kicked at the water stream, and then turned when he saw Todd.

"Daddy!" he shouted, and kicked water at him.

Past the wall, there was a shower room with a metal pole in the middle that had three nozzles on top. It was darker inside, covered by a high ceiling. Jack stood in front of the pole as the water shot down onto his naked body. He was standing on one foot, brushing the cascading water off his golden thigh and the other foot. He was bent over slightly. His entire body, right there.

"Finally!" he shouted, and his voice bounced off the shower room walls, doubling itself. "He wakes up!"

Todd sat on a bench outside the shower room and noticed another one of his towels and Jack's bathing suit on it. He would wait here and then confront Jack. He would punch him. Anthony continued to play with the water pouring from the wall. The shower turned off and Jack walked toward him; Todd took a breath and opened his mouth to say something, but then Jack's naked body was right at his eye level, inches from his face. Instead of speaking, Todd looked down quickly. Jack reached for the towel, he was so close now, and began to dry himself up and down.

"We walked all the way here," Jack said. "We swam, we built a castle, we dug a moat. We were wondering if we were going to have to walk back and find you still in bed."

Todd stared at the floor. Jack's feet were broad, with a bit of hair on the toes. The bones running through the tops of them were perfectly splayed, like the strings of an instrument under the skin.

"I was . . . I slept in. You can't just take—"

Todd looked up to confront Jack, but Jack's dick was still there, inches from his face, circumcised with blond hair above it, balls hanging heavy below. Jack's hand reached out and patted Todd's cheek affectionately.

"Admit it, you timed your morning perfectly to see me naked." He laughed a little and then pulled his bathing suit off the bench and stepped into it.

"Daddy, you are tooooo sleepy," Anthony said.

"Do you want to stay or do something else or go back?" Jack asked Todd. He knelt to wash Anthony's sneakers off under the rushing water. "Sorry, he didn't know where his flip-flops were, so he got sand all over his shoes." Then he picked Anthony up with one arm and turned the spigot off with the other. They stood there under the sun.

EIGHT

They're all gathered in the thin space between long lab tables watching Jack try to stomp Todd's mouse to death. Every time Jack misses, a bunch of the kids howl with disappointment. The mouse runs, white and frightened, across the tiled floor, but the kids are packed tightly and it can't find a path through their feet. Todd is shouting, "No! Jack! Stop!" Kids are laughing. Ms. Bidlen is down the hall, missing the entire thing, and Jack lifts his foot and slams it down on the floor, missing again.

Todd is stuck behind the rest of the kids, blocked out by Logan and Rick. They all have their own mice in little containers on the tables in front of their seats. For this part of the curriculum, all the different biology classes crowd together in the big lab room.

Jack's foot comes down again, misses. Todd wants to bust in and scream and push Jack, but then he would have seemed to care too much about his mouse, which he'd only gotten yesterday. If the mouse survives he'll have to run it through a maze the teacher made and observe dispassionately. People can't know he cares too much.

One of the girls next to Todd says, "This is so fucked up," but she doesn't do anything, why doesn't she do anything? He wants to think that none of the kids know that this is his, Todd's, mouse. He wants to think that all they know is that a mouse has escaped, and that Jack is after it. But he doesn't think that's true. He senses Jack has become their point of attraction, turning everyone against Todd and toward himself. Or maybe it's that Jack's anger, Jack's ridicule of him, has become an irresistible current sweeping everyone along with it.

Todd had named the mouse Brinker. To himself, but still, he'd named it.

The classroom door starts to open, and Jack's foot comes down one last time. It connects, splattering guts and blood around his shoe. Suddenly this is real, and it's reflected in the faces of some of the students. He really just did that.

"What's going on?" Ms. Bidlen asks.

Rick Barnes quickly says, "One of the mice got out, and Jack stepped on it."

"By accident," Jack added.

She walks over to them, short and always a little frustrated. "First of all, everyone sit down," she says.

They all go back to their seats.

Jack remains standing and lifts his foot up. The mouse is flattened on the floor, its insides pressed out. He shows the bottom of his foot to Ms. Bidlen.

The other mice are searching the sides of their plastic cages; any opening, the tiniest hole, might offer escape. But there are none. The only way to escape was offered by Jack, holding the cage upside down and dumping the mouse out, only to obliterate it.

"Whose mouse was it?" she says, and scans the cages. A few of the kids look at Todd. They knew. Maybe not all of them, but some of them. Todd raises his hand.

"Go wash your shoe off," she says to Jack. On his way out, he walks by Todd and pats him on the back.

"Why did you let it get out?" Ms. Bidlen says to Todd.

Hannah Grace is a table away and says to another boy, "That is so fucked," under her breath, and Ms. Bidlen turns her way.

"I heard you, Hannah. And don't talk like that in my class. What's going on with everyone today? You know what?" She's getting angrier and angrier. "You can't talk in here that way. Go to the office, I don't have time to punish you myself."

Todd thinks that now Hannah and Jack will pass in the halls, and then what? What will happen?

"Why did you let it get out?" Ms. Bidlen says to Todd again, this time sternly.

He doesn't speak. He's learning, slowly, that there's no point.

EIGHT

The parking lot, the office, the lockers, the classrooms, the essay, the doorway to the house he grew up in, his mouse. Hawk Mountain. How he fell forward. How the other boys and girls were up ahead with the teacher. How Jack was standing there above him. The images from Todd's life that last year in high school gathered around him; not diffuse like a cloud, but layered like a crystal.

He wanted to go home. It was the day of the school district meeting and Todd sat in the auditorium of the elementary school. The teachers had stickers with their names on them pressed to their clothes. Yellow stickers for elementary school, blue for middle school, red for high school.

He'd almost forgotten about this meeting, lost in the flurry of Jack's presence. Todd hadn't thought about finding a babysitter. Jack had been sitting at the kitchen table as Todd stood, hunched over, looked at sitter listings on his computer.

"Anthony already knows me," Jack had said. Todd kept scrolling. Jack had stood up behind him, then, peering over his shoulder. "Do you feel okay leaving these random teenagers with your son?"

"That's how babysitters work," Todd had said. There had to be someone who could do this. "It's a stranger who watches your kid. And you depend on them to not, you know. Why am I even talking about this, you know how it works. Even if you don't have kids, you must. Besides, these sites have them all rated."

"That's not what I mean. I mean one of them might end up being your student this year. That could be weird? Someone weaving their way into your life and you have to see them at school every day?"

Todd had straightened and turned around. It was just an hour, an hour and a half. If Jack were going to do something terrible to Anthony, wouldn't he have already done it by now?

Now Todd was in a row of metal folding chairs with teachers and staff seated like students.

"Not all districts have meetings like this," the superintendent said, "but we try to be as much of a family as we can." He was behind a podium, flanked by the three principals; two of them were whispering to each other and the other was looking straight ahead and smiling. "We share the most important burden in the world. And we see the work that we've all done. Those of you who have been here with us have heard me say this before, but when a student comes from one school to the next, from one classroom to the next, we can see how he or she was handled, what lessons they learned, what kind of person they've been made into. When you're seeing a child, you're seeing all the other teachers in their behavior. It takes all of us, working together, to change a child's life."

Todd noticed his own leg bouncing up and down, restless, a teenager's movement. He looked around the crowd and saw Ms. Paige in profile, a few rows back. The elementary school teachers had it the hardest and the easiest, he thought. They were the constant face for the kids in their class, aside from the music teacher, art teacher, gym teacher. They could make a child feel safe or unsteady for an entire year. He should talk to her. He'd meet all of them, he supposed, as Anthony grew up through their influences, passed from one classroom to the next, making his way to Todd in the high school. Todd closed his eyes tight against the thought of Anthony growing up, and then there was the sound of clapping, then shuffling, as the sixty or so of them rose to greet one another.

He headed toward Ms. Paige, but was stopped by a man with a red sticker. "Most of us know each other already," said a man with a red sticker. "But you're . . . the new English teacher?"

Todd pulled his lapel forward, brandishing his sticker, and recited, "Hello, My Name Is Todd Nasca. And you're . . . Sah-her Ay-zahr?"

"Sahir Azar," the man said, emphasizing the first syllable and making more space around the *h* in his first name. "Like, It's-ALL-Here!" gesturing grandly to himself.

Todd laughed. "That is a terrible joke."

"True, and not as funny as listening to people struggle saying my name." Sahir paused, then tried to start over. "I'm the librarian. We're the two people in the high school who like books. Although it's mostly computers now. For me, anyway."

"Aren't there two other English teachers?" Todd asked.

"Yes, but"—he made a furtive move with his hand—"they don't really read much."

Todd saw Ms. Paige on the other side of the auditorium, standing near the superintendent but looking their way. "That's going to be my son's teacher," he said.

"That?"

"Her," Todd said, and pointed her out.

"Oh, Elaine," said Sahir. "Hold on."

He took his sticker off his lapel and pulled Todd's off too, and switched them hastily, smoothing his tag out on Todd's lapel. Then he waved. "Elaine!"

Elaine came to them from her conversation.

"Hi, Sahir," she said, and turned to Todd. "Elaine Paige, I teach here. You're at the high school?" She looked at Todd's tag. "Wait, your name is . . ."

"Todd," he said. "But I think Sahir gave me his tag because he knows It's-All-Here." He pointed to his face and smiled.

They both laughed. "That is so dumb," Sahir said. "I taught it to him, of course."

Elaine looked at the tag on Sahir's shirt, then turned to Todd. "Todd Nasca?" she said, and shook his hand. "Is there a joke about that too?"

"Unfortunately, it's a serious name," he said. "You could make a NASCAR joke, but please don't."

"Don't worry," she said. "I don't know anything about NASCAR, so I can't."

"It's just around and around," Todd said. "I think that's all there is to know."

"Like the speech. He gives us the same speech every year, but he means well." Elaine paused, then asked, "Did you grow up here?"

"Lanchester," he said. "Actually, you're going to be my son's teacher. Anthony Nasca?"

"Oh," Elaine said. "Did you and your family all move here for your job?"

"Just me and him," Todd said.

"I didn't see you at the parent-teacher meeting."

"Oh, I figured we'd talk here anyway," Todd said. He'd had no memory of receiving a letter about the meeting. Nothing.

"Do you want your tag back?" Sahir said.

"My tag? I think I'll remember my name."

"It's your first school event, your first time meeting me and Elaine. Who knows who you'll be after today?" Sahir said.

"Hopefully I'll still recognize myself after this year," Todd said. And suddenly he felt dizzy. Something overcame him, smudging his thoughts together.

"Is he here with you?"

"He?"

"Your son? Anthony?"

"No. No, he's at home."

"Oh, you found a babysitter? Must have been hard, given that they're all out right now babysitting for everyone here."

"No, I mean . . . yes."

Just for a moment, laughing like this, he'd forgotten who was home with his son.

"I'm sorry, I actually have to go because the babysitter can't stay." He was already moving away from them.

"Well, goodbye, Sahir," Elaine said, joking.

"Goodbye, Sahir," Sahir said too.

"Goodbye, Todd," Todd mumbled, and headed out.

And when he got home, Jack was downstairs, but was it the same Jack? Should he treat him the way he always wanted to, or treat him as if he were an entirely new person? Did Jack think Todd was the same Todd?

"He's upstairs sleeping," Jack said. "How was it?"

"It was—"

"*Daddy?*" Anthony's voice called from the second floor.

"Well, I thought he was asleep, he must have woken up when you came in."

"He never wakes up. When he's out, he's out."

"Well, he was asleep when I left him there."

"*Daddy!*"

Todd went for the steps.

Anthony was under the covers, but squirming in bed.

"Can you read me *Wolf Story*?" Anthony asked. He'd left the book downstairs.

"Did you try to trick Jack into thinking you were asleep?" The words didn't feel like they were his as they came out.

"Daddy, can you *please* read me *Wolf Story*?"

"Did you fall asleep or did you just tell Jack you were sleeping?"

"I woke up," Anthony said.

"When?"

"When you came home, Daddy."

"You never wake up," Todd said. "You always sleep like a log."

"Logs sleep?"

"Never mind," Todd said, and shook it off. He headed over to the bookshelf and looked through. "*Lamont the Lonely Monster*?"

"No," Anthony said, and folded his little arms.

"*Be Nice to Spiders*?"

"Can you get it from downstairs?" Anthony asked.

Todd thought about Jack on the couch.

"I'm not going downstairs. But I'll read *Be Nice to Spiders*." When he sat on the bed, he saw that his son was clearly still upset. He started to read anyway.

"Daddy," Anthony interrupted, "will Jack be here tomorrow?"

"Well, yes. I guess so," Todd said. "Are you . . . worried he's going to leave or are you worried he's going to stay?"

Anthony considered for a bit, then replied, "And did you used to be best friends?"

"No, not really."

"And, and, is he here instead of Mommy?"

Todd felt dizzy and tried to regain himself. "No, no. That's a silly idea."

"Why?"

"Because . . . because Mommy is your mommy. And she's . . . still away. Did. Did Jack say he was like your mommy?"

Anthony pulled the covers over his head, and Todd shook him lightly.

Muffled, Anthony asked again, "*Wolf Story?*"

Todd started reading *Be Nice to Spiders* again.

"Please, Daddy," Anthony said, buried under the blankets.

NINE

Todd comes out of the Ben Franklin convenience store with licorice and a comic book. It's a Sunday. He doesn't like comic books, but he's trying to train himself out of watching television. He's lonelier than usual lately and finds himself filling his life, slowly, with disciplines. Writing in a journal. Doing push-ups in the morning. (This he'd given up after a week.) The comic book was meant to wean his attention away from the TV. Not quite as difficult as reading a book, but not as mindless as sitting there. Slowly, he noticed too he had been retreating to his bedroom more and more, avoiding any spot where he'd interact with his mom and dad, pulling into the room of the house that was most like the inside of his own head. The comic books are cosmic; they could be about saving the entire universe. They feel expansive, as his world contracts.

He finds the weak point in the edge of the licorice wrapper and pulls at it, and when he opens it, he sees a red pickup truck in the parking lot, not far from where he's standing. The front windows are rolled down, and in the small wedge of space that makes up the backseat, there's a white German shepherd turning, turning to him and barking against the little back window. In the front seat is Jack, and, just past him on the driver's side, a man dressed in a flannel overshirt and a white undershirt, fat in the face.

The man smacks Jack in the back of the head. Jack's head jerks forward with the blow, and he keeps looking down. Todd can see it from where he's standing, sea-glass-green eyes. Jack's father is saying something to Jack, but Todd can't make out what.

Todd's first instinct is to hide the comic book. He rolls it up and reaches around to put it in his back pocket. He doesn't like to bend them up like this, but he can't let anyone see him reading one. He should turn to go, he thinks. He should walk away.

Jack's father hits Jack again, then grabs him by the short hairs on the back of his head. He draws closer and starts saying something into Jack's ear. The white German shepherd starts to snarl angrily, slobbering, as if to defend the scene in the truck from Todd. *Look away, look away.*

Jack pulls his head from his father's grasp and averts his eyes, right to Todd, standing there, holding his licorice in one hand in an absurd stance. Jack's face trembles, more than that first day, more than when he pressed Todd against the lockers, angrier than the growling dog barking spit against the glass. This is the angriest face Todd has ever seen.

"*What are you looking at, you fucking faggot?*" Jack shouts out the car window.

His father laughs a little. Maybe he didn't know Jack had this in him. He pushes Jack in the back playfully, jolting him forward.

And then Jack opens the door and rushes Todd, and the dog pours out behind him. Jack pushes Todd to the ground. Will he punch him now, is this it? Todd turns his head and closes his eyes, he lifts a hand up to shield himself, but instead of a fist, he feels a sharp pain in his hand, accompanied by a deep pressure, and Todd feels his own blood hit his face, before he realizes the dog is shaking its head back and forth with his hand caught in its mouth.

"Jack! Please! Jack!"

Jack is to the right of him now, watching in awe. Jack's dad gets out of the truck and stands there for a second; he doesn't seem displeased. Finally—it's only seconds, but it feels much, much longer—he strides over casually and kicks the dog's back. The dog's demeanor changes entirely. Its emotional self collapses into a whine. It lets Todd go and cowers, wheezes a few times. Jack's dad grabs its collar.

"Come on!" he shouts, and leads it back to the truck, tugging on the collar. The dog is forlorn, afraid and reluctant now, so that even though it's moving with Jack's father, it's still being dragged to the truck. Then it jumps back in.

Jack still stands there, and Todd is pushing himself backward, hand bleeding from punctures who knows how deep, scraping his butt against the asphalt, tearing the comic book in his back pocket, the licorice still settled in its bag a few inches away.

"Todd—" Jack starts to speak, but his dad has come back and takes him by the arm. His fingers pushing deep enough, Todd can see, to leave bruises. Jack gets back in the truck and his father slams the door, then goes to the other side. They pause for a moment; maybe they'll do something. But then the engine rolls over and the truck begins to pull out of the parking spot. For the first time, Todd realizes that nothing and no one he's been told to depend on can be depended on to save him. Jack looks at Todd as they go. Jack, stuck in the moving truck with the adult who did nothing to help Todd. There's a nothing expression on Jack's face, like he's not even breathing.

Todd stands and rushes back into the store.

"Can I please wash my hand, please!" he shouts, as blood drips onto the tile. He feels stupid and scared and tries to conceal the depth of what just happened. He's afraid of the wound, afraid of Jack, afraid of Jack's father, and even afraid that the man who works at the shop won't help. Will he think, *Who is this dumb dramatic kid, running into the store, shouting, "Can I please wash my hand"?*

NINE

In the glow of the television, Todd rubbed the two small oval scars on his hand. Almost unnoticeable now, smooth and white in the thick flesh between his right thumb and forefinger; sometimes whole months would go by and he wouldn't think about them.

Jack was on the other end of the couch drinking a beer, and Anthony was between them. He was asleep, breathing quietly, leaning against Jack. The movie was nothing noticeable, it was on regular TV, broken up by commercials. Neither of them was invested in it, but it was something to watch. There were four empty bottles on the table.

Jack looked over at Todd. The cold blue light waved over his face. Sorrow, worry.

Jack put his bottle on the table slowly, then reached over to pick Anthony up.

"I'll take him to bed," Jack said.

At first Todd kept staring straight ahead, still rubbing his right hand with his left. Then he came to. "What? No. No."

"Don't worry, I'm not that drunk," he said, and picked up Anthony's limp body. "God, it's like he's dead," Jack said.

Todd watched him go, watched Jack turn the corner, and heard the footsteps up the stairs. He sat there, his mind filled with Hawk Mountain and senior year and the dog, and the fact that Anthony would be starting school in two days, and that Livia had texted again. This time she'd been more insistent. Not rude, though she was capable of aggression, he knew. But pleading.

Maybe he should change his number. *She wouldn't be able to find us at all then*, he thought. He wondered if he wanted that. She'd basically abandoned them. And anyway, wasn't it a relief to have shed her, to become who he wanted to be with his son and no one else? *Fuck her*, he thought, *let her think I'm dead*. But it was a thought, he noticed, that was not in his voice.

On the TV, someone pushed a man who fell forward and hit his head on the edge of a coffee table. The noise brought Todd back to the present and he realized, fully, that Jack Gates had taken Anthony, taken his son, up to bed.

He got up and shook his head in a no motion, as if to shake free of something, and paced quietly to the lip of Anthony's room. Jack was on the edge of his bed, reading *Wolf Story* to him. Perhaps he'd woken up on the way to the room, but if so, he was asleep again now. Jack's voice was calming as he read, which was unnerving to Todd. Jack touched Anthony's head, then turned the lamp off and stood up.

"Are you going to bed?" Jack whispered when he was in the hall.

Todd nodded.

"Okay, me too," Jack said, and as he walked past, he patted Todd on the shoulder. Todd stepped back in a small, almost unnoticeable flinch.

Livia's text had read:

> You're not the only parent. Even if you are a good one, he needs a mother.

Todd looked in on his son again. There wasn't a sign of movement or violence in him. Though he knew that would change after school started. He wanted to pretend, like all the other parents, like his parents before him, that going to school was natural. That being a child in one room after another, imbibing information at such a dizzying pace that it couldn't possibly be held, so that it would almost all be slaked off, was somehow better than a child staying at home, growing and thinking at his own pace with his family nearby. But it wasn't natural, he thought. All that a parent, or a teacher, could do was mediate the harm.

After a moment, Todd stood and went to the bathroom and then looked at himself in the mirror. His face didn't have the calmness of his son's. He'd grown into the lines of concern. He wondered what he looked like when he was asleep, if anyone would ever be able to tell him.

At Hawk Mountain, he'd fallen forward. He could hear the other boys and the girls up ahead with the teacher. There were yelps and laughs ahead of him, but he stayed behind. It was the end of school, and he wanted to be alone. After all those years together, they weren't his friends anymore, like everything had been erased. They all wore plain clothes and talked to each other about it. He'd fallen forward as he was listening to them, a tree root was raised from the ground as if to meet him, as if the world itself wanted to trip him. And as he sat up and brushed himself off, Jack had been there. Jack must have stayed behind too. But why?

Todd dried his face and hands and went downstairs. The TV was off now. Jack was asleep on the couch on his side with his back facing outward. Todd sat on the floor in front of the couch and listened to Jack's breath. He reached forward, slowly, and lightly touched the edge of the couch and rubbed the cushion with his fingertips, feeling its texture.

"How long are you going to sit there?" Jack said, apparently not asleep.

Todd pulled his hand away.

"Sorry, sorry—"

"It's okay, it's nice having you there," Jack said. There was a pause between them. Then Jack went on, "Are you going to do that every night? I mean, it's okay, but there's not enough room on this couch for both of us." He rolled over and looked at Todd and laughed a little.

Todd stood up and gathered the bottles left around the room in his hands, two from the table, one near the statuette of Heracles on the side table.

Jack started to sit up, saying, "Todd, do you want to—"

"How did you find me, Jack?" Todd said, standing up, bottle necks between his fingers. He stood there impossibly long, with no response. Like a photograph, no movement, just a hovering, everyone stuck.

"I told you," Jack said. "It was just a coincidence. Or fate? However you—"

"I don't believe that," Todd said.

"Which one, coincidence or fate?"

"Either," Todd said, then fumbled around with his words a bit. "Not fate, not fate. I believe in coincidence. But not this time. It's *too much* of one. You, what, took the bus to the town I *happened* to live in and walked on the beach I *happened* to be on right to the spot where I *happened* to be?"

Jack didn't say anything.

"Yeah, never mind, Jack. No big deal. Nothing's a big deal."

"Todd—"

"You've got to go soon, okay? Okay? Anthony's starting school and I'm starting school, and things are going to get busy."

Jack, sitting upright now, too close to Todd to stand, said with concern, "I think you're stressed out about Livia texting you."

"What? How did you know she texted me?" Todd was defensive, confused. Had Jack checked his phone earlier?

"The other day," Jack said. "You told me? In your room?"

"Oh. Yeah."

"Did she text you again?"

Todd didn't respond.

"Are you okay?" Jack asked, as Todd walked out of the room.

TEN

The red cover of *The Catcher in the Rye* is the same color as their ties, Todd notices, as he pulls it off the school's library shelf. He's been getting permission to come here lately during study hall; sometimes here or sometimes the media lab, anyplace where he can be away. The library is usually empty, and Todd wonders why no one comes here when there are so many books. But he also wonders that the library has still managed to be here at all, not gutted and replaced with a computer room or another gym.

He holds the book in his right hand. The bandages came off a couple of weeks ago. He had to get four shots over two weeks with a thick needle piercing into the meat of his arm, because he'd lied to his parents and said a stray dog had bitten him. Jack has mostly left him alone after the attack. In English class, he doesn't look back anymore. In the hallway, he doesn't taunt him. After school, he walks by silently.

He must have told some of the other kids about the dog, though, because Rick and Logan bark at Todd in the hall sometimes. He'd worn a large bandage for two weeks, but no one asked him why, not even the teachers. He feels his presence receding into a place where even a wound won't find sympathy. He'll pass by and they'll bark and snarl at him and then crack up. Once, Logan knocked Todd's books out of his hands in the hall and a few of the other kids saw and laughed. When he knelt down to pick them up, a few of the students barked at him, and someone, though he didn't see who, kicked his biology book down the hall. Hannah Grace saw. She was there but didn't laugh, and didn't do anything to help either.

He scans the first two pages.

If you really want to hear about it . . .
. . . two hemorrhages. . . .
—I'm not saying that . . .
. . . madman stuff . . .
It killed me.

He's read it before. It's one of the few books he wants to reread. He feels—is *obsessed* the right word?—with Stradlater, and has read the parts with Stradlater multiple times, always missing his presence when he disappears from the book. Todd doesn't understand what the feeling is or why he feels it, but he always goes searching for him again in the pages. The book feels different without him.

There's a rumor at the school that if you read the novel too much it distorts your brain and makes you kill people. Someone read it and tried to shoot the President, he thinks. He can't remember the details. Just that it will drive you crazy. But he doesn't believe that. It's a curious book that keeps him company; he likes to find it on the shelf in the school library, even though he has his own copy at home. It's doing fine here among the others, less lonely than the characters inside the covers.

But he's dimly aware that there's something off about the books that he reads, that they all read. Every one of them is meant to elicit some feelings of sympathy based on . . . similarity. They don't read any books about other cultures or any other kinds of people. He would've brought this up with Hannah if they were still talking, but now he doesn't talk to most people, just some of the teachers and some friends from another school. Everyone was supposed to look the same and the school reinforced this with its uniforms. Later in the year, they are scheduled to read *Crime and Punishment*, which he supposes is about a different culture, but only sort of. He thinks, maybe when he's a teacher, he'll change this. He can teach novels about people that no one seems to understand. Thinking about the future like this, when he's away from Jack and everyone, keeps him feeling vital. Like when he gets older he can treat this as a bad dream, one you can wake from with a start, then close your eyes and go back to and repair. As an adult, he'll undo every bit of this.

He puts *The Catcher in the Rye* back on the shelf and walks along the aisles. He sees a few of the other boys here today, including Logan and Justin, at the far end of the library where the computer and magazines are, and he tries to avoid them.

From around the corner of the last aisle, he hears a punctuated sound that he realizes is crying. Muffled. He turns and sees, halfway down the aisle, Jack, with his face pressed into the crook of his arm, which is against the edge of a shelf. He's sobbing quietly.

Todd is frozen again. This is a condition of his life now: momentary paralysis. He steps forward and lets out half a word, then manages to say a little more.

"H . . . hey. Are you . . . ?"

Jack looks up and there are tears swelling up his eyes, one of which is bruised and purple, and Todd scans Jack fully and sees bruises on his arms too. Todd flinches backward. Isn't anyone else noticing that this is happening? He remembers what he learned when Jack's dog attacked him: Nothing could be depended on to save anyone. Maybe not even

Jack. He thinks about *The Catcher in the Rye* for a second. The redness of the cover, the loneliness of the characters and of reading it.

"Are you okay?" Todd says.

"Leave me alone, Todd," Jack says. He puts the center of his forehead up against the shelf and tries to slow his breathing. And then, more quietly, "Please."

Todd moves forward a few steps and is standing next to Jack now, can hear his breathing, can feel the warmth of being close to him.

"What happened? To your eye?" Of course Todd knows what happened, he saw it in the Benjamin Franklin parking lot, and of course Jack knows Todd knows. But Jack probably told everyone it was something else. A fight. A fall. Something tough or funny. Todd reaches out with his right hand, unbandaged, scarred, and puts it on Jack's shoulder. Jack closes his sea-glass eyes again and tries to contain the feelings spilling over.

They stand there and Jack starts to calm. Starts to breathe normally and turns his head, still leaning against the bookshelf, toward Todd. Todd pulls his hand away, but there's no malice in his eyes. Just a questioning look: maybe the world is not the same as they both thought it was. Then they hear boys talking. Boys approaching. The voices draw closer from the end of the library and Jack stands quickly and wipes his face with his hand, wincing as he touches the bruised eye.

"Oh-ho-hoooo," Rick Barnes says elatedly, and Logan Krevanchy claps his hands.

Jack backs away from Todd as the other two boys advance, so they're all in a row now, and then Logan Krevanchy barks at him. Rick moves forward and pushes Todd backward. He stumbles, almost falling.

"Is this where you come during study hall?" Logan says. Todd turns to walk away and feels a hand grab his shirt and pull him back.

"Hey, three guys on one," Rick says. "This is probably what Todd wanted, right?"

Todd looks at Jack, into his eyes. *Help.*

Jack steps forward. He's looking into Todd's eyes. There's no questioning anything now, there's only a clarified need.

He punches Todd in the stomach.

The other boys are barking as Todd collapses, the feeling of the punch and the shouting and the humiliation in him unfolding and clenching and unfolding. *Finally,* Todd thinks, *this is what it feels like to be punched, this is what it feels like to be punched by Jack.* Like a bolt shot through him, still blunt and painful in its absence. He was surprised it hadn't happened earlier. He starts to wheeze and pant and his eyes well up, and he's afraid he'll vomit now, on the ground again with Jack above him, and the barking and snarling and the gnashing of teeth.

TEN

"Do you still talk to anyone from school?" Jack asked.

"No," Todd said.

"So you disappeared too," Jack said.

"What about you?" Todd asked. And then his phone rang, and it was Livia, so he wasn't paying attention when Jack said, "Just you. You're the only one, Todd."

Todd stared at his phone without answering; it blinked at him again and again.

"Do you want me to . . ." Jack reached for it, and Todd pulled away, answering it reflexively.

"Hi . . ." Todd said. He was apprehensive. Jack walked out of the kitchen and up the stairs. "Listen, before you start, I've been meaning to call."

"*Before* I start?" Livia said, and laughed a little. "Start what? I've texted and called I don't know how many times and you're not responding—"

"Hold on, hold on. Let me finish. I've been meaning to call you, but the school year is about to start—"

"You're working again?" Livia said. She sounded almost sad about it. Probably upset Todd wasn't living off her separation money anymore.

"Yes, at the high school . . ." Todd heard feet running down the stairs, and then his son was with him.

"Can I talk?" Anthony asked, and reached his hands out.

"Do you know who it is?" Todd said, confused.

"Todd, is that . . . Can I please? He wants to talk to me. Anthony, it's your *Mommy*," she said urgently, her voice audible in the room.

"My mom," Anthony said, as if he were lost.

Todd gave up, angry, and knelt. He held the phone to his son's ear. He couldn't make out what Livia was saying but saw Anthony nod bashfully. "Yes," he said. He realized he should've put the call on speaker mode, but it was too late. When Jack walked in, Todd looked up angrily. "Okay, Anthony, that's enough, say goodbye."

"Goodbye, Mommy," he said.

"Okay, text me in a few weeks when you're ready . . ." Todd said. "No, I don't think that would be good . . . Not before you get back, he's already . . . Livia, he's already confused enough without you checking in all the time, wait till you get here . . . Okay. Okay. 'Bye."

"Anthony," Todd said sternly. "Go play in the yard." But Anthony just stood there.

"How did he know who I was on the phone with?"

"He did?" Jack laughed. "How did you know, Anthony?"

"I thought I heard Mommy's voice," Anthony said.

"Anthony, you've never even heard . . . Daddy isn't asking you, I'm asking Jack. *Jack*, how did he know?"

"I don't know, I—"

"I did hear her voice when I was a baby," Anthony said, protesting.

"Anthony, go play outside or upstairs."

"I did hear—"

"Somewhere else, okay? You're not in trouble, but I need to talk to Jack."

Anthony wandered out of the room, slowly.

"I don't know, Todd," Jack said. "I think kids just *know* shit like that sometimes. Didn't you know stuff like that when you were a kid? But listen, don't you think he should know anyway? That his mom wants to see him?"

Todd settled into thought for a minute, then reared his head back. Jack had two of Todd's ties wrapped around his neck. "Why are you wearing my ties?"

"Oh!" Jack said, feigning surprise. "I needed to see if you had a tie, I was going to go for a job interview somewhere."

"Where? What? You went through my stuff?" This was too much to take in at once.

"No, I walked by your room and your closet door was open and these were hanging there, so I was comparing them," Jack said. "I didn't go through your stuff. Do you have a body stuffed in one of the closets or something?"

"You have a job interview? Around here?"

"Well, not really. I was thinking about it, getting a job here."

"Jack, you can't . . . You . . . you have to leave. On Tuesday. Tuesday is the last day. You don't have to leave tonight, and I don't have the time to help you tomorrow. But Tuesday."

"Not *here* here," Jack said quickly. "I want to find a job in the area. Maybe in Newchappel? Or something? And then I can call Linda and we can sort everything out, but I want some stability. I mean, unless you're okay with me staying here."

Todd closed his eyes.

"You've got a lot on your plate right now," Jack added. "I won't get in your way, okay? I think . . . Livia is . . . well, maybe she won't even show up. Or maybe she'll realize you don't want her to intrude on this life you're making for yourself. You said she pretty much just let go before, maybe she'll let go now. Come here," Jack said. He moved forward and gave Todd a hug. Todd didn't move, he didn't hug back, but slowly, he rested into the embrace. Jack put his hand on the back of Todd's head to hold him there.

"You know what's weird?" Jack said, still hugging him. "This red tie is almost exactly like the ones we wore in school! Did you mean to get a tie like that?"

You have to leave, Todd thought. *You have to.*

ELEVEN

The prom is coming in a month, which is one month before the end of school. It's a midwife to the disaster of adulthood, and Todd doesn't have anyone to go with. He doesn't really want to go, and he's never even imagined himself going. But he always assumed he *would*. Everyone would, that was what you did. Everyone paired off, even if it was with a friend, one of these kids that they've known now most of their lives.

He didn't know anyone he could ask anymore, though. The world had drifted away from him. His guidance counselor had sent a note to his parents.

Todd seems to have gone through drastic changes this year. He's become a loner who doesn't have many friends and doesn't show interest in the other kids. His grades have dropped, not into the danger zone, but they could still use improvement. We understand that he's already accepted to Keene State, so maybe he's letting himself go. This may just be the typical senior year condi-

tion of losing track of what matters, but he should push harder, or he may carry these habits into college with him. The more disturbing thought is that boys who withdraw like him may be involved with drugs, so we recommend looking around his room to see if there are any drugs or paraphernalia. We've enclosed a brochure for you to show you what they look like. The drugs teenagers use today are a far cry from the drugs teenagers used back when you yourself were in school, so this is not a matter to be taken lightly. Better to find them at home and have "the talk" with your son than to have us find them here and have to have "the talk" with the police.

His mother showed him the letter after he came home and found her searching through his room. She must have known he'd walk in on her in that moment, wanted to be caught so they could have "the talk." Why had the guidance counselor put quotes around that? Shouldn't standards for good punctuation be as high for staff as for the students? Mostly he was stung by the embarrassment of the phrase, "He's a become loner who doesn't have many friends . . ."

He'd only had one meeting with the guidance counselor this year. Who did she think she was? How did she presume to know or understand *anything* that was happening in his life? The phrase turned in him like carsickness.

He told his mom that he wasn't on drugs, that he'd never tried drugs, and that he just wanted to get out of school and be done with it and go to college. She'd accepted his explanation without resistance, and his father never brought it up. No one was interested in anything other than the surface, and this at once saved him and condemned him.

This isn't just how things are, he wanted to say. *Things have causes, they happen for a reason, and yes, yes, something has happened,* something is happening to me! But he would never say any of this.

At lunch, he mostly sits alone now or near the small cluster of kids who don't talk or say much. Maybe they've felt the way he feels this year but had felt it all along. He wasn't popular before but he blended in with everyone, he had his friends, his light friendships, he was one of them. Now he was . . . he couldn't think of another way to say it to himself: blended out. Like he'd been taken apart, smoothed into something that was more like a void, like the ocean.

But the prom is coming. He sees Hannah Grace emptying her tray and getting up to go. She's far away from him now. She's still composed, still herself, he's just not part of her life anymore. She doesn't turn around toward him in class anymore. Doesn't walk in the halls with him. Doesn't ask for gum. Still, he thinks, *She hates the prom.* Maybe they still understand each other. *Maybe she'll go with me.*

"Hannah," he says.

"Oh, he-ey, Todd." She looks around nervously as they walk out of the cafeteria.

"Can I ask you—" he says. "Can we stop so I can ask you?" And they both stop for a moment. "Are you . . . would you go to the prom with me?"

"Oh, Todd. I can't. I'm sorry."

He takes a breath.

"I'm going with someone," she says. "He asked me a few weeks ago."

"Are you . . . are you going to the prom with Jack?" he asks, and his face gets flushed.

Hannah's face scrunches toward the center and then it relaxes when she sighs. "Todd, it's really none of your business who I'm going with."

Todd closes his eyes tight, then opens them again, and Hannah sees what's happening in him.

"If it makes you feel better: No. I'm not. I'm going with someone from Liberty," she says. A boy from another school. Someone who doesn't know him, doesn't know anything about what's happening to him or who he was or could be. "Fuck Jack. If I went to the prom with Jack, Justin and Logan would probably say I was pregnant with his twins."

Todd smiles. He's happy to hear someone say something about the boys that isn't merely the praise they're always receiving. For being okay athletes. For being sort of funny. For getting slightly above-average grades. For being young. For being boys.

"I don't really want to go to the prom," Todd says, "I just, I thought maybe we could go."

"I don't want to go either," she says. "Trust me, there's nothing uglier than a beautiful prom dress."

Todd smiles again.

Hannah peers into the cafeteria and sees a few girls she knows busing their trays. Soon they'll be approaching: popular girls who have eased up on the hierarchies in senior year, who have accepted Hannah because they're interested in her flat tone and over-it-all-ness as an accessory. Hannah can't like them, Todd thinks, she can't. But he knows she probably can't refuse them either.

"Listen, though, Todd, no offense, but I wouldn't go with you even if I weren't going with someone else."

Kristen and Steph and Fiona are coming this way now.

"You're . . ." She considers her words quickly. "You're, like, a problem now. I don't want to get barked at in the halls or . . . I don't want to have to carry whatever it is you're going through. I've got enough to deal with."

"But school is almost over," Todd says. This feels as bad as the note from the guidance counselor.

"It's not over yet, though," Hannah says quickly.

A problem, friendless, lonely. It feels like everyone is saying out loud what he thinks about himself now, which is, everyone knows, the worst thing anyone can do to another person.

Hannah starts walking forward, pretending she wasn't talking to Todd at all.

Doesn't she see that none of this will matter in a few months? Todd thinks. He clings to this when he can. He'll move away from Lanchester and be something else. *Can't she remember we were friends just a few months ago?* And in a few months all these fears and hierarchies will be totally gone, he thinks. *None of this will even affect us; we'll go to school and live in different places. It will all disappear.*

The three girls pass him and call out to Hannah.

I promise, he says in his head to himself. *I promise it'll disappear. I promise.*

"Why were you talking to him?" Steph says, and Hannah says something Todd can't hear. Then, in a voice loud enough that Todd is sure she means him to hear it, Kristen says, "Which one of you would wear the dress if you went?" and the group laughs.

They're trying to protect themselves; they're all trying to protect themselves, which is the best way to be sure they'll always be hurting each other.

ELEVEN

The car was parked but still running on the drop-off roundabout in front of the elementary school. Todd looked through Anthony's little backpack.

"You've got your lunch box in here, right?"

"Yes," Anthony said quietly.

"And what's in your lunch box?"

"Pear. And sandwich."

"What kind of sandwich?"

"Turkey, and potato chips."

"Okay, and what else?"

"Juice."

"That's right," Todd said, and messed up Anthony's hair a little, then fixed it again, comfort and stress. "Come on, let's go, this is a big day!"

He got out of the car and went to Anthony's side to let him out. Ms. Paige stood nearby, talking to another boy, who skipped away happily before she strode over to Todd and Anthony.

"First day for both of you!" she said. Then she noticed Anthony sheltering himself behind his father's legs. She met Todd's eye. "Don't worry. He's doing what a lot of them do on the first day, especially if they don't do kindergarten. After today he'll be excited to come back, I promise."

She knelt, her head near Todd's waist, and leaned to the left to say hi to Anthony.

"Hi-ii. Do you want to come in and see the sandbox inside?"

Anthony shook his head no, and Ms. Paige looked up at Todd.

"Then he'll grow up and get to high school and feel this way all over again. Not wanting to go to school."

"Thanks," Todd said, smiling. He stepped to the side to reveal the school to his son; Anthony tried to follow and stay behind his legs.

"See Ms. Paige's bracelet?" Todd said to Anthony.

Anthony leaned forward to look, and Ms. Paige held her wrist out. The bracelet was thick and polished, the color of coral and pearl. Anthony touched the bracelet quietly. Todd widened his eyes at Ms. Paige to indicate that now was his moment to leave. When she noticed, she put her hand on Anthony's shoulder, and Todd hurried back into his car, slipping out of the open air.

Something broke in Anthony when he saw this, and he began to cry, loudly and with increasing desperation, "Daddy! Daddy! *Daddy, PLEASE! PLEASE! PLEASE! DADDY, DON'T GO! PLEASE!*"

Ms. Paige stood by Anthony's side and waved at the car as Todd drove away, their forms becoming smaller and smaller until they disappeared behind a curve. He was crying at the wheel, and a little way down the road he pulled over and sobbed. He leaned forward, he needed to get to work, he was already late. He was crying. He couldn't stop. A car slowed as it drove by him and he turned his head and measured his breath; what would they think if they saw this man, parked by trees on the side of the road, crying in his car?

When he got to school, he had a few moments to breathe, still and slow, at his desk. This was a new space. A desk, a blackboard, a projector hanging from the ceiling like a heavy surveillance camera, five rows of six seats each, and storage closets behind them. The sun would not come into the room through the windows till the afternoon, so the mornings would be lit by the harsh overheads. He laid his grade book, his lesson notebook, *Lord of the Flies*, and a roll call sheet on the desk. The room was his, but it would rarely be his alone.

Students entered, talking to each other, and he tried to smile at each one as they entered. He remembered how, at the beginning of each class when he was a kid, the teachers always pretended to not notice the students coming in, as if these teenagers were none of their business until the bell rang.

"Hi," he said to each of them as they passed, making eye contact whenever he could.

When they sat, he read off their names one by one, sometimes receiving a quick correction. It was Gabrielle Gree-WEE, not GREE-vee. Collin Dole's last name has two syllables.

He did the same with each class; English, then English again, then study hall, then lunch, then English again. In the third English class, saying hi, he recognized one of the students. It was the taller boy from the Pizza Palace parking lot. The one Jack had threatened with a broken neck. *No, wait*, he remembered, that was only a joke. Jack hadn't actually *said* that to the boy, had he?

What was Jack doing? he wondered.

What was Jack doing right then, in his house?

"Hi," he said to the boy, who didn't show any signs that he knew who Todd was. When they did roll call, he found that the boy from the parking lot's name was Banner Bolland, which was, Todd thought, a stupid and cocky name.

He knew them all now, in this way. How he felt about their names, the way they responded when he called on them. He felt which were his favorites, though he knew that that always changed by the end of the year. He felt he could tell, with nothing other than the impression made in their first hour together, who had read the book over the summer and who hadn't. This must be the way a student felt moving to a new town, coming to the school, learning to know these people who all knew each other. Whatever their differences, though, they all knew exactly how to act. At this point, they'd been trained. Show up. Be quiet. Look to the front of the classroom. Don't waver. Don't check phones. Wait till class is over. Whatever happens between classes will be up to them.

At the end of the day, Todd stood at the urinal in the bathroom down the hall from his class. The urinals were closer to the floor than usual, for the kids who were still short and the ones who were all done growing but whom the world at large considered to be the wrong height. The door swung open and two boys walked in, laughing and talking to each other; Banner Bolland and another boy Todd didn't recognize.

"Hold *on*, faggot!" Banner said to the other, before they both noticed Todd at the urinal looking at the over his left shoulder. The other boy's eyes went wide when they saw Todd, knowing they'd been caught out.

"Oh fffff . . ." Banner said, holding in the word *fuck*. "Hi, Mr. Nasca."

Todd finished and zipped up and the other boy added, "We were just joking with each other, he didn't mean it, like, as an insult."

"Yeah," Banner said. "Everyone says that now, it's just like a thing here. But, yeah, sorry, sorry."

Todd walked toward the pair and looked at them with anger. "Well, you'd better be fucking sorry," he said. His face trembled, and he slowed his breathing. They'd never heard a teacher curse at them, Todd was sure. The teachers, like the students, all knew exactly how to act.

"It's not okay. Okay?" The two boys were stuck in their spots, not moving. "Okay?" he said again, and finally the two boys nodded in assent.

Todd moved to the sink to wash his hands and watched them in the mirror. They stood silently next to each other in front of the urinals, both staring at the wall.

"*PLEASE!*" his son had screamed this morning, when Todd had condemned him to twelve years of this. "*PLEASE! PLEASE! DADDY, DON'T GO! PLEASE!*"

TWELVE

At Hawk Mountain, Todd can hear the other boys and the girls up ahead with the teacher. There are yelps and laughing, but he's stayed behind.

It's the end of school now, and he tells himself he wants to be away from them. To be alone. But the truth is he has no choice. After all those years together, they aren't his friends anymore; it's like everything has been erased.

And the clothes they're wearing today are different—they're all permitted to wear plain clothes on the field trip—and that's conspired to erase their connection too. Rick Barnes, who is up with the rest of them, has a shirt with a giant rooster on it, and has told everyone it's his big cock shirt, but Todd only hears that from afar. He's not allowed to be in on the jokes.

They move forward and up the mountain ahead of him, and his foot gets stuck on a tree root and he falls and knocks his shin painfully, as the voices sound smaller and smaller in the woods. The distance grows between them. The front of his pants leg is torn, and his exposed leg is scraped and bleeding, covered in forest dirt.

When they see this, he thinks, they'll make fun of him. Pain soaks his leg. *When they see this, they'll laugh at me again.*

He brushes away the dirt, and then, noiselessly, there is Jack, a few feet away. Jack, who must have stayed behind too. But why?

Jack gets closer, closer, till he's standing above, looking down at Todd, who is scraped and vulnerable on the ground, with no one else around.

TWELVE

This was going to be Jack's last night at the house and the three of them went to the boardwalk after school, late in the afternoon. Todd wouldn't have to confront Jack with anything now, he could just walk and walk until the afternoon was over, then the evening, then tomorrow morning. Then Jack would be gone.

The memory of pain, Todd thought; so hard to recall something that used to be so intensely present.

"Did you like school today, Anthony?" Jack asked.

Anthony nodded in an exaggerated motion. He was holding his father's hand.

"Ms. Paige said you did," Todd said. "She said you didn't cry at all."

"I didn't cry," Anthony said.

"Well, not like yesterday," Todd said.

"I didn't cry yesterday," Anthony said.

"It's okay to cry," Todd said, and stopped walking. "But it's not okay to lie. You cried and you should just admit it."

"Whoa, Todd," Jack said.

"I don't want him bottling everything up."

"He's six," Jack said.

"Almost seven," Anthony said.

"Yes," Jack said to him happily, "six and a gigantic half!"

Anthony made a playful noise and ran ahead a few paces.

"She scolded me for not sending him to kindergarten," Todd said. Around them the summer was finally, finally dying. The ice-cream stand was having its last day, and a few people were gathered around for it. Two teenage girls, whom Todd didn't recognize, a family walking away, and an older man and woman with a German shepherd. The dog was big and completely innocent; it could knock someone down and never know it had done the wrong thing.

"Scolded you?"

"Well, suggested maybe it was an issue for him. It wasn't easy for him yesterday or today."

Anthony turned back to them.

"Daddy, can we get ice cream?"

"That's where we're going," Jack said.

Todd's phone went off in his pocket with a message from Livia.

> I don't find that funny but if it were true it would explain a lot ha ha will call you tomorrow

"What is it?" Jack said.

"I got this weird text . . ." But then Anthony was running ahead of them toward the ice-cream stand, and they moved faster to catch up.

"Anthony," he called. "What kind of ice cream do you want?"

Anthony turned to look at his dad, but he didn't slow down. He went right over to the couple and their dog, Jack and Todd not far behind.

"Hi-i," Anthony said, and immediately the dog snarled at him. The gray-haired man had a poor grip on the leash, and the dog lunged at the boy.

Anthony screamed and Todd saw it all unfold, one action after another. The woman turned to see what was happening, too late to act; the dog opened its jaws; the man scrambled for the leash. And Jack moved in and pulled Anthony back, then smacked the dog across the face. The dog was stunned, and Todd too was dizzy.

"Don't hit my dog!" the man shouted, finally getting hold of the leash. "He was looking my dog right in the eyes, you can't do that!"

"That dog almost killed my son," Jack said. "You're lucky I didn't kick its skull in!"

"Come on, Mitch," the woman said. "Come on."

Anthony was crying, and Jack was holding him.

The couple led their dog away and Todd could see Jack whispering into Anthony's ear, slowly, slowly, until the boy stopped crying, and then looked at Jack. Finally, when the couple was gone, Todd ran forward.

"Jesus Christ, are you okay? Give him to me, Jack, give him to me."

Jack handed Anthony over to Todd, who buried his head in Todd's shoulder, where Todd held his head close.

"He's fine!" Jack said. *No thanks to you.* Jack hadn't said it, but Todd could hear it nonetheless. As surely as he had heard Jack say, *That dog almost killed my son.* "You're fine, aren't you!"

Anthony made a muffled sound into Todd's shoulder. Two syllables sent into Todd with a shiver.

"What?" Todd said.

"Woof! Woof!" Anthony said, raising his head and laughing.

"Woof!" Jack said back. "I wanted to make sure he wasn't afraid of dogs after this," Jack said. "So I just said . . ."

Todd set his son down hurriedly and took a step back.

"What?" Jack said.

"Woof! Woof, Daddy!" Anthony shouted.

Todd felt a turning feeling in his gut, like his stomach was in his chest and his heart had dropped low.

"Woof!"

"Stop it!" Todd yelled. He knelt in front of Anthony, and Anthony woofed again. Todd reflexively covered Anthony's mouth. "Stop doing that! You hear me? Stop!"

Anthony was stunned for a moment; his father's hand was big enough to cover his entire face. It had cut off his mouth, trapped the air inside of him. Then he started to cry again.

"Todd, he didn't—"

"Would you just fuck off!" Todd shouted at Jack. "Keep out of it, you're leaving tomorrow, anyway!"

Jack faltered.

"Let's go," Todd said, and took Anthony's hand and led him, faster than his small legs could take him, back to the car. He buckled Anthony up in the back and then got in.

"You're leaving tomorrow," Todd said in a low voice beneath Anthony's sobs, looking at his own eyes in the rearview mirror. The sentence felt like an amulet that could protect him. He said it again. "You're leaving tomorrow."

"What is going *on*?" Jack said at the passenger window, then opened the door and got in.

Todd drove them home in silence, slowing his breathing, trying to calm himself.

When they parked, Todd looked over the seat at Anthony. "Listen," Todd said, "I'm sorry."

"It's not a big deal," Jack said. "Sometimes grown-ups get angry."

Todd looked over at Jack. What was this? What was he doing?

Todd got out and opened the back door and unbuckled Anthony and hugged him.

"I'm sorry, I'm sorry," he said.

"If you keep apologizing, you'll mess him up," Jack said, still in the passenger seat.

"Can you go inside?" Todd said, and handed Jack the house keys. Jack took them and went out, up, and in.

"I was scared, that's all. I didn't want anything to happen to you."

"It's not a big deal," Anthony said, parroting Jack's words.

"It *is* a big deal if you get hurt, okay? I don't want you to get hurt."

Anthony was quiet for a minute, then said, "Is Jack leaving?"

"Yes," Todd said with a sigh. "Yes. Tomorrow."

"Okay," Anthony said.

"Okay?"

"We'll have more room," Anthony said. And Todd smiled, his eyes welling up with relief. They would be okay. Jack would be gone, and Anthony would be okay with it. There was no protest.

"I love you," Anthony said casually, surprising Todd. The words came out as if they were a mere fact, a shrug of unassailable truth.

Todd hugged his son.

"I love you too," he said.

Then, in the same tone, Anthony added, "And I love Jack. And I love Mommy."

THIRTEEN

On graduation day, all the kids are in their seats. They are stationed alphabetically by last name, on either side of a stage in a football field. Behind them are bleachers filled with parents and other family members here to celebrate their own emancipation, the moment they'll be free of their children. Some of the children, not children anymore, will go to college; some will stay in town; some, soon, will marry; some will die; but this time is over.

The speech is done, and now names are being read.

"Rick Barnes," the principal reads, and Rick Barnes walks up onto the stage in his gown and everyone cheers, and some boys' voices and an adult voice shout his name. He stands there for a dumb moment, holding his diploma and shaking the principal's hand, and then walks off.

"Kelly Crawford."

Todd thinks about the way the students cheer for their friends, and how, when he walks up onto the stage, no one will cheer. No one will shout his name out, and his parents, sitting behind him in the bleachers, might not notice this, lost in their own celebration.

"Jason Farringher," the principal says, and some adults shout his name.

His parents are completely out of touch. When they all got out of the car in the crowded lot, Hannah was walking by with Justin Geiger, and Todd's mom called Hannah's name. "I hope you kept Todd out of trouble this year," she said.

"He got through it," Justin said. Hannah's brow furrowed and she saw Todd's face, red with shame.

"He'll be all right," Hannah said. "He's so excited to go to college," she said.

His father laughed. "Well, I hope so!"

Maybe they will notice. Maybe when they cheer for him, they'll cringe inside when they notice they're the only ones applauding. Like a mote in the eye of silence; a noticeable, irritating speck.

"Jack Gates," the principal says.

Jack walks up and a bunch of the boys cheer, and Todd looks over his shoulder to see if Jack's parents are there, but he can't spot Jack's father. He remembers, then, the line from Jack's essay: *now that Mom's not around.* The boys are cheering, but do they know him? Do they know anything about him? What happened to his mom? Todd looks back to the stage as Jack, his smile already faded, steps down and heads back to his seat. He doesn't look in Todd's direction.

They are all called. Justin goes, then Hannah goes. He sees them on the stage one after the other. For a moment, even though they're right there on the stage, he misses them.

Gwen Hofmann goes, Courtney Hudock goes, Jason Kelly goes, Jen McGinley goes. Names of kids he knew his whole life but had drifted away from him before this year. Faces he wouldn't ever forget, not really, even though they had, at some point, turned away from him.

Todd looks back one more time to see if there's any sign of Jack's dad, which there isn't. But Todd's mom spots him looking back and waves. Todd waves weakly, and soon it is his turn.

"Todd Nasca," the principal says, and Todd stands and walks up the steps. Now he can shake a hand and get a piece of paper and be done with it for good. As he ascends the steps and approaches the podium and principal, he can see his mother and father stand in the bleachers, cheering. He's almost startled by the sight of them, here, now, at the end of his year of feeling alone and terrified. As he shakes the principal's hand, a girl's voice shouts his first name. Was it Hannah? And as he takes the diploma, he hears a bark, like a dog's, from the audience. Then another, then another. And he tries to smile, for that moment he is supposed to stand and smile. But he hears the boys barking at him. Logan and Rick and the others; Kevin and Scott and Jason and Mike and Joe, all barking from the audience, and the principal pauses for a moment and smiles, unsure what this means. Todd sees Hannah in the audience; she's not barking. She pushes Justin and he barks one last time, but stops before the others do. The chorus of dogs erupting, one final goodbye. And then the moment ends, one last bark, and another name is called.

Todd tries not to cry as he heads down the steps on the other side of the stage; he looks to Jack's seat and sees it's empty. Has anyone else noticed? And at the end, when they throw their caps to symbolize the severing of their youthful heads, and as they take photos to capture the moment, Todd searches and searches. But Jack is gone.

Except the impression of Jack will never be gone, not really. He's in the dark behind Todd's closed eyes, like an afterimage from staring too long into burning light.

And then, fifteen years later, Todd will open his eyes, and Jack will be there above him again, blotting out the sun.

THIRTEEN

The voice message from Livia came at one p.m. Typical, really: she'd called without taking a second to think that at that time Todd would be working.

"Todd," the message began, "why won't you *answer* when I call? It's not as if I call often. And yes, I know that that's part of the problem. But another thing is, if . . . well, it's weird to say this in a message, but . . . if you are *gay*, then you could have told me. It actually clears a lot up. Why you were so distant, and why you didn't want to touch me anymore. When my brother made that joke, how you were so upset. I mean, he shouldn't have used that word or . . . Anyway. I understand. I'm glad you have this guy. This guy Dave? He was little aggressive, but I'm sure he's nice. I suppose he knows Anthony well, but I just need to say, neither of you are Anthony's mother . . ." There was a pause. Then her voice began again, "It's time for us to set a date. And maybe you think it's been too long for me to be a mother, but people change. I've changed. You've . . . well, I don't have to say *you've* changed, do I? Anyway, the important part is . . . I'm coming. I'm in Rome now, but . . . let's set a date for next week. I know this might be a surprise, but, well, I was surprised too, when I called and your . . . partner? I'm not sure what word you both use. Anyway, I was surprised too. So I guess we're even. What's life without a little surprise, I suppose. Anyway, Todd? Call me back. And try to answer when I call, Todd. Try."

He listened to it in the car, hazards blinking, about to get Anthony. As Ms. Paige walked the boy out the front of the school toward his car, Todd found himself mumbling, "*My* son."

"Daddy!" Anthony said, running toward the car. "I got a sticker!" There was a sticker of an eagle on the end of his index finger. "It can fly!"

Ms. Paige opened the door and knelt as Anthony got in. "He did well today," she said, and Anthony tapped Todd's face with the eagle sticker, saying, "It got you, Daddy!"

"Yes," Todd said.

"He's very clever, I'm going to have to keep an eye on him," Ms. Paige said, and then cast a look to Todd. "And on you too!"

"Close the door, Anthony," Todd said, and Anthony did, and waved goodbye to Ms. Paige from the other side of the window.

"Is Jack home, Daddy?" Anthony asked. "Is Jack home?"

Todd didn't answer.

But he was there, sitting on the porch steps when they returned. He was wearing a button-down shirt and Todd's red tie. He stood as the car approached and smiled in an almost bashful way.

"I locked myself out," Jack said. "Maybe you should give me a key!" Then he laughed weakly.

Todd strode past him and opened the door. Anthony went to hug Jack, but Todd intervened, and told him to go to the backyard and play. Todd noted inwardly, then, that this was becoming a common move, telling his son to be somewhere else so he could talk to Jack, so he could deal with Jack, so he could manage Jack.

"How was school?" Jack asked as they walked in together.

Todd put his keys down next to the statuette. "Jack . . ."

"Sit down," Jack said. "I want to talk to you." Jack sat on the couch.

Todd remained standing. "You talked to Livia."

Jack let out a breath. "Yes, but—"

"You told her—"

"Hold on, hold on. Sit down, okay?" He patted the side of the couch.

Todd remained standing for a moment and everything held its place.
Still.

Still.

And then, finally, he sat.

"I went out, I walked to that store across the bridge. Um . . . what's it called? You know what I mean. The one I mean. I went there and I got this shirt and I . . . well, it sounds stupid, but I didn't know where to go. I wanted to find a job. I don't really need a job, but I wanted to show you I had a reason to be here, and then as I was walking, way past that store—Gerson's, that's right, Gerson's—I walked past Gerson's, dressed like this and I realized I could just . . . *talk* to you. You know?"

Todd could hear the sound of his own heart in his ears, the life in him reaching its outer edges. "Jack, you told Livia we were boyfriends? *Boyfriends?* You answered my *phone*? *When?*"

"You were . . . showering yesterday morning. I didn't like the way she was talking to you. She was harassing you and Anthony. I didn't even give her my real name or anything, I said my name was David. You can just tell her it was a joke if you want."

"Are you *fucking crazy*?" Todd asked. He covered his face with his hands and shook his head. "You are. You're fucking crazy. Why did I even let you stay?" And now, along with his heart, he could feel his breath, warm, against his own face. He was breathing in the air that came out of him, he was being turned inside out.

There was a gentle tug on his left arm.

"Todd, Todd. You were right. You were right. That's what I'm trying to tell you."

Jack pulled Todd's arm down slowly, and Todd lowered the other one. Jack ducked his head down to meet Todd's eyes. "I found you. You were right. It wasn't a coincidence. It wasn't. I looked you up. You had an old profile that linked me to your old school, and it had a bulletin saying you were moving here. And right by Hawk Mountain . . ." He took a breath. "So, I found you. That sounds so stalker-y when I say it out loud, but it wasn't that hard except that you didn't have any recent info up online anywhere. But me finding you on the beach, that *was* . . . well, that was the fate part, I think. I just, I don't know. I knew you'd be there. Like how birds know where to go, like that. I knew. There was this . . . feel-ing. *Go this way.*"

He put a hand on Todd's knee. Todd looked at it, then back at Jack's face.

"The last time I saw you, I thought, *Talk to him.* At graduation, you know? But my dad was there, under the bleachers, and he motioned to me to come over, and then told me, 'Congratulations, now get the fuck out of my house.' That was what he said, as soon as I went over to him. He . . . Well. Listen. It's not important. But I *wanted* to talk to you. After graduation. I know it was fifteen years ago, *fifteen years.* But suddenly I was in my own life. And I felt, like, *good. Let the guy live, let him go do his own thing.* And I didn't know you had a *son!* A wife. Well, an ex-wife. And a *son!* And she has . . . she has no right to intrude. Not on you. But something is missing. I can tell that. Something is missing here. You're not yourself. And I knew it as soon as I saw you. And something was missing from my life too. So, after years of Linda and that not being right. Well, then she slapped me a few times, and I thought, *What am I doing?* And I thought, *The person I want to . . . I want to be around . . .*" Jack took a deep breath. "This is probably too much at once . . . I'm say-ing too much at once . . ."

Todd sat silently, he didn't feel he could speak until the right words appeared, didn't feel he could move until the right movements rose up.

"But what I want to say . . . I . . ." He looked in Todd's eyes, into Todd, with his sea-glass eyes. "Todd, I—"

"*Jack, don't* . . ." Todd said, in total desperation.

And Jack leaned forward and kissed him, quietly and gently, on the lips.

Todd didn't kiss back. Then their foreheads were touching. Then their breaths were so close that they were tangling, going into each other's lungs. Then Todd's eyes were open and Jack's eyes were closed.

Todd stood. It was all set in motion then. Todd went to a window and pulled the curtains closed. Set in motion. To the next window. He closed the curtains there too, the room was darkening, the light was set back now, made to wait for everything that now was set in motion, that had to happen. He walked back to the couch and stood before Jack, who was eye level to his waist.

Jack looked up at him, his eyes filled with hope.

Todd picked up the statuette and with a single line of motion swung it at Jack's face, connecting with his cheek, with his skull beneath. The sound came, of impact and cracking and the air and spit flying from Jack's mouth. Jack let out a sharp moan and turned his head to look at Todd in disbelief. Then Todd hit him again, this time above the cheek, hammering his face with the head of the lion, whose bronze mane split open Jack's left eye, the meat of it unfolding from its severed membrane. Jack covered his face and screamed now, in understanding.

"*Todd please!*" he pleaded. "*I—*"

Todd swung at him again and the impact strangled the words so that they came out as a gurgle, and Jack tumbled to the floor on his hands and knees. And the statuette went up again. Up and down and up and down again. Todd's breath was racing, racing, and his heart. Blood flew from Jack's skull and neck onto Todd's face, and a sound started to come from Todd's mouth and echoed in his veins as the blood inside rushed through him faster than ever before, as if every tiny passage in him were awakening, a moan, deep and loud. Up! Down! Jack's brain exposed and the flesh on his neck exposed and Todd crushed the bones there, the vertebrae, the tendons split and splayed like fallen wires. And Todd was alive with the act, covered now in Jack's blood and flecks of the meat of Jack's body, and finally he dropped the statuette to the floor with a loud but unheard sound, for nothing could be louder than how he now felt. He fell to his knees and pushed Jack, Jack's body, over till he, it, was on his back.

Jack's dead face. One eye open and green and unmoving, the other split, the curdles of it filled with blood now. Jack's dead warm blood, which was pooling around the crown of his head, which was also dead now, lying at a strange angle, uneven on the floor. Todd's breath was deep but slowing. He moved his fingers and touched Jack's dead lips, which were already losing color.

Everything was quiet for a moment, except for his breathing. He closed his eyes. He put his hand on Jack's dead face. Then opened his eyes again and looked up.

There, huddled against the frame, standing in the doorway, looking onto them both, was Anthony.

PART TWO

In a book in the front room, a poem starts with the words,

> the last winter will arrive
> with the sound of bells

and that book is wedged between the others, its pages pushed shut, holding the tension of the full shelf. No one will read that book again, and not because things have turned from their path now, a perversion of a normal life. No one will read that book again because that is the nature of most books: read once, if at all, then shelved with the words locked inside.

Maybe every murder is a pin in the map of time, yours, mine.

It's not winter yet, so the bells have not arrived. It's barely the fall. Outside, the leaves have only started to turn, the branches driving death toward their edges. Todd, with the body, with Jack on the floor, the blood pooling, and Anthony standing; six eyes, five whole and one split open.

The day is letting go of the sun as Todd rushes up to Anthony, tramping blood into the carpet, and grabs him by both shoulders.

"What did you see!" he begins with a shout, but his son does not respond.

Behind them, Heracles and the lion are covered in flesh and warm blood, cooling like the day. Todd picks his son up and rushes into the kitchen and puts the boy on the edge of the table. Above them are the empty bedrooms where before today they've slept like nothing was about to happen. Made beds. Drawers with folded clothing. Books on the shelves and nightstands and a scattered toy here, a shoe turned on its side in the closet next to its mate. Above those rooms and the roof float the seabirds and the ravens whose voices are like metal against stone, and the hawks and eagles cry out.

"He . . . was hurting me," Todd says. "He was hurting Daddy. Jack was hurting Daddy." Anthony swings his legs a little, off the edge of the table, like he's taking a break from play. He is, in fact; minutes ago, he was in the backyard, where his father sent him. In the bare grass, a space where he imagines himself to be different people. Knights and wizards and other animals and superheroes and a host of things he will never be. In that way, he lays a revealing veil across the ground and the world becomes a different place too. A tree becomes a castle. A pale beige spot where the grass is dead becomes a portal. A stick becomes a bone or a wand or a cane.

"Do you understand?" Todd says, and then hugs his son, and as he hugs him realizes there must be blood on his face, Jack's blood, spattered across him like a swipe of freckles.

Past the yard, down the hill, a lost dog is ambling through the grass. There's a collar around his neck and a tag that clinks as he moves. He was fat once, but he's skinny now, a yellow Labrador. The food he finds—worms in the mud, killdeer eggs, Popsicle wrappers—makes him sick. The birds fly up as he trots past them. A family misses him, but he will never know it. Life, now, is this starving path through the grass.

"Do you understand?" Todd says again, then turns and wipes his face with his sleeve, which also has blood on it, he realizes. There might not be a way to clean his face now. He pulls back and looks his son in the eyes, trying to look into Anthony's eyes the way Jack used to look into his.

Anthony's brow furrows. "What do you mean?" he says.

Away from here, the water reminds the sand, again and again, of its sound, like rushing thunder. The waves make the same sound as breath against your ear.

A crow on the hill above the beach is eating a plover chick, its down shredded, tufts of it blowing away, and one orange leg kicking as the black beak digs for its beating heart, its brain, pulling out the hesitant intestine. The plover cries out once, a tiny, hopeless bleat.

Todd does not know what to say. For a minute he stands there, looking into his son's eyes, and his son, legs swinging idly, stays with him. Their eyes are on each other. There has not been a moment this still between them since Anthony was born, or never when he was awake anyway. Todd can't cry now. He thinks that to himself, it's the first thought. *You can't cry, you have to move forward, you have to get him to do what you want.*

"You can't tell anyone about this, you understand? Ever ever ever ever ever. You can't. Promise. Promise."

"Okay, Daddy," Anthony says with a shrug. Like nothing has happened. Like life hasn't just stopped in the next room.

The sky starts to deepen and the sparrows that wheel around the house stop looking for seeds trapped in a wedge of shingle. Spiders crawl up the walls and turn webs in drain gutters. A mouse finds its way into a crevice by the porch. Worms move underneath, aerating the earth.

Todd wants to ask what Anthony saw. Maybe he didn't see, maybe he'd walked into the doorway just as Todd was finished . . . doing . . . that. Doing that with Jack. Jack, who is still in the other room. Lying there, oh God. Oh God, Anthony. Maybe, though, he'd only seen a blur, a scrap of something before Todd rushed forward and seized him and blocked his view and picked him up and moved to the kitchen and put him on the table and talked to him and held him with a promise. You can't tell anyone about this.

And all the while with blood on his face. His arms. His shirt. His shoes. Maybe all Anthony knows is that his father is frantic, covered in blood.

"Daddy," Anthony says.

"Yes?" Todd asks breathlessly.

"Can I go back outside now?"

On the beach is a jellyfish, spit out by the ocean. It's nothing now. An almost clear bubble that can't move or breathe or eat. A splayed film that will dry into the grains. What was the point of it being alive if no one will even step on its carcass and be stung?

"You can," Todd says. Anthony slides himself off the table edge and turns to the door when Todd grabs him again. "But stay outside, stay out there. If you stay out there till I call you, I'll give you a surprise later."

"What is it?" Anthony says, excited.

Todd knows he'll have to come up with something. But it could be anything. It doesn't have to be special or exciting. Or he could just fail. Could just say later, *I lied.* He could tell his son he's a liar. He could do anything now, he realizes. It's a thought that flashes through him like heat lighting: *I can do anything now. There's no reason not to.* The thought doesn't leave so much as it burrows deeper in.

Todd hears a car go by on the road, but it doesn't stop. He can hear so much more now; his senses are on edge. It's almost the time of year when the monarchs put themselves into chrysalises to dissolve and re-form. Some of them are doing that right now, a little too early, so they'll emerge and freeze to death. They'll never make the journey south, never land on branches with tens of thousands of their kind, so many of them that the tree branches break under their beauty.

So Anthony heads to the backyard, and Todd moves to the front room. He walks around the body. Jack. He will have to touch Jack. And this strikes Todd deeply, a high-pitched hum seems to run through his head with the thought that this is something possible now. No objection, no invitation, just touching this body. Jack's body. Head lolled to the side, the split eye closer to the floor, the good eye half open. Todd does not know much about bodies. He's never seen a body this newly dead, not like Jack has, who saw his mother on the floor blackening with lividity.

Standing by the body, he finds himself holding the statuette again. He doesn't remember picking it up, this thing that he got when he was with Livia, a remnant of their time together, he thought it would please her to have it in the house, Heracles and the Nemean lion, cast in a mold in Delaware, hot liquid metal shrinking into ripples of muscle and struggle. He'd brought it home and put it on the table, and she loved it for a while and he loved it for a while and then they forgot about it. Now it could never be forgotten.

He will have to lift Jack up and take him to the basement. He hunches and brings his arms under Jack's armpits. Todd's cheek is warm. It touches Jack's cheek, which is going cold like the year. Jack is heavy as Todd pulls him up. He's never held a person this way—a person gone slack, a person limply seeking the ground.

Jack's chest is against Todd's. Jack's head is on Todd's shoulder. Their bellies are touching. At first, you might think they were dancing. Then, maybe, that Jack was grieving, and that Todd was holding him up. Then you'd see that it was neither of those.

He steps backward into the kitchen. They're so close now, and Todd thinks that he might slip, that he might fall backward and feel the blood's heat on him, all over him, along with Jack's weight and death. Jack's inside, out. On him. But he doesn't slip. He holds Jack up. At the lip of the doorway, at the top of the basement stairs, it's hard to see the world is still happening, all at once.

By the rocks in the ocean, tautog swim with vacant eyes open in the water. White in belly and stone gray above, they turn to look at mollusks. Their throats are lined with teeth to grind them down. Seals slip through the rolling waves and poke their heads up like lucid thoughts. Then down they go again, into the water with the mako sharks. The dolphins. The sea cucumbers. Farther, toward the deepness, things find strange ways to survive without light. Not a world away from the house, just a few miles out, that's all.

Jack's feet fumble on every step, so that Todd holds him tighter as he descends. Slow, close. Each step into the basement is careful and deliberate. Then he's there. In room without light, he lays Jack, Jack's body, down on the floor, but he can barely see; there's a flat rectangle of light coming in from the top of the stairs, like a god, he thinks. Like a two-dimensional god of orange-yellow light and straight edges and angles. For a second, he wonders if this is what the angel of death might look like.

He goes to the top of the stairs and pushes the switch. The light blinks on, and Todd goes back down and sees Jack on the floor, as if he's sitting down, his back against the wall.

"You can't sit if you're dead, you're just positioned that way," Todd says in a whisper. He doesn't notice that he's said anything, though. Perhaps he didn't say anything. Perhaps it was only a thought, or, less than a thought, a possibility. He goes to the other side of the basement and finds the giant plastic container. Airtight, light blue, artificial, the color of a pill you'd take to cure or prevent something. He unclasps the lid; a short hiss, then a pop, then it's open. It's filled, he sees, with decorations. A plastic tree. Shining bulbs, rolls of plastic lights, and there, there, another angel. Also plastic.

He pulls them out and puts them on the floor, along with a card Anthony made, construction paper with cereal O's glued to it. He's got to make space for this body.

The statuette, Todd thinks. The image of it up there in the living room interrupts all his movements. Heracles and the lion. Heracles killed the lion as an act of love. No arrows could penetrate its fur, so Heracles wrestled it, choked it to death intimately, with his bare hands. Heracles wore the lion's skin, its mouth like an open hood on Heracles's scalp, as if, in remorse, he'd decided to let the lion devour him. Why did Todd correct Jack, he wonders, when Jack said Hercules? It could be Hercules, up there, locked in that embrace. It could be. Todd's up the stairs, he's looking on the floor for the statuette, before he turns to see it on the stand by the couch where Jack used to sleep. He'd forgotten he put it there.

Todd picks it up, heavy and bloodied, and takes it with him. Back to the basement door. Two steps down, a voice calls. Anthony calls him. "Daddy!" he shouts. "Can I have my surprise now?"

In the woods behind the house, a coyote rolls to its side, beige fur blending with the ground beneath half-fallen leaves. It breathes and winks away the gnats trying to drink the watery film from its eyes. Maybe the coyote hears Anthony's shout, for it stirs, just a bit; the world disturbed in a tiny ripple.

Todd leans to the basement doorway and yells harshly, "No!" Then, finding he is holding the statuette tightly, he relaxes himself and says, "Go back outside, now. I'll get you when it's time."

I'll get you when it's time. He pauses on the stair, but no door opens, so Anthony listened. Who doesn't love a surprise?

A tick has found its way into Anthony's flesh, inside his ear. It snuggles itself into the curve, where the blood is thin and scarce; it will have to wait awhile to be fed, and so it won't become fat and found and killed. It will take what it wants and fall away. Slowly, it will drink Anthony's warm blood, through a nick it makes with its mouth. It's a good home for this little thing, which lives on the life of the living.

Todd sets the statuette on a worktable, where the tools are in a metal box, and next to that a bag with gardening instruments. Hammer.

Weeder. Jigsaw. Hacksaw. Spade. Lock cutters. Garden shears. Screw-driver. Rake. Awl. Everything you would need to fix a problem or clear a plot. He goes back to Jack, Jack's body, and drags him up to the bin. Then Todd gets under Jack's weight and lifts Jack's legs, so now Jack's torso and head (with one good eye, one split eye) rest on the floor, and his feet are over the edge of the container, like he's stretching. But there's no tension in him. There's no blood rushing anywhere except the slow honey of dark blood thickly leaking out the back of his head past the air-clotted scab. Todd gets under Jack again and heaves up, holding him like a baby, like a fallen friend in war.

At the same time, a hawk comes to rest in a tree and watches Todd's son, playing on his own. Pretending to be something, making erratic movements. The bird tilts its head one way, then the other. Anthony is watched by the hawk and eaten by the tick, and tiny mites live in his eyebrows and lashes, and his father is holding a corpse now, in a cave in the ground beneath him.

When Jack is in the container, his knees bent, his head to the side, Todd stands and looks at him. This is the quietest peace he has ever seen. The moment when he looks upon Jack, and Jack's face does not stir.

and there will be
no resurrection

is the last line of the poem, which through all of this has sat in the book pressed shut on the shelf. It might be true, about the resurrection. No sunlight will reach the eyes of the dead to wake them. Then again, what does a poem know? It's only words in a book that will never be read again.

But as the night shows like spilled ink, like blood sinking into fibers of the carpet and settling there deep to stay, something has become true.

Things will be darker now, much darker now than they were before.

PART THREE

ONE

Where was Livia?

Well, the driver told her, she was passing through Springfield, and she'd be glad that she didn't have to stop there.

She knew Springfield. It had a Basketball Hall of Fame. It had a downtown that was always trying to do new things that never took. It had an old friend of hers who, in her fifties, had decided (her word) to become a lesbian. But it didn't look familiar, not on the highway away from the Hartford airport, not even in her memory.

"Why not?" Livia asked. She'd detected a twist of racism or classism or somethingism in the driver's comment; she wanted to push him into saying it.

"Oh, uh, no reason," he said to her from the front. "It's just not a place of note."

"And New Granard is?"

"Why'd you fly into Hartford instead of Boston if you're heading to

New Granard?" the driver said, changing the subject. "Out of curiosity. Is it better? Cheaper?"

It's none of your fucking business, she thought, and remained silent. But really, it was because she'd bungled the ticket. Now she was stuck in this long car ride together with a driver she'd committed herself to not talking to for the next three hours. She was tired and wanted a shower and had no idea what she'd do when she arrived in Todd's town.

She pulled out her phone and called Todd and it rang and rang. So she looked at pictures of the Basilica of Saint Anthony instead. She was drawn to it because of its name. Standing in the basilica she had realized that she didn't know what Saint Anthony was the saint of. Then she thought, Todd wouldn't know either. But her son might be a holy person when he got older, if holy people still existed by then. The basilica had three domes, like a family. It had a huge interior and a shining floor and solemn candlelight, all reflecting something.

"O Holy Saint Anthony, gentlest of saints," she whispered as the darkening New England woods rolled beside her, "your love for God and charity for His creatures made you worthy, when on earth, to possess miraculous powers. Encouraged by this thought, I implore you to obtain for me the custody of my son."

A prayer couldn't hurt, unless God actually existed and knew she didn't believe in Him. But it was something to hold on to. Something to do till she got there, a way to atone, with a wish.

They'd gone home together after meeting at Cavalier's Bookstore and Todd had been polite, almost, when they had sex. He looked up at her and seemed thankful. It frustrated her but also drew her in; she'd been overwhelmed by her attraction to him, but he didn't know how to use that. He never consumed her, there was no intensity or coarseness, no shock. But that was the sort of man she was supposed to be with, she'd thought back then, someone who couldn't hurt anyone.

But in the doldrum between meeting and pregnancy she found herself wanting to be not just held, but *overrun* with feeling. Again and again, this desire to be consumed would show. And the way it came was also the shape of what it wanted: waves. As she grew, he dwindled. He loved the thought of the baby then, and his mildness, she felt, was between the three of them. Sometimes she'd fight with him just to remind herself that he was holding something back. He'd close his eyes and clench his hands and open them all the way. Close, open. Close, open. What would happen if he showed her what was happening? She knew it wasn't right to push him to extremity, but she wanted him to be himself. Todd would touch her stomach and she'd recoil. *Hurry,* she'd thought each day to her baby. She wanted to have Anthony so she could leave Todd. But when Anthony came, tearing his way out of her so violently that she had to be sewn up after delivery, she couldn't connect to him either.

She couldn't blame Todd for letting her go; she'd suggested it from the dull and hollow cave of her constant depression, and when she left, urgeless, she didn't even kiss her son's big newborn head goodbye.

Outside, it was all woods. Dark green and orange this time of day. Blurred. In New England, none of the cities were big enough to make an impression. They were saturated at the edges with trees, until you hit the water, where you could look across to Europe.

After she left Todd and Anthony, she was off to Lisbon. Off to Venice. Off to harsh sun in the center of Nicosia. It wasn't a crime to run away, was it? Off to places that moved her, that introduced new faces, where consuming passions were the default, not something she had to provoke. She'd had the money, she always had. She should've done this instead of marrying Todd; staying with him for two years of dating, pregnancy, birth, divorce proceedings. But it wasn't until after she divorced Todd that she realized that she could've done it alone. She wondered if she could be thankful for that realization. But now he was raising her son with his boyfriend, she thought bitterly.

It wasn't that he had a boyfriend that bothered her. Or at least, if it were, she wasn't going to mull over her prejudices. It was that he didn't even think to let her know or to involve her. He didn't tell her that that's why they'd had sex so infrequently. He didn't say, *I deceived you.*

Sometimes when she would think about these things, an inner voice would rise that said it was all okay. Okay that she'd left, okay that she hadn't reached out almost at all, okay that he hadn't reached out to her very much either. She could reflect on the mismatch of the pieces. She wanted to be with her son, and she wanted to confront Todd for not letting her go before they conceived. She could even sometimes think that Anthony was better off, even though she needed him now. But that calm yet chiding voice had to be banished: she was already in motion. The car was on its way. Her son, raised by two people who didn't believe in consequences or honesty.

"I'm not stupid," she said quietly to the window. "I know I'm selfish, but I'm not stupid."

"What?" the driver asked. "Do you need something?"

Livia had no answer.

TWO

It's cold in the basement, and the container is airtight. A cold vacuum would slow things down. It would give Todd time to think.

The first thing he thinks is to get a pillow for Jack's head. Otherwise, Jack's cheeks and forehead and lips would darken from their current pallor into a full-faced bruise. Todd doesn't know how he knows this, but he can't bear the thought of Jack's face becoming unrecognizable. More unrecognizable. He goes up the stairs.

When he enters the kitchen, he peers into the backyard, and Anthony is gone.

The movement through slow time, the in-between of one heartbeat to the next, feels like a chasm. There aren't any thoughts, not like when Jack took Anthony to the beach and Todd woke to the empty room. Nothing fills him this time; he just moves. His body turns to the back door, a shudder runs him through. As he reaches for the doorknob, no. No, there is Anthony again, ducking under a small spice tree near the back, too low to the ground to be easily spotted. His son pops up like a plank held underwater, boisterous at the surface. Everything is okay. These are his nerves now. Will they always be? Todd turns around and goes upstairs and into the bedroom.

Will I cry? he thinks.

He pulls a pillow off his bed. It's the one with the differently colored pillowcase, the one with red stripes across it that he's had since childhood. He doesn't know why he picks this one, but halfway down the stairs he realizes that he will never use it again. This is Jack's pillow. He thinks, *I'll have to destroy it*, knows in his heart that he means, *I'll have to destroy everything.*

In the cold basement, he kneels down by Jack's side and slides one hand under Jack's head, which is not warm, not cold, but lingering in the mild and heavy. It's sticky where the blows were struck. The coagulating scab will cling to the pillowcase. It doesn't matter.

"Here," Todd says, lifting Jack's head, and with the other hand he puts the pillow underneath. "Here's your pillow." He stuffs it there. It's too wide for the container, and the edges curve against the sides, cradling Jack's head, as if Jack were sleeping and had wrapped the pillow around his ears to keep noise out. Jack's head is still uneven. Todd moves it toward himself a bit, trying to get Jack's face to turn slightly to the left so the split eye is less visible. He smooths the pillow. "Is that better?" Todd says, and hears it. A voice in the dark talking to Jack's body. It should sound out of place, but it doesn't. "Nothing is better," Todd says, trying out the voice in the dark again. "Nothing will be better."

He wonders again if he will cry right now, in this moment. What would that sound like? But the wondering exiles the possibility.

Instead of crying, he stands and walks over to the worktable and gets the pruning shears, then turns back, gets down, and holds up Jack's right hand. He puts his forehead against it and sits with this, the intimate knuckles of the dead. The forehead and the hand, like a prayer. He puts the hand down, reaches to the other side, and lifts up the left. Jack's body is getting stiff. Rigor mortis. The way the dead resist any movement, he thinks. As if the body needs to prove it's dead. And then he thinks of the times he's scolded Anthony for making faces. "If you make a face, it'll get stuck that way." It's what Todd's mom said to him when he was a boy. Is that saying an allusion to this? The dead stuck face? Jack's face is serene. It will stay this way till it melts.

On the ring finger, a pale circle where a ring once was. There's a movement, a slight movement, a tremble from Jack, and Todd jumps.

Hum. Hum. Hum.

No, not from Jack, from his own pocket. He doesn't look to see who it is or press the button to stop it, he lets the call terminate itself.

A reminder, though: Todd feels the front of Jack's pants. Jack's crotch has a small dark stain of piss on it. The phone is in his right pocket and Todd pushes his hand in, feeling the tightness of Jack's thigh against the fabric. Jack's legs are turned to the left, knees slightly bent, to fit him into the container. The phone glows when he withdraws it. It wants to be a living thing.

Linda. Linda. Linda. A glowing rectangle that doesn't belong here.

Fuck her, let her think I'm dead.

Todd takes it over to the workstation and grabs a hammer. He brings it down on the phone halfheartedly. He doesn't have the energy to strike a hard blow anymore, that energy has already found its form, like a flower opening into fruit. The phone bounces as he hits it. The screen cracks. The light still glows. He hits it again and shards scatter. Again, and its non-guts are exposed now. The little card inside nestled among the back half is revealed, a square fetus or brain, or both. He smashes it again. No one else is allowed down here. No one but Todd and Jack will ever be down here. The phone has always been lifeless, but now more so.

Back at Jack's body. Todd holds pruning shears with one hand, Jack's left hand with the other, and sticks Jack's stiffening ring finger between the bladed beak. He squeezes the turquoise-blue rubber handles and the finger comes off with a punctuated sound like *huck!*

Todd fishes the finger from where it's fallen. He's never held a finger in his hand like this, on its own. It looks like it wants to be sheltered, a little mouse, a little curve of flesh, of nail and soft blond hairs below the knuckle. A pale place where a ring was, above the pulpy site of amputated root. He puts it in his pocket.

"I'll come back soon," he says reassuringly. Then he pulls the lid on, pushing on it to evacuate the container of as much air as possible, and clasps the clasps.

There's no pause, there's no deliberation. This is what you do, that's what he knows without even thinking it. You say goodbye in pieces.

Later, when Anthony is sleeping, he takes the pieces of phone and flesh, mixed together in a bag, and he walks into the ocean, straight in, with his clothing on. The bag looks unworldly; he's been at it all with the hammer. The ocean doesn't reject him, but it might not want him either. It pushes on him, like it pushes everybody who enters. The ocean asks the questions in rhythms, "Are you sure? Are you sure? Do you want this? Do you want this?" until you're far enough out that it does the opposite, it pulls you in or floats you and holds you there. The ocean wants commitment.

He opens the bag and throws the blood and plastic and glass in all directions. He thinks of sharks and how they come out at night and how if one smelled this blood and traveled for him like a bullet, if it caught him by the leg, it would be all right. That would be the way of things, what was arranged for him here in the water.

But nothing comes for him. It's just a tiny bit of Jack, after all. A test to see if Todd can do this again and again until there's nothing left.

The pieces sink or float. Some will be taken by fish, others will dissolve.

"Okay," Todd says to himself breathlessly, standing in the ocean in his clothing at night. "Okay."

THREE

Todd collapsed at three; passed out on the couch with a toothbrush in his hand clutched to his chest like a cross. He'd soaked the carpet with cleaner and scrubbed. He'd mopped up the floor. He'd paced. He'd washed his face in the kitchen sink and washed his hands and changed his clothes and bagged the old ones. He'd opened the basement door and closed it without going down.

That is a separate time, he thought about the world beneath the house. *That is a separate place*. Keep it to itself, to its own. And keep the aboveground life running.

Up here could be sun and grass and work and breakfast and birds. Below would be Jack. The beach would be the meeting place of the two worlds, sprinkled with blood. If anything could handle two lives, it was the ocean.

The toothbrush had scoured the statuette, invading every groove of mane and muscle. He'd held the demigod and the lion under the tap, but they needed his help.

After washing the blood and flesh away, he reset the statuette again. He stopped noticing the toothbrush in his hand, the hand with which he'd struck the first blow. He didn't feel the toothbrush or the hand as he walked upstairs to Anthony, who was calling him.

"Daddy! Daddy!" Not urgent, but needy, as always. Of course, of course, that's what a father was for. He glanced at the clock in the kitchen and hiked the stairs, grateful, ultimately, for this morning call; he might have slept through and been late for work. But it was six-thirty a.m. There was still time, but he had to be quick.

Anthony was standing in front of the bathroom door in his pajamas.

"Go ahead," Todd said, "brush your teeth! You don't want stinky breath." It felt weird to say *stinky*, a child's word. It didn't fit anywhere.

Anthony stood on the bathroom sink step stool and pushed a coil of paste onto his brush. Then he turned and held out the toothpaste to Todd, who realized that the brush was in his hand. The bristles were stained pink now. He took the tube and put toothpaste on the brushes and waited for Anthony to finish.

"Bruff yur teef wiff me, Daddy," Anthony said as his mouth foamed up.

"No time," Todd said. "We're late, hurry up and go get dressed, Daddy has to take a shower."

Anthony spat and rinsed and ran back to his room. Todd set his toothbrush down and took his shirt off. He rinsed under his arms and used the bar of soap. He smelled like salt water, but not like blood and struggle, that had been washed away. He picked up the toothbrush again and put it in his mouth, then realized what he'd done. He stood in front of the mirror with it hanging there for a bit, hesitating. But he could only taste the mint paste. Life was normal, aboveground. It had to be. Quick now, quick. Move past the hesitation. No time to regret taking Anthony to school today. *It's a spiral*, Todd thought. *Don't spiral.* Anthony was a boy going to school and there was blood in Todd's mouth. He threw the toothbrush in the garbage and gargled with mouthwash.

He had to rush away from Anthony and Elaine Paige to get to work on time. *Is rushing like this suspicious?* he thought. Fear crept from the ground up into him. But no. People rush all the time in the morning.

He arrived and checked his mailbox on his classroom door, and before he'd sifted through the notices of sporting events and sign-ups and announcements he was supposed to make, the door opened, and in came the kids.

There wasn't a break until midday, in the extended quiet period for lunch. One of the papers instructed Todd to announce to each class that there were auditions for the winter play. But he hadn't seen this till just now. If he read it off to the rest of the classes, the morning ones who hadn't heard would complain that he hadn't read it to them. Better to lie. He folded up the sheet and put it in his backpack, so that the janitor wouldn't find it in the garbage can later.

He pulled out his phone and started to type, then it occurred to him that he should go to the library and use their computers instead.

He was lucky, there were only a few kids there. There was a mirror on the wall by the row of computers that reflected what was on the screens to the rest of the room. The kids would look at pornography otherwise, which was thought to be the worst thing a kid, especially a boy, could do with a computer. If there were no images, he doubted anyone would pay attention to what he was reading. He typed.

how does the body decay

First the larynx, he read. The gristle of it would dissolve away underneath the neck skin. Then Jack's stomach, which would take longer. Jack's intestines and spleen, his liver, his brain. His heart. All of this would be happening at once, with small simultaneous notes, but the dissolution would be shifting its emphasis as it went, from one part to another, from the lungs to the kidneys to the bladder.

He was right, he discovered, that it would all take longer in the container—which he realized must only be partially airtight, but not fully—in the cold of the basement. But he would still have to be quick.

how to cut up a body

This revealed less. All the accounts he found about doing what he needed to do said the same thing: It was strenuous work. It would take a certain kind of determination. But all of the sites were about doing it quickly, mostly detailing people who had done it in a hurry to avoid being caught. He wouldn't be able to be fast. He had a life; he had a job. He couldn't do it all at once; he had a son.

One of the resources he found explained how to cut up a body for food. (Did sticking that toothbrush in his mouth make him a cannibal?) They were a nihilist group who sold pins and bumper stickers that read SAVE THE PLANET, KILL YOURSELF. They also advocated mandatory abortions and starvation.

Someone was walking over. Sahir waved to him. Todd leaned forward to obscure the text from the mirror behind him.

"Hi, Todd," Sahir said. "How are you settling in?" He was taller than Todd but seemed smaller.

"I'm fine, fine. I left the computer at home. My computer."

"Do you need help with these?"

"No," Todd said, and smiled. "I think everyone knows how to use a computer now."

Sahir frowned. He was wearing a fall-colored checked shirt and light khakis. "You're right," he said. Then he gestured to the rows of books. "Those are what people don't know how to use."

There was a pause.

"The English teacher and the librarian," Sahir said. "It could be a novel."

"Hey, Sahir, can I get back to this, I've got to finish up a few things here? Let's talk sometime soon, though?"

Todd glanced down at the screen. *We are Jainist Extremists, but where the Jains still preserve their own lives . . .*

Would it be a lifetime of these moves now? Using the school computer instead of his phone, lying to his colleagues, concealing his thoughts, erasing his steps.

"Ah, it's fine," Sahir said. "Anyway, the English teacher and the librarian couldn't be a novel. It's not interesting enough!" He laughed low and lonely as he walked away.

. . . we advocate sitting in a corner and fasting till you blink out. Give the rest of the world a chance to live: make way. The website looked outdated and clunky, maybe they'd all followed through. What a shame for them, then, that the planet was still going as it was.

There was a tab that read "MURDER" and Todd clicked on it.

Readers may find it surprising that Planetary Cleanse Organization does not support murder. Murder is unethical not because it ends a human life but because it tends to promote the drive to live more, to populate, to strengthen the desperate need to celebrate life.

He'd have to break the bones first; he couldn't just saw Jack's limbs off.

He'd have to break the bones by standing and pulling on Jack's legs till he made a small fracture, or by fixing them in place and hammering them, and then sawing at the spot of the break. He could twist the arms out of their sockets, the way a kid would pop his shoulder out in football.

As always, he left early, right after his last class, because he had to pick up Anthony. Exhausted, he hoped to leave unnoticed, not thinking of what was ahead but internalizing the feeling: it needed to happen, it needed to be done.

At his car, his phone rang. Livia again.

"No fucking thank you," he said to it, and tossed it into the passenger seat, where it continued to hum.

FOUR

Livia watched Todd decline her call. She was sitting in the red rental car, which she realized she'd need soon after the driver dropped her off at the Shrewsbury Hotel. She would learn to be better with thinking ahead, with organizing, with taking care of things, she told herself at the rental car office, two towns away. She'd need to.

When he threw the phone into the car seat she saw, for the first time, the unambiguity of Todd's dismissal. That wasn't something you could teach a child, she wondered, was it? She'd made a mistake leaving Anthony those years ago, but he wasn't so old that he would remember it and hold it against her forever, was he? She could change the course of things now, if she tried, if he hadn't been turned into someone like Todd: mild, unenthusiastic.

Todd's car turned left from the lot and she pursued slowly. It was pretty in New Granard, but not beautiful. The trees were dense. One could only see a little way in. It was odd, after Venice and Grado and Positano, to be on a coast like this. Maybe it was a good place for a child to grow up. She'd been moved and moved and moved by her parents. From Detroit to Coney Island to Mill Valley, second-tier places, she felt. That's where her mother bought and sold big real estate and then abandoned ship. She remembered thinking her mother would never slow down until she died. But it happened sooner than anyone wanted, when Livia was fifteen, and she stood at the edge of Mount Tam with her father and threw the ashes into the wind. So even in death, her mother didn't stop moving. Livia sometimes thought of her molecules, still in the air, becoming people's breaths, first and final. Maybe she could stay close to Todd, sometimes. But she wanted Anthony to see the world with her. The good cities. The beautiful ones.

Todd's car slowed in front of her. They'd come to a stop sign. The two cars lingered, and she knew that he could look into his rearview and see her idling behind, and that everything she was going to start would start here, now, on the street. They could even make eye contact in his rearview. She turned her head to the side. She could get up right now and walk to his driver's side and knock on his window, she thought.

Then, thankfully, as Todd's car went on past the intersection, a white car turned from the cross street and moved between them.

Maybe she would take Anthony in the summers.

She had no plan. She knew she should have one, but she didn't, except to make something happen that would lodge Anthony back in her life. Then she'd figure out the rest.

She could stay close to Todd *if* he was honest. *If* he told her—finally!— that he was gay, with David, whoever David was; all she knew of him was that he was rude and he had talked to her like she was nobody. She supposed Todd would have to be honest when she showed up, it wasn't like he would hide David away, not now that they'd spoken.

Todd turned left ahead and when the white car went straight along, Livia turned left too. She saw him pull into Sheckel Elementary and hang there with other parents as the kids moved from the school doors to the cars and buses. She drove past smoothly, then turned around and waited on the other side of the street.

A woman with blond hair, holding a little boy's hand, approached Todd. Livia was struck by the fact that she didn't recognize the boy at all. He skipped but somehow still looked sullen. He slowly hugged the teacher and then waved. She saw him get in the car. Todd didn't get out of the car to meet him. *I would have gotten out,* she thought. *That's how you greet your child.* She would have hugged him. She would have said hello to the teacher. She would have shown this boy she did not recognize excitement to see him, not just waited for him to open up a door and then speed away. She would've, she would've, she would've.

Instead, she sat in the car and cried.

FIVE

In the basement, at night, in the room beneath the world, Todd is regarding Jack's body in a bin.

"Hi," Todd says quietly.

He puts his hand where Jack's heart is. There's no beat, of course, that's the promise of death, it gives the body its first and last and only chance to stop moving entirely. Every movement now would be caused by Todd and whatever bacteria made their way into Jack, or the ones that were already in his body, exploring new possibilities. Todd realized that he was bringing his own microorganisms down here with him in his breath and hands and hair. And that was part of why Jack would decompose: because Todd touched him.

He undoes Jack's tie. It's his own tie, he remembers. Though it seems now to really belong to Jack. He pushes into the knot and slides his fingers into it until there's leeway and then he tugs till the tie slides through Jack's collar and Todd is sitting with the tie dangling in his hand, like a flat dead red snake.

"It's yours now," Todd says, and holds the tie to his face. He'll have to burn it. He'll have to burn all the clothing.

He sets it down and leans over and reaches into the bin and unbuttons Jack's shirt, slowly from the top down. When he opens the shirt, he sees Jack's body is pale, only flushed with color in the arms and neck and face. Anywhere the sun touched while he was alive. The little golden hairs on his body are soft, and Jack's belly is soft because he can't flex now, can't show the ripple of abdominal muscle. But Todd can feel it underneath as he runs his hand up and down Jack's belly and chest and then into the right sleeve of Jack's shirt to pull his arm out of it. Todd struggles with the weight.

"Help me with this," he says. Then he laughs a little, then closes his eyes so tightly against what is happening that a quick pulse of headache runs from his temples forward into his face. He braces himself and pulls Jack's body toward him, releasing the right arm from the sleeve.

And then, while he's holding on to Jack, Todd pulls him forward. Just for a moment, just so their foreheads are touching. Just so Todd's breath is warming Jack's body's face so that Todd can feel his exhale circulating back to him. He blinks and feels his right eyelash brush the crushed-up and thick patch of Jack's left eye.

"We're going to do this together, okay?" Todd says. "We're going to do this. You and me." He rocks a little, like he's comforting a child, or someone in mourning.

"You and me, okay?" he says quietly.

Todd puts his cheek against Jack's cold cheek and his hand on the back of Jack's head, which is uneven now, smashed as it is. Nothing is jagged, but it's mottled, unnatural.

Holding Jack, he slides the other corpse arm out of the shirt, and then pulls the shirt so it comes out from under Jack's belt.

Todd thinks about how Jack hadn't even yet untucked his shirt when it had happened. How he'd looked so handsome, sitting on the porch when Todd came home.

There is a saw nearby. There is a hammer. There are the shears. There are bags and scissors. This will be the last time Jack's body is composed.

He lays Jack's shirtless body back down in the bin, careful, like putting a child to bed. He reaches in to take off his belt. When he pries the buckle backward and unhooks the prong, he starts to talk, only dimly aware of the story, how it undoes itself from his voice.

"Do you remember," he begins, "when you laughed at me? In the shower at gym class? When our classes were merged together?"

He unthreads the belt from the loops.

"I was . . . scared of you," he says, much more quietly. "I knew we'd be in the locker room together, and I knew Mr. Wolfe would make us shower."

He pictures the baseball field across the street from the school, how on nice days they'd cross together and play. Todd didn't hate baseball. And the good thing about it was that when they weren't waiting to bat, they were all far away from each other. There were a few too many boys when the two classes were merged, the boys outside playing baseball, the girls doing something else, wherever they were. And the class lasted almost two periods. So some boys were stuck in useless positions. Right field. Umpire's assistant. Alternate pitchers.

It was muggy and they all ran back sweaty together, laughing and spitting on the street. In the locker room where they stripped, Todd felt a nausea of anxiety, as he often did, about getting undressed. Some of the other boys were totally at ease. Brian Young would walk around with his ass out sometimes as a joke, and guys would fall out of their front boxer flaps and they'd tease each other. It was always a place of potential humor or trouble or both. The shower room wasn't big enough for all the boys, and Mr. Wolfe walked in with them at first, telling one team to wash first and the other to wait. Todd sat on a bench as the first group, Jack's group, stripped and got in together, loud, their voices echoing off the tiles. Some of the boys left their underwear on, which wasn't uncommon, no one said anything. Afterward, they peeled their dripping underwear off under their towels and threw them in plastic bags in their backpacks.

Todd pushes Jack's legs back, so that the bottom half of Jack's body is raised up now, and then he reaches beneath the back of Jack's pants waist and pulls. No, no, wait. The shoe first. He unties the right shoe, like Jack is drunk again. Like he needs to be cared for. When he tugs the first shoe off, he looks at it and slips his hand into it. It's warm. It shouldn't be, but it is. Todd hurriedly takes Jack's right sock off and touches Jack's foot. Cold. How the shoe held a false warmth in its hollow is beyond him, but he checks it again and now it too is cold. He undoes the other shoe and slides the left sock away from Jack like snakeskin.

In the locker room, Todd looked down at the floor, and then stood with the rest, who were all naked but him, in his gray briefs with a white waistband. The warm shower water ran over his head and his pale skin and his closed eyes and he was trying not to think too much about what was happening, surrounded by boys, water firing across them, all the showerheads on at once, so loud that it was one flash after another, after another, like the ocean. He was trying not to think about how they'd all been forced in there by Mr. Wolfe, to be around these other stripped boys, and how it would be over in just a few minutes, and then a voice found its way through the shower room doorway and filled it, bouncing off the walls over the punctuated hisses of shower water.

"Hey, why is Todd in his underwear!" Not a question, but a shout. Jack's voice. Todd's heart turned over. A few of the boys looked his way, but it wasn't picked up and didn't catch. And then everything was back to normal again except Todd's heart pounding and pounding. He wasn't sure it was over until he was dry and dressed and had escaped back into the school hallway.

"I always wondered why you said that," Todd says. He raises up Jack's body and reaches beneath the waistband, sliding his hands beneath the pants and underwear, and pulls. Jack's thick thighs and muscled calves slowly come out of the pants legs, and Todd sees that there's some shit on Jack's ass. And Todd thinks about standing over Anthony when he was a baby and lifting his son's legs and pushing him in half like this to clean him. And he will, eventually, go get a towel with warm water. He will clean Jack's body slowly and with care. But for now, he finishes removing Jack's pants, and Jack's legs fall one by one, dead, into the container. Jack is naked, and Todd regards him.

Jack's feet. His toes. The hair on his legs. The discoloration on the back of his legs, a shade that cradles the sides of his thighs and lower back and shoulders, not fully creeping up the sides of him, but not hidden either. Jack's scrotum and penis; not *balls*, not *dick*, that's not the name for them now. The pubic hair above them. Jack's belly button. His chest. His ribs where his heart isn't beating. His nipples and neck. His shoulders. Jack's calm dead face. His hair. His naked body. Todd breathes. Something is threatening to overwhelm him. But then the feeling goes away.

And then he steps one foot into the bin and stands it on Jack's right shin to brace it. And he bends over and holds Jack's right foot and then at the same time brings his own foot down on the bone and pulls upward, again and again until there is a small squealing sound of tiny fracture. The birth of a jagged crack inside for the teeth of the waiting saw.

SIX

On the road to school there was a dead groundhog, and then, a little later, a part of a raccoon. Anthony spotted both and stared at them, enthralled, turning his head to see more. Todd, after the raccoon, stopped the car for fear that he'd throw up. He'd rolled the window down. He was tired, his arms were so sore that he could barely lift Anthony into the car.

The images of the groundhog, on its back with closed eyes to the sun and its long, yellowed, front teeth, followed him to his desk, where he sat with a copy of *A Separate Peace*. The book had a different cover now than when he was in school. Now it lacked the image of a sullen boy standing by a tree. There was a cartoonish tree instead, a silhouette of two boys, and the title floated across the top in a banner. No indication of the war in the book, the failed operation, the ways that boys cleave to each other.

Todd's head ached at his temples. The kids in his homeroom told them they were here as he said their names. He barely looked up. Then the bell, and they left loudly, and a few minutes later his students came in with their bags and phones and gum. They took their seats loudly, the metal legs of the chairs groaning as they scraped across the floor. They would all talk till he talked, he knew, they would never be silent on their own, they were laughing and would keep laughing. *I should've cut the leg off at the thigh instead*, he thought, considering his sore shoulders.

"Tell me about chapter eight," Todd said. They told him about chapter eight. It resonated with them when Finny said that there was no war happening, that it was all a conspiracy. It resonated because, they told Todd, they don't trust anything anymore.

"How can you know if anything exists?" Colleen Miles said, and someone behind her groaned.

"Yeah, what if Colleen doesn't exist?" another student said.

"No, think about it," she said, "everything is, like, not real. On screens. If someone wanted to delete all the books and the music and everything, they could just do it."

Todd listened to them go on with each other. This was something that had come up before. How everything they knew could be erased. With magnets, or by going to the bottom of the sea to cut the cables of the internet, or by sunspots. They're worried or excited that nothing will last or that nothing exists in the first place.

"They love each other," Todd said suddenly, and the kids went quiet. "Gene and Finny. But they have no idea how to handle it. That's real."

Banner Bolland laughed a little at the unbearable thought of it. Todd looked at him.

"You think it's funny to be in love?" Todd said. "Have you ever been in love?" Banner laughed again.

"Come up here," Todd said.

The class shifted, and one of the other boys put his head into his hands. Banner stood with a smirk, tall, maybe dumb, and walked to the front looking at Todd.

"Face the rest of the class," Todd said, and Banner did. "Tell the class you love them," Todd said.

They all erupted at that; it was the funniest thing that could have happened.

"I loooovvvve yooouuu," Banner said in a gooey infantilizing voice.

Todd stood through the subsequent laughs, waiting for the last of them to drip down. Finally Banner Bolland looked at him.

"Now say it seriously," Todd said. A few giggles from the rows.

"And you all?" Todd said, and took a step forward. "You can be quiet. Because it's just as hard to hear it as it is to say it. So you can shut up and listen to him."

One of the girls, Abby Colm, still had a smile on her face. "You can stop smiling now, Abby," Todd said. Her face turned red, then they were all still. There was nothing but the room of them breathing with each other. Todd looked at Banner Bolland again and raised his eyebrows. Banner's face scrunched up and his head moved back a little.

"Go. Ahead," Todd said.

Banner looked across the field of eyes. He looked at them, into them. They needed him to say it to move on, to resume class, otherwise this moment would hold. Banner Bolland welled up. He breathed them all in.

The room was quiet and waiting. Todd closed his eyes. He reached to put his hand on his desk, dizzy.

SEVEN

Once, in Bologna, in an apartment down a crowded alley, Livia had a tarot reading, and the card reader kept pulling the coins. Two cards in a row, *Pentacolo*. But Livia had all the money she needed. She told this to the reader, who sneered at her and then looked up to the ceiling. When she looked back, she said, *Fondamento*. Home. And then she pulled another card, and it was a maiden holding open the jaws of a lion. Todd had brought home a statuette like that once, except it was Heracles, not this woman. The room wasn't dark or decorated with anything, it was austere. A plastic table with metal legs. The woman was smoking. The next card, coins again.

And here, now, there were groups of sand dollars drawn on the board in pink chalk. Each one had a number above it: 3. 5. 7.

Anthony and the other children spoke in unison, responding as if at mass, as if they were echoing the words of something holy.

"Sand. Dollar."

"How many?" Ms. Paige asked, and pointed to the number.

It would be *dollaro di sabbia*, she thought. An animal named for grounding and coinage. A living pentacle. There were little workbooks on each child's desk, and each was open to a page with a drawing of a sand dollar. Each desk with a book with a pentacle on it.

Their eyes were on Ms. Paige. Anthony was fidgeting, and Livia stood in the silent hall, looking through the window in the door. He was so big, she thought, but so little too. The little chair he sat on, the little shirt, the little pants. That smallness caused a *longing*; overwhelming.

The sand dollars were a sign, she thought. From Saint Anthony? She wanted to hold him. She thought about opening the door. They all started to write letters in their workbooks, the way children do; not really writing so much as drawing each character carefully. The little girl with tight braids sitting next to Anthony saw Livia and stared.

Livia waved, folding her hand in half and then opening it again three times, a child's wave. The girl waved back once, shyly. Then Livia pointed at Anthony. The girl looked to her left, then looked back, not understanding.

"Can you *get* him," Livia said aloud, impatient. The girl looked dumbstruck for a second, then turned and tugged on Anthony's sleeve.

"Can I help you with something," a strong voice said to Livia, and she jumped. She turned to the man in the hall with her. "Do you need something?" He was taller than her and intense, with a patchy beard. Livia wondered how they could let a man like this in here with children.

"My son is in there," Livia said, surprised, proud, to hear it come from her own voice without hesitation. "Anthony. Nasca." She said his last name with some irritation.

"I haven't seen you here before," he said. "I'm Ed Williams."

She didn't say anything.

"The principal," he said. "And if you don't know that, you need to come with me."

Livia glanced back into the classroom, and Anthony was looking up, right at her. She put her hand on the doorknob, and Principal Ed Williams reached out to stop her.

"Don't put your hand on me," she said in a strained whisper. She didn't want Anthony to see her face in anger or desperation. It wasn't fair.

"Do you want me to call the police?" he said.

Livia let go and said, "I'm his mother."

"Mr. Nasca is a teacher in the school district, and we know he's a single parent."

Single, Livia thought. So Todd hadn't told them he was living with a man either. She followed the principal down the hall.

EIGHT

"You know, I used to have dreams about everybody, Logan and Rick and Justin Geiger. And some of the girls too. I used to have dreams about them. The . . . locker room. Or being in class with them, the parking lot. Still a teenager. But, I don't know why, you never showed up in my dreams. You never made an appearance. You were just . . . gone. I guess I knew I'd see you again."

Todd looks over his shoulder at Jack's face. Todd is sitting with his back against the container, on the cold basement floor. His muscles are too tired to do much work. There's a flat, almost plant smell now, not overwhelming, but there, a faint acrid urine scent. Jack's body is missing a leg now.

"So maybe that wasn't . . . I mean, maybe that's why I let you in. Because I knew you were going to show up at some point. Life couldn't keep going on without us bumping into each other. Or you finding me, I guess." There are cuts on Todd's hands from when he slipped with the saw on Jack's left wrist. He was holding Jack below the elbow, trying to saw into the tendons. The hands, he knows from every crime show he's ever seen, would be identifiers. The hands, the teeth, the face. They all had to be totally pulverized. Todd's arms were so weak from the night before, and he was so tired, that he pushed the saw forward blindly a bit too far and grazed his opposite index finger with a tooth of it. His blood opened up and rolled down Jack's forearm, the rivulet of it pooling in the gash Todd had cut there. His warm blood pulsing in Jack's cold body. That's when he stopped, sucked on his finger, and sat down.

"But I went to our ten-year reunion and then the dreams just stopped. Livia made me go, although she wouldn't go with me. At a fire hall, of all places. I didn't stay long, I stepped in, said hello to a few people. They all seemed sort of sad, I guess. Fatter, mostly. Older. A lot of them still lived there. I walked in, said hi, then walked out and called Livia and said, 'Mission accomplished,' and then, you know, I stopped thinking of them." He sighs. "Livia gave that to me. She . . . helped me with that." He thinks of the phone, thinks of how Livia's been calling, thinks he will have to deal with her at some point, and how his anger with her has been rising, but why? Maybe it's not fair. "Maybe I'm only mad at her because you were mad at Linda. Or something. I wonder what Linda is doing now. Maybe there's a search out for you. That's why I have to be thorough. Have to be thorough, Todd."

He picks up some pliers and looks at them. A finger or two; he could do that tonight.

"Hannah Grace died," he says sorrowfully. "They talked about her at the reunion. She'd died maybe five, six years after we graduated. She was with some guy who was beating her up. They were married, I think. I don't know who he was. He was hitting her, and I guess one night she went to sleep and just didn't get up. That was it. Maybe organ failure because he hit her, I don't know. Someone said to me that they were sorry to hear it, that it must have been hard for me. But I didn't even *know*. So I just said, yes, it was sad, it was horrible. I pretended I'd found out

158

just like the rest of them. They must have thought that things were . . . normal? For me. That everything after you showed up was just *normal*. That I went back to hanging out with Hannah and Justin or whatever, even after school ended. Even before it ended. Justin was there, he said hi, no big deal. When I got home, I looked Hannah up online and there was one of those old clunky websites. A memorial to her. And I saw that and I felt . . . you know? I didn't feel much. And I didn't really think of her again. I started to look you up then, I remember that. And I stopped myself. I couldn't even be *sad* anymore because all those people weren't even real people anymore. They were just dreams, and then at the reunion they were like strangers. You eclipsed all of them, you took up all the space."

He stands and looks at Jack and raises his voice.

"All because *you* were fucked up. Because . . ." Then he realizes he is shouting at the person he killed. Then he forgets that too and sits down.

"I didn't know about your mom. I wish I'd known what happened. My parents are still alive, though I don't really talk to them anymore. I mean, where *were* they my whole life anyway? And then when I got married to Livia, they came to the wedding and Dad said he was 'relieved.' At the fucking wedding. And then when Livia left me, they got angry. So life since then has been this big ocean with me and Anthony in it. Floating on a raft together. Which is fine. Or maybe like a play. You know how plays only ever have a few characters, and everything that's happening in them happens in . . . real time. It all unfolds and unfolds and unfolds. Just those few people. That's what it was like on the beach. The play was running, and you walked onstage."

He trails off and takes a breath.

He picks up the shears and stands. And then cuts off a finger on the hand below the sliced-open wrist. And then another. And then another. They pop off and are ready to be smashed to pulp and fragment.

Everything, now, has its own horrible gesture of drama.

NINE

Banner Bolland's head emerged past the doorframe. He knocked lightly and Todd looked up. It was one-thirty. His body was still sore, but he knew he could do more tonight. If not, maybe in the morning.

He didn't say anything, and Banner walked in.

"Mr. Nasca," Banner said. His typical obnoxious tone was gone. Todd's desk was a confused scattering of papers, which he started to gather as Banner approached.

"What?" Todd asked. "What's up, Banner?"

"Nothing, I . . ." He stopped. "Never mind."

The papers all came together in a pile, and Todd grabbed the side and stood them up and leveled the edges. There. It was in order now.

"No, no, go ahead."

"Listen," Banner said. "The other day wasn't . . .

Todd waited.

"It wasn't . . ."

Sahir stepped into the classroom then, cutting everything off.

"Oh, sorry," he said. "Bad time?"

"No, not a bad time," Todd said. And then, to Banner, "Is it?"

Banner looked to Todd, then to Sahir. There was a small, shaking moment.

"I'll wait in the hall," Sahir said.

"No, no, it's okay, go ahead," Todd said, hoping that Banner would let it alone, until it dissolved in him like a splinter.

"I think it was *fucked* up, okay?" And his eyes got heavy with tears.

"Whoa!" Sahir said. "*Banner.*"

Todd stood. "You know, it's your own fault. I'm trying to teach you this book, and I know, *I know* not all of you read it. I'm not an idiot. And the kids who did, they might actually be invested in it. Did you stop to consider that? That you laughing takes them out of the experience? And how many of you even feel anything about any book anymore, and there you go, erasing the feeling."

"But—"

"So I balanced it out."

"What did you do?" Sahir said to Banner, trying to find a foothold.

"They all think I'm . . . they all think it's so funny now," Banner said, deflated.

"They'll get over it. You'll get over it too," Todd said. "Anyway, what do you want me to do about it? You're dealing with the consequences of your actions." *Consequence*, he thought, and then sat back down.

Banner was frozen, there was nothing to do but take it. Finally he shook his head and said, "This is so fucked up. This is so *fucked up.*"

"Hey!" Sahir said, but Banner hurried out. Just the two of them, then. Sahir laughed a little. "I guess it *was* a bad time."

Todd didn't say anything.

"This is normal. You're new, they're going to see how far they can go."

"Sahir, I think I'm losing it," Todd said suddenly, and then regretted how much that gave away.

"Losing what?" He put his hand on Todd's shoulder. After a minute, he said, "Up until high school, I went to school in Sri Lanka. You wouldn't have ever spoken to a teacher in . . . any way, really. You sang the Christian songs in the morning, you listened to the lectures all day, you did your work, you took your tests. I'm not sure if that was better or worse. But it's different now, I think sometimes the kids, they think of themselves as customers or something. And the parents do too."

"I don't know," Todd said.

"How was he in here?"

"What?"

"I mean, he can't have had a hall pass that lasts that long. I can go find him and have him sent to the office for that if you want. I'm the librarian, so I don't have to see him every day. It doesn't matter if he likes me or not."

"No, no. It's fine."

"What happened?"

Todd shifted a little, and Sahir withdrew his hand, as if he'd just remembered it. "I heard him say 'faggot' a little while back. I've been holding it against him."

"He said—"

"I guess it doesn't mean anything anymore. He wasn't calling anyone that, it was just a nothing word. He said he was joking."

"Even if it was a joke, it wasn't a joke. Obviously the word has a history, but besides that, it seems harmless, but last year we had to scrub a swastika off the side of the building. The whole, um, structure of these things is that people think they're not happening, or that when they happen, they're not hurting anyone, really. But there's always something right beneath the surface."

"Sorry," Todd said vacantly.

"For what?"

"Ah, I mean . . . Well, did you want something?"

"Oh, just to see how things were getting on," Sahir said. "You seemed—I don't know if stressed is the right word?—in the library."

Todd let out a quick exhale, like a laugh, and shook his head faintly.

"You don't have to forgive all of them just because they're kids," Sahir said. "That sounds harsh, but it's true. I know you were a teacher before, but middle school, right? Here they're sort of deepening who they are. So they all have their own personalities."

"We should help mediate the damage," Todd said.

"Yes, well. For some of them it will take years before they find a better version of themselves, you know? No matter what we do. We only get this short little stretch to be around them. Not all their personalities are forgivable."

The bell rang out, and Sahir patted Todd on the shoulder again and the school day went on, running itself aground.

When he got to Sheckel to get Anthony, Elaine asked him if he could get out of the car.

"Sorry, I know it's weird, but could you? Could we have a moment?"

Anthony was in the passenger seat, and Todd and Ms. Paige stood behind the car to talk.

"I don't know why they didn't tell me until today," she said.

"What?"

"And I don't know why they didn't call you. They wanted *me* to say something. It's typical . . ."

"Elaine," Todd said impatiently. His jaw hurt.

"Sorry, sorry. Well. I guess your wife? Livia? She's been here. You didn't tell me that you were married . . ."

She continued talking, but Todd could barely hear the sounds, much less make out the words. There was only so much, only so much, he thought. The other children jogged by, happy to meet their parents. Nothing was happening to them; they were on some track from here to teenage years to adulthood to marriage to death. There would be no interruptions like this, no murder and the need for another murder now, to find Livia, to dash her head against some stone or push her from a precipice, to hit her with his car—

"Todd?" She touched him, like Sahir had touched him earlier, on the shoulder, with her one free hand, the other holding papers. Everyone wanted to console him without even knowing what was going on.

"Sorry," he said. "Ex-wife. She's . . . she's nobody."

Elaine reared back a bit.

"No, I mean. That sounds so harsh. She . . ." He poked his head around to be sure Anthony couldn't hear him. "She ran out on us right after he was born. Did he see her? Did he talk to her?"

"No, no," Elaine said. "At least, I don't think so. I guess she was lingering outside, and Ed saw her."

"He wouldn't recognize her anyway," Todd said.

"Well, Ed threatened to call the police on her, then she said she was your wife, and he was so confused, I guess, that he let her go. At the end of the day, he told me, and I said you didn't have a wife. I'm sorry to have to tell you about this. But now I know what she looks like and so does the staff and Anthony's other teachers. I don't think she'll come back. Is she . . ." Elaine fumbled for a word. "Is she safe?"

"She's a bad person," Todd said. "She's not a monster." And as he said this, the tension released. It was true, after all, wasn't it? The images of pushing her, of hitting her with his car, left as quickly as they had arrived.

"Okay," Elaine said. Todd turned back to get in the car. "Oh wait." She handed a few drawings to Todd. "His drawings. You never get a break, do you? From your school to our school, then home with a kid. I don't have any. Never married," she said, and laughed a little hopefully. "So I guess I get a break when I get home."

Todd looked at the drawings. First a fish and a sea urchin and what looked like a sand dollar, under a line of raised points, the blue crayon surface of the water, jagged like saw teeth. The second drawing was of a dog, a Scotty scribbled out in black.

"Do you have a dog?" she asked.

"No," he said.

"Oh, I was hoping to meet him," Ms. Paige said, and laughed. "*And your little dog too,*" she said in a witch voice, then said, "Oh God, dumb, Elaine. Sorry. I don't mean to invite myself over."

Todd ignored her. He was looking at the next drawing. He was frozen.

A boy. A man. And another man.

"Oh yes, who *is* that anyway?" Elaine said.

"He's . . ." Todd couldn't finish.

" 'Jack, I know," Elaine said. "He's shown up in a bunch of drawings. But who's Jack?"

TEN

Livia sat up in the bed, legs stretched out across the dull maroon comforter, the TV on. She hated this place. The maroon was to cover up shit stains and blood from fucking, probably. Why were hotels in small American towns like this? The lights were fluorescent, never really illuminating the room, just giving the illusion of it.

On the TV, a hyena stood in front of a dead wildebeest and growled at circling lions.

It was too much, she knew. Today had been too much. The normal thing would be to talk to Todd. But he wouldn't talk to her.

It was the same when they'd fought during their marriage. She'd be screaming and he'd shut down a bit, and she had to explain that screaming was *normal*, didn't the Italians scream at each other all the time? Didn't she and her ex-boyfriend from Lebanon shout until they were spent? But Todd would walk away. Once he even said, "I'm not going to validate your moral universe." It sounded like something his therapist told him, if he had been in therapy. She didn't know if he'd ever gone, sitting in a room with another person, talking as if no one were there; she wasn't sure it would do Todd any good. But provocation hadn't worked either. What, now?

Her own attempts at therapy had been halfhearted until this latest therapist, the one who told her to watch her own thoughts without judgment, to see how they rose and fell. Instead of *rise* and *fall*, though, Livia decided to see which thoughts made her want to run, and which ones she could sit with. Therapists, tarot card readers, books, prayers. All of them worked on the idea that something was missing. She was unhealthy and needed to be healthy; or she was unequipped to deal with the future, and she needed to be equipped; she didn't know enough; she wasn't innocent enough. *He's my son*, she thought. It was okay to let that override all the questions, wasn't it? What could make more sense than her wanting her son?

She stood and went into the austere yellow bathroom and looked in the mirror. Maybe she would go out? No. No. And anyway, where would she go?

She had his address now; she could stop by his house.

The principal had unwittingly shown it to her, when, in the office, he'd opened a file with Todd's info and said, "Tell me your address." But he was pointing at it on the paper with his index finger! He had done it for the same reason, she knew, that he had chosen to believe Livia was Todd's wife, and why he hadn't called the police. He'd rather give the address away with his errant index finger than continue the confrontation. People would do all sorts of things, unconsciously, to avoid trouble. When she was pregnant with Anthony, she'd read a story about a family whose child went missing and, years later, welcomed an adult into their house who looked nothing like him, just pretending to be their kid. It was a mutual delusion.

She didn't want to be deluded anymore. Maybe it was hard to know, as her therapist had said, if she was seeking in Anthony something she felt her life lacked, or if she really should be there for him. But it didn't matter anymore. The feeling wasn't delusion, the feeling was what mattered: a longing to be there for Anthony.

Who was she, who could she be, if there were no good options?

She changed the channel. There was a dog show on, and a man leading a pure white German shepherd around the ring. People in the room next to her were talking, their voices coming through the wall as a low blotched hum.

In the information box on the screen, by the text next to the dog's name, there was a little star in a circle, indicating he'd won an award before.

Call again, she thought. *Call right now.*

And just like that, her phone rang.

"Hello—"

"You came to the school?" Todd said harshly.

"Yes, I'm sorry, I—"

"You want me to get a fucking restraining order? *What are you doing here?*"

She tried to be calm. "You wouldn't return my calls."

"What do you want, Livia? You want your life back? You *left*. If you're going to keep coming around, I'll have you arrested."

"Arrested? Todd, don't you think it's funny that the principal thought we were married? Are you hiding your boyfriend from him?"

"My . . . Livia, I don't have a fucking boyfriend."

"No?"

"No, I'm . . . I'm dating somebody, a woman."

"Who?"

"It's none of your business, leave us alone."

"I don't believe you," Livia said.

"It doesn't matter if you believe me or not anymore, don't you get that?"

"You want Anthony to grow up being bullied," she said.

"What?"

"Two dads," Livia said. "No mom. No one to even teach him how to . . . have feelings . . ." She couldn't articulate anything anymore. She was trying to hurt him, trying anything now. It wasn't fair that it had to be this way.

"It's not like that at school anymore. It's . . . Nobody cares . . ."

"Oh, so there *is* someone, then—"

"No, Livia, there is no one else," Todd said. Then, quickly, "Except the person, the woman, I'm dating—"

"People always care, Todd, even if they say they don't."

Everything was quiet for a second except the low-volume announcements on the TV and the mutter of voices through the wall, the world going on around this pause in the center of it.

"You stay away from the school," Todd said finally. "You stay away from *my* son. You had your chance."

"Or what?" Livia said. "Or fucking *what*, Todd?"

But he'd hung up.

Livia threw the phone across the room. *"Fucking faggot!"* she shouted. Then she rushed toward the phone, saying, "I didn't mean it, God, God. I'm sorry. I didn't mean it. I didn't mean it." She looked at the phone again, nervous that even though she'd heard the call go dead, Todd was still on the line. Of course he wasn't. But now a long thin crack ran across the screen.

ELEVEN

"Do you ever wonder," Todd asks Jack, "what would have happened if the other guys hadn't come into the library that day? When you were crying from the black eye your dad gave you? It was the biggest black eye I'd ever seen, I think. He must have really, really gone for you."

Across Jack's belly, a faint light green has spread, almost indiscernible in the darkness of the basement, but there nonetheless; the color of a fading, pallid leaf.

"Once, when Anthony was four, we were at the playground and I saw a man grab his daughter—she was probably Anthony's age—by the arm. She was, I don't know, running where you're not supposed to run, whatever. He walked up and grabbed her and *pulled*. I saw her feet lift, suddenly, off the ground. And I yelled. I don't know what came out of me, but something came out of me. I got up and walked over and I told him to take his hands off her, and this guy—I think he was taller than me; he was definitely bigger—he let go of her right away, and I looked and saw the rings where his fingers had made marks in her arm. Her little arm. But then she started crying and grabbed her dad's leg. And then Anthony started crying too, he'd stopped to watch me. He's so observant, you know? He sees things. So I had to go back and go get him and he didn't stop until we got into the car together.

"I guess me stopping that man from hurting someone else was scarier than someone being hurt. It's like it doesn't matter what's actually happening. It only matters what seems the worst. What feels the worst to see."

Below Jack's greening belly, his penis and testicles have swollen up, and a line of semen is drying over them, forced out by the pressure of thickening blood, bacteria, the dead erection. Todd reached in and held it, once. Nothing could be a violation down here, not to either of them, not to God, not anything. Jack's body feels like his own.

Jack's left leg, halfway down from the thigh, is missing. Jack's left hand is missing all its fingers. Todd brushes his hand along Jack's left side. "I had this acupuncture doctor once, who said that the left side was your mother, and the right side was your father." He shakes his head. So what? Then he remembers what he wants to say.

"Do you know that my son has been *drawing* you? Writing your name. He doesn't even really know how to write yet. I had to tell his teacher you were imaginary. That you weren't real. And then I said that the best thing to do is pretend you don't exist. That's how I said it, 'Pretend he doesn't exist.' So she said, 'You have to *pretend* his imaginary friend doesn't exist?' I said to her you know what I mean. She said okay, but said that's not what people do now. Now people say, you're supposed to encourage the imaginary friend. You're supposed to . . . talk to it . . ." He trails off. His head is always aching now. When he wakes, before he sleeps. He's been clenching his jaw. His teeth hurt.

"Anthony had an action figure once, some green muscular guy. And it came with a sword, it was part of a whole universe of action figures. And Anthony had torn its arm off, and I had to glue it back in to get it to stay. And he said, 'But the arm doesn't move anymore, Daddy.' Because it was glued in, you know? I couldn't pop it back. So I asked him if he wanted to throw it out, and he said, 'No, I want it to move again so he can use his sword.' He was so sad."

He stays quiet for a minute and thinks about what to do next and realizes that there's no way he can do this alone, so he speaks again.

"I'm going to cut off your arm tonight, okay?" he says. "I'm going to pull on it and twist and pull and twist until it comes out of the socket at the shoulder. I don't know if you've ever dislocated your shoulder. My dad did once, I saw it when we were playing Frisbee and he fell. It was so weird, his arm suddenly a little longer. Well, anyway. It'll be like that. I'll pull and then your arm will be longer, and then there should be this space. This won't be as hard to do as your leg. It'll come off quick so most of the time with it will be over there at the worktable instead of sawing at it. But I'll be right there. Right nearby."

TWELVE

Anthony should have a normal childhood. He should be at a friend's house, maybe the girl from his class he talked about, angrily at first, but then happily. She'd taken an orange-colored pencil and refused to give it back. He hadn't pushed her, but had shouted, *I'm so mad*, which surprised Ms. Paige. The day after that, he'd still been angry at the girl, but Ms. Paige asked her (Corrine? Colette?) to give Anthony a mint, and that she could have one too. A little peace offering was all it took, and now Anthony brought her up. Corinthia, that was her overwrought name. "Maybe Corinthia will give me mints again," he said.

The house had a smell to it now. A slow but sharp veal smell there in the background till it faded. There had been a small amount of liquid, some sort of liquid, which Todd had emptied out. Then he'd sprayed under Jack's body in the container and wiped it up.

Anthony should be over at Corinthia's house, Todd should be talking to her parents. Anthony could be in their backyard eating dinner with them, falling asleep at the end of the night. But there couldn't be friends in their lives right now.

No one will find out, he said to himself. And then a knock at the door, quick, hard, multiple.

They were in the kitchen, Anthony was at the kitchen table drawing. Todd was staring into assignments. "I'll get it," Anthony said, and jumped up.

"No!" Todd shouted. "Let Daddy get it, okay?" He walked to the door and looked back to see if Anthony had stayed put. But he was there in the archway between the living room and kitchen again. That seemed like his space now. The place where he left the realm of the everyday—or not? Seeing or not seeing Todd smashing Jack's skull. In the frame, on the threshold, what had he witnessed? That was it; Anthony between one realm and the next.

Past the opened front door, Livia stood in front of him, holding the screen door wide, ready to come in. She looked the same, almost. No change in her face or her weight or her hair. It looked like she'd just left yesterday, and now was here again on his porch.

"What—" Todd said, and then looked back to see where Anthony was, realizing he didn't want to be too loud or dramatic or angry. "What are you doing here?"

"You know what I'm doing here," she said, and looked past him, though he moved with her, blocking her view. "You want me to shout for him?"

"I'll call the police if you do," Todd said.

"You'll have me arrested in front of him?"

And then Todd realized he couldn't call. He couldn't ever call the police again. This would have to happen another way. Why hadn't he taken Anthony to Corinthia's house?

"Where's your boyfriend?" Livia said.

"For fuck's sake, Livia, I don't—"

"Daddy? Dad?" Anthony said, and then he felt him at his leg, sheltering behind him.

"Oh my God," Livia said, performatively, Todd thought. "Oh God," and she knelt. "Do you know who I am, Anthony? Do you know who I am?"

Todd picked Anthony up and turned into the house.

"Todd, you can't!" she said desperately.

"Come in," Todd said through his teeth.

She followed him in slowly, like an animal walking into a clearing.

"It smells in here," she said. "What's that—"

"Raccoons," Todd said quickly, "under the porch." He sat Anthony down on the table. "Anything else you want to say about my house? Is that why you're here?"

She remained silent.

"Listen," he said to Anthony. "Can I talk to you?"

Anthony nodded.

"Do you know who this is?"

"Can I have *Wolf Story*, though?" Anthony said. He looked at Todd and looked at Livia.

"It's not story time," Todd said.

"I know, but I want it anyway." He put his hands out.

Todd gave Livia a stare, then took a breath. "It's on the back porch," he said to her. He pointed to the door.

"Oh, okay, Anthony? Anthony? Would you like me to get your book?"

Anthony nodded. "Yes, please," he said.

Livia walked to the door, looking like she was holding back tears. "I'll be right back, Anthony, okay?"

Todd wanted to shout at her, *You weren't here for seven years, he's not going to care if you leave for a minute.*

"Listen," he said to Anthony in a hurry. "You don't have to do anything she says. You don't have to do anything you don't want to do, okay?"

Anthony reached his hand into the back of his mouth. "Daddy," he said, "there's a tooth loose." He wiggled it and Todd remembered the sharp and twisting feeling of turning a baby tooth out of place. Not unlike twisting an arm out of its socket. "Can I put it under my pillow?"

"Anthony, are you listening to me?" Todd said. "Listen. Listen."

Anthony looked at him, stricken, as Livia walked back in. "Here it is," she said. "I know this book. Did you know that I used to have it when I was a little girl?"

"My tooth is loose," Anthony said to her.

She set the book on the table. "Wow, will you give it to the tooth fairy?" He didn't respond.

"Anthony, does Daddy have a friend here?" she asked.

The thought flashed through Todd to strike her, and it was so overwhelming that he felt, for a moment, that he couldn't trust himself anymore. Then he thought, *But I didn't hit her, did I?* and his face went hot and a shiver vibrated through him. And as all this happened, Anthony spoke. "Yes," he said.

"Livia, he's a kid. Stop asking him questions you shouldn't even be asking me."

"Where is Daddy's friend now?" Livia asked, but Anthony just shrugged.

"All right, Livia, it's time to go."

"Is Daddy's friend David?" she asked.

"No," Anthony said.

"Livia. It. Is. Time. To. Go."

"No?"

"No, it's Jack," Anthony said.

Todd grabbed Livia's arm. "I will throw you out of here myself," he said.

"Don't hurt Mommy," Anthony said suddenly.

"Oh God," Livia said. "Oh God, did you hear that? Yes . . . Mommy. I'm Mommy."

"I know," he said to her.

"*Livia, goddamn it!*" Todd shouted, and she straightened, and so did Anthony. "Jack is Anthony's imaginary friend, and we've been trying to—"

"We?"

"—get rid of him for months now, and we're not supposed to keep bringing him up. You're *hurting* him by talking about it. And I don't have a . . . I'm dating someone. A woman. So stop this. Or do you not want to see him again?" She was quiet, and Anthony shuffled himself off the table and sat underneath it, wiggling his tooth.

Livia went to kneel down to him, but Todd maneuvered in front of her, blocking her view and stopping her from crouching.

"You can't come in like this. You can't come over and make demands. Do you understand that this is not how you do things?"

"I've been trying to call," she said, standing again, stern but desperate.

"And I was *busy*, people have *lives*," he said. "I'm teaching, I'm in a new place, I'm trying to raise him. I'm . . . There's no time! There's no time for you right now. Do you understand that other people *exist*? That our lives can't all just set themselves down and get ready for your grand entrance?"

"You're dating someone," Livia said.

"Yes," he said.

"Can I just . . . be close to him?" Livia said. Todd was confused but then understood she meant Anthony, and when she said this, their son tottered out from under the table and to her.

"Can I?" she said, but didn't wait for an answer. She picked him up. She held him close. He put his head on her shoulder. Todd watched her search for her feelings, it was an expression he'd seen in her before. A sort of pause to check what was there, what was happening, what she was supposed to display.

He sighed. "Listen, you can come by Tuesday." He sighed.

"But that's almost a week away," she said, exasperated.

"Do you want to see him or not?" he asked.

She nodded. "I'll come pick him up—" she began.

"No, I don't trust you. You can spend time with him here."

"I wouldn't take him, I'm his mother."

She set Anthony down on the edge of the table. "Mommy will see you soon, okay? Soon," she told him. He looked at her and didn't say anything.

Todd walked Livia to the door.

"I'll be here," he said. "At seven. You can . . ." Todd said slowly, "meet the woman . . . I'm dating. And you can play with Anthony while you're here."

She looked into the kitchen again and waved at Anthony.

"Thank you," she said finally.

When she left, he pulled out the school district directory. A laminated sheet of phone numbers. He called Elaine Paige. He said would you like to go out on a date.

"I thought you'd never ask," she said. "I was going to ask you myself, but then I thought, no, no, let him show interest. But then I thought that was the *old* me thinking I could show interest first, why did it have to be you asking me out. But—"

"Tuesday?" Todd asked.

"Sure, that works," she said.

"No, wait, Sunday. Sunday first. We can walk on the boardwalk, okay?"

And again she said yes.

THIRTEEN

In the morning before the robins tilt their heads to hunt, it goes like this: Todd in the basement with Jack again. Lower, lower than where the worms burrow, surrounded by plastic air fresheners shaped like mushrooms, the tabs pulled from the tops so that the whole place smells like strawberry gum overlaying the course of death.

Todd rises early now, does what he can, then goes to the beach and releases it into the waves. Then he comes back to wake his son as the day opens. Like work, a schedule, a rhythm, till the friend, the lover, the brother, the enemy, is gone.

He's starting on the other arm.

"You know, when we were together, Livia pushed me against the wall of the bedroom. Just," he says, pulling up on the arm and twisting and failing and pulling up again to dislocate it, "right against my chest. She was pregnant with Anthony. Right against my chest, and I fell backward. I stood up and turned around and faced the wall and then I punched it, like the wall was the problem."

The sound of the shoulder popping, the way the arm stops short, won't realign, the way of bone abruptly hitting bone.

"She said she was sorry later, that it was the pregnancy. But it wasn't," he says. "I mean, she used to get *mean* when we fought, before she was pregnant too. Insults. Needling, jabs. She wanted me to respond, 'the robot,' she called me." He comes back with the saw and gets down in the container. He'd be straddling Jack's legs, if Jack's legs were there. Without the second arm, Jack's body really won't look like a body anymore. His face is still there, although the color is changing, mildly, a creep of ash. His torso is still there, his abdomen, his penis and scrotum, his buttocks and back, though his legs are gone, his feet are gone. Todd breathes. Artificial strawberries. The saw sinks into the soft flesh. Blood doesn't pour out, but some dark liquid oozes slowly.

"I remember thinking that it was all bullying. The push, the insults." He pushes and drags the saw through more flesh, a knife cutting through steak. Till the arm is held by sinews, which he cuts with thick-handled metal scissors. Then he takes the arm over to the worktable and starts, with knives, to cut the muscle and fat and skin off. When it's off, he cuts it into smaller pieces. Smaller. Smaller. Reducing it to something unrecognizable that can be swallowed by birds and fish and crabs and whatever else can claim it, putting the flecks and scraps into baggies, pulling on fat and muscle till it comes hesitantly away from the bone. He holds the hand. Angled on the palm with lines of fate and love. The life line, which one is the life line? If he knew, he could tell if palmistry was true, if the body knows when life is going to stop.

He's held this hand once before. Not in a handshake, but in help. Hawk Mountain. Jack got closer, closer, till he stood above Todd, looking down at him, scraped and vulnerable on the ground. He reached his hand out. He took Todd's hand. There was no one else around. "Come on," Jack said, as sunlight spilled through the leaves.

Todd walks back to the container and puts a hand on Jack's cheek. "You're never going to say anything ever again, are you?" Todd asks. "You're never going to talk?" And for a moment, he falters. A thought shows its edges: maybe this is all a prayer.

The thought is opening, and then, instead, a sound, common but unfamiliar anyway, a creak, a gesture, a letting in of things.

The door at the top of the stairs opens.

Todd drops the knife.

The knife clangs as it hits the floor.

Pieces of flesh fall from the edge of the blade.

What's left of the arm lulls to its side.

Todd turns to the stairs and runs.

He sees the figure at the top, diminutive.

He rushes toward it, backlit, eager to enter this world.

It steps toward him as he hits the stairs.

He's up one, two, three, to the top until he reaches out with his arms and

he grabbed Anthony and held him tight to his chest and pushed from the dark into the kitchen.

"What are you doing awake?" he asked, and then asked again, as if once weren't enough. "What are you doing awake?"

"What's down there?" Anthony asked. He was startled now. He was in his pajamas, startled at how fast his dad was, how decisive. This was a moment for Todd to say the right thing.

"A monster," Todd said.

Anthony started to cry, the fear welling up in his tired mind.

"So you can never, ever, ever go down there," Todd said. "I'm so glad I got you before you went down."

"What does it . . ." He tried to speak through the sobs. "What does it . . . what does it look like?"

He couldn't be too descriptive, because he couldn't have Anthony asking about it. A lock, why didn't he have a lock on the door, it wasn't like anyone was coming to the house and would ask, *Why is there a lock there?* But Elaine might when she came. There was so much to keep together.

"Listen," Todd said, and walked his son to the other set of steps, then up those, too. "Listen, it's not like I saw anything, I was afraid that there was one. And the more you talk about them, the more likely they are to hear you if they're around."

Anthony buried his head in Todd's shoulder. According to the clock in Anthony's room, it was almost five. He put Anthony into bed.

"So you can't talk about it, okay? That's how it works." He figured if Anthony ever brought it up, he could say that this was all part of the imaginary friend thing. Todd could explain it away: *A monster? No, no, he has an imaginary friend that he talks about and I've told him we shouldn't bring him up anymore, that's the latest consensus with these things. He's delusional, really.* And then he'd laugh, the way parents did when they made a mean joke at their child's expense.

"Why were you awake?" And then Todd noticed the blood for the first time. The blood on the front of Anthony's pajamas. Specks of it. And on the bed too. It must've been on him as he rushed up the stairs, Jack's blood on his son, on Todd, and then he got it on his son.

"My tooth, Daddy," Anthony said. And then he opened his mouth wide and one in the front from the bottom row was gone now, a sallow hollow of gum where it'd been pulled away in a turn of nerves. And when Anthony pointed, Todd saw that the tip of one of his fingers was bloody. Then he lifted the pillow up and the tooth was there, too, with a smear of blood around it on the sheet.

"There's blood," Todd said. The obvious, out loud, was like a protection to him. "From your tooth."

"Will the tooth fairy come?" Anthony asked.

"Yes," Todd said. "But you have to go back to sleep. And if she doesn't come while you're sleeping, it will be tomorrow when you're at school, so don't move it."

This was normal blood. Normal blood, from a normal pulled tooth.

In the morning, upstairs time was normal.

Downstairs the time was immediate, but up here everything had already happened. By the time anyone noticed what happened, it was already over.

FOURTEEN

The ocean was colder each time Todd walked into it. It was time, again, now, for sweaters and jackets against the season. Elaine had a long red coat on, and Todd long sleeves, and they walked along the beach, each holding their shoes in their hands. Her toenails were painted, and the sand was darker from where a thin layer of water washed across it. Anthony was running, stopping, throwing up sand in the air, and running again.

"He lost a tooth," Todd said.

"Oh, believe me, I know, he was very excited to show all of us the five dollars the tooth fairy gave him on Friday," she said, smiling. "They were all impressed by the drawing she made of a tooth on it."

"Yes, well," Todd said. A bright fog held above the sand in the distance. Up the hill, the boardwalk was mostly empty now. "I hope you don't mind that he's here with us," Todd said.

"If I'm going to go out on a date with you, I have to acknowledge that you have a son."

"And that he's your student, I mean. I hope it's not like working."

"Look to your left," Elaine said, "does that look like work to you?" Todd stared into the ocean that he had been visiting each night. The salt water exhaled another wave at them, and then pulled back into itself, exhaled again. It knew him.

"Okay," Todd said.

"I grew up here, and I don't think I could go anywhere else. The woods and the ocean and the mountains nearby."

"I didn't know you grew up here," he said.

"Well, since this is our first date, there's probably a lot you don't know about me. That's what dates are for."

"I haven't been on one in years."

"I can see why, with your ex-wife like that."

"Can we—if it's all right, can we not talk about her? I'm trying to forget she's around."

"Sorry. So there's not been anyone since her?"

Todd stopped walking and closed his eyes. He breathed with the waves.

"Are you all right? Todd. Todd?"

"I just . . . I don't want to think about it."

They walked again for a while, not saying anything.

"What about you?" he asked finally. "When's the last time?"

"Well, I don't think mine is as bad as yours, but I went out with a guy I grew up with. We were friends. Friendly, I mean, we stayed in touch. We went out to dinner, and he was a little boring, but I thought, that's okay, sometimes people are boring at first and they take a little time to open up. But I looked him up after. I mean, I shouldn't have, probably, but I did. And there were all these photos with him and another woman, and I guess they'd been dating for a few months. So I called him after the first date and he said, 'Oh, her, that's not serious.' But it definitely *looked* serious. They were even on a trip together. A beach. Not like this beach, a tropical one somewhere. They'd *traveled*. So. That was the last time. Over a year ago. I know it was only one date, but I felt so deceived. Why even ask me out?"

"I'm sorry," Todd said softly.

"It's okay, it's not your fault," she said. "I guess I have trust issues. But doesn't everyone?"

He put his hand on her back and rubbed her shoulder blades lightly. The first time he'd touched her this way, she turned her head to him slightly. Ahead of them, Anthony fell forward into the sand. Todd ran forward and leaned to his son.

"You're okay," he said. On the ground. He reached his hand out. His son took it, his own tiny hands now covered in sand, like the front of his shirt, like his feet.

"I'm okay," Anthony said.

"That's what I said," Todd said.

"Anthony, are you all right? Are you o-kay?" Elaine said, and Anthony laughed.

"Here," Todd said, and picked his son up, his body aching, always aching now from the work. He walked toward the water and held Anthony horizontally, his face above the water, and lowered him, offering his hands and feet in the surf. Anthony moved his hands around rigorously.

"You want to go to the store?" Todd asked.

"There's something I want from there too," Elaine said. "Promise not to think it's dumb."

"I won't," Todd said.

"Promise, or think it's dumb?" She smiled.

"I guess you'll find out," he said.

They walked up the sand and onto the boardwalk and into the store with bare feet. Anthony ran off into the aisles. "You can get one thing," Todd said. He turned to Elaine. "And what about you? What did you need to get?"

"Hold on," she said, and disappeared around a corner.

He should get some shirts, some shirts for the basement. At the end of a row of them, mostly with designs of comic book characters and catchphrases from TV shows, there were plain ones, bundled in threes and wrapped in plastic. He pulled white ones off the shelf. No, no, obviously he needed something darker, even if he was going to burn them right away. He took two packs of navy blue, which Jack's melting and revealed stickiness would be indistinct against.

"Okay," Elaine said, appearing again, holding something long and flat in a prism of plastic.

"What?"

"Just remember you promised." She laughed a little, and showed him the label. "A kite," she said.

"A *giant* kite," Todd said.

"It's for my niece," Elaine insisted.

"With a . . . is it a dragon on it?"

"All right, I'd be lying if I didn't say I was going to fly it first a few times. I'm not even going to see her for another month or so."

"It won't be kite-flying season by then," he said, and they walked toward the counter.

"Okay, okay," she said. "It's *mostly* for me. I think—don't you think?— that that's why we work with kids. Everyone wants to relive their childhoods."

"I guess," he said.

"Did you wear lots of blue shirts in your childhood?" she asked.

"I don't really want to relive it."

Anthony came up to them and on tiptoes pushed a box with a doll in it onto the counter. Stiff and lifeless like a Barbie, the doll's hair was blond; her clothing was strange and exaggerated. The clerk, a man with a sparse gray beard, looked at it, and then down at Anthony with a small grunt.

"Is there some sort of problem with that?" Todd said warily to the man.

"No problem here," the man said. "He's your kid."

"This too, Daddy," Anthony said, and handed another box from the same toy line to Todd. In it was a plastic white dog. It looked like a German shepherd, covered in tufts of fake white fur. Todd looked at it in his hand. No.

"I said one thing. One."

"But she needs a dog to lick her face when she's buried."

"Buried?" Elaine laughed.

"In the sand!"

"No, put it back."

"I want it, though," he whined.

"Put it back," Todd said again.

"*I want it!*" Anthony shouted. And Todd handed it to Elaine.

"Could you take this back for me, I need to talk with Anthony for a—"

"*Jack would have got it for me,*" Anthony said suddenly.

It struck out at Todd. He froze, dizzy.

"Anthony, Jack isn't real," Elaine said.

"Yes, he *is*," Anthony said, and then Todd was grabbing Anthony's arm and pulling him away from the store, from Elaine, from the white plastic dog.

"Todd?" she called from behind him.

"Hey, don't forget your son's doll," the clerk shouted after them.

"You're hurting me! You're hurting me!" Anthony screamed, but there was no one around to care as Todd's fingers pressed deep into his son's arm, pulling him down the boardwalk toward the parking lot. When they got to the edge of it, he knelt in front of him.

"Do you know why that clerk laughed at you?" Todd said forcefully. "Because people think it's funny when a boy gets a doll, that's why. Dolls are for girls." He could feel the rotten turn in his words.

"Todd!"

He turned, and Elaine was behind him with two bags, one with the edge of the kite peering up out of it. "Your shirts."

"Hold on," he said. He took Anthony to the car. "Get in," he said. Anthony got in and Todd closed the door behind him.

"Listen," she said.

"Are you going to tell me it's too much?" Todd said. "Because, Elaine, I know it's too much. And Livia is trying to get back in his life now and he keeps talking about his . . . friend, and now he's talking about monsters, too, like they're real, and—"

"No, Todd, no," she said, and set the bags down and then put a hand on his shoulder. "I mean, yes, maybe you scared him a little, but . . . I was going to tell you during the week. I didn't want to tell you on our date. But since that's over now, I guess—"

"What?"

"Well, when he brought in the five-dollar bill that you gave him, one of the other boys came up after and said could he see it. And so Anthony showed it to him. And he—his name is Ethan—Ethan said, 'The tooth fairy didn't give that to you.' And Anthony pointed to the tooth you drew on it, and Ethan said, 'No, she didn't give that to you because she's not real.' And he—Anthony, I mean—he pushed Ethan to the ground, and then . . ."

"What?"

"He kicked him."

"Kicked him?"

"Yes, in the side. Ethan cried at first. Ed . . . well, I'm starting to think Ed doesn't want to ever have to talk to anyone's parents, even though he's the principal. He said, 'Did they work it out?' And they did. But it took a lot of work to get them to calm down and to get Anthony to apologize. That was, I think, the worst part."

"That he wouldn't apologize."

"No, more like . . . Well. It's like he knew it wasn't right, but he didn't care."

Todd looked back into the car window. Anthony was lying facedown in the backseat with his head in the crook of his arm.

"When they turn seven, like he will in a few months, they go through things that can be intense. But add to that the extra stuff, I think it's his mother coming around. It's putting pressure on him."

"She came over," he said. "The other day."

"Oh no," Elaine said.

"I should get him home," he said. They were silent for a moment, wondering what was next. He looked up to the sky. It was easy to forget it was there when you spent so much time below the surface. A huge expanse, never-ending. The seagulls were there, exploiting the currents.

"This was not a good first date," Elaine said. Then she laughed. "But, believe it or not, it wasn't the worst I've been on."

"Jesus," Todd said, and they laughed. Relief. "You'll have to tell me about that." There was a pause, and then he said, "Will you? Let's try this all over again. On Tuesday? Come over and I'll cook."

"You cook?"

"Well, I'm okay," he said.

"You don't have to cook for me to apologize."

"No, no, I was going to ask you anyway. To come over on Tuesday."

"Okay," she said.

"I'll do something that I can't fuck up," Todd said.

"There's a low bar after today," she said, and they laughed again.

He picked up the bag. "Thank you. Thank you for being understanding." The bag held the shirts and doll. And he saw, also, that she had also bought the white dog for Anthony.

"I owe you for these," he said.

"Don't be silly," she said. "Just make sure dinner is good."

He hugged her, lightly, and when he pulled away, he could feel her holding him a bit, expectant. He walked to the driver's side.

Before he got in, she said, concerned, "If he saw Livia at your house . . . well, he can't *unsee* that. Stuff like that stays with a child, even if he doesn't talk about it."

"I know," Todd said. "I know."

FIFTEEN

The inevitable encounter with nature was coming. What else would she do? She could drive to Boston, but it would take hours. She could drive to Provincetown, but that was all gay men, with their laughter at breakfast and riding bikes in their shorts and walking along pointing at everything; they wouldn't even see her. The woods, however, would take her, without question.

On the hotel bed there was a pair of boy's lemon-yellow shorts. Anthony would like those, Livia imagined. And there were sneakers—so small!—with a painted tiger on each side. She had no idea if either would fit him, but she wanted him to be *in* something she gave to him.

She lifted her hiking shoes out of the box and laced them on. Her feet felt heavy. She pulled the tag off her raincoat. That was the thing about New England, she remembered, everyone was always ready for different elements, and there were outdoor goods shops everywhere. They were invariably wood-colored inside, with a kayak or a canoe hanging on a wall. They had a row of backpacks, dried food by the counter, maybe the head of a dead animal or two if they catered to hunters, which was less and less. No one wanted to kill animals themselves anymore, or to think about others doing it. People wanted death served to them, which was fair. In America, the butcher shops that hung the carcasses in the window were few and far between. That was a sort of repression, wasn't it? In Italy, as in Spain, the fucking and the butchery were all on the surface. Maybe, she thought, that was her problem with Todd and whatever his name was that he was hiding. And the men in Provincetown. They didn't know how to behave properly in public because they were so used to hiding. Everything they did, she felt, was distorted by what they'd held back. She tried to reason through these feelings but then forgot she was trying and gave up and walked down the hall to the front desk.

There was a boy there who looked about fifteen, but she figured he must be older. He sat on a swivel chair, staring into space. Was he unhappy?

"Hi," she said. He nodded.

"Hi," she said again. "Where can I go hiking around here?"

"Mount Lock," he said.

"Not anything strenuous, just a walk through the woods."

"We have some maps." He pointed to the little plastic display of maps. She pulled one out. There was a picture of a hawk and a chipmunk and a bear with a cub on it. She did miss this aesthetic. The way that animals evoked a warning or a promise: in the woods you can bump into something you aren't prepared for. The way they evoked cold air and rushing water; green shadowing canopy above, or the flames of autumn.

"Maps?"

"Well, your phone won't work there," he said. "Nature, you know?"

"How old are you?" she asked. He was pale and skinny and had glasses. She would never let her son look like this.

"Seventeen," he said.

"Why aren't you in school?"

"I finished early," he said.

"Good for you," Livia said. He shrugged.

She tried again. "If you're smart enough to finish early, why are you working here?" He handed her a map without saying anything.

Why was it that people in America didn't know how to just *talk* to each other? "Sorry, that was rude."

"It's fine," he said.

"No, it's not. I lived in Europe for a long time, I forget what's rude and what's not anymore. Have you been there?"

"No," he said again.

She looked at the map idly, but she felt the urge to shake him.

"Have you seen a bear?" she said, pointing to it on the map.

"Yeah. Not a bear and her cubs, but I've seen a bear. You don't want to see a bear and her cubs anyway, if you do you've got to run," he said, finally showing interest.

"I used to live here," she said. "Well, New England, I mean. You know where Mystic is? I grew up there and then lived outside of Manchester for a while."

He didn't say anything.

"Why am I saying that? I'm saying that because I remember about the bears and the cubs and so on."

"Oh, okay."

Was he not interested in *anything*? she wondered.

"Are you going to work here the rest of your life?" she asked. "Don't you want to see the world?"

The boy stood up and walked away, into the office behind a wall. A minute later, a person, a manager, came out.

"Can I help you?" he said. He was fat and friendly-looking. Unlike the boy, he had a name tag on. He had the same color hair as the boy did and Livia wondered if he was the boy's father. He spotted the map in her hand. "Oh, going hiking?"

She put it down on the counter. "No, I . . . Can you have some towels sent up to the room?"

"Sure," he said jovially. "Need any soap or shampoo?"

"No."

"You know you can always call down here if you want. Press the button with the little front desk icon above it," he said jovially. "No need to come all the way down to the desk!"

"I know how it works," she said. She would switch hotels tomorrow, she thought.

"Okay, great."

She walked back down the hallway, fluorescent lights humming them through with a stale yellow. When she got back to her room, she threw away the shorts and shoes, stuffing them into the little garbage can under the work desk.

SIXTEEN

"I have to pull your teeth now," he says. Todd's been resisting; of all the parts of Jack he had to get rid of, the face had felt inviolable. The first look Jack gave him, in the classroom, when he laughed at Jack's voice. Jack's face on Hawk Mountain, backlit by the filtered light. Jack's face on the beach. On the couch. On the floor. Even with the split-open eye and the gray that wraps itself around him now, even with this dead calm, the face was more Jack than anything.

The basement, the part of it that's usable, is the size of the dorm room Todd had had during his first year in college. Todd would lie on the top bunk, not far from the ceiling. Most of the other students in his hall had unstacked the bunks so that there were two beds on either side of the room, but Todd liked this little strip of air between him and the opaqueness above. At night he would masturbate slowly and quietly so that the bed didn't shake and alert his roommate, and he supposed his roommate did too. The close proximity shielded them from each other.

"It's stupid," Todd says. "But when I went to college, I always thought you would show up one day. That you'd be going there too, and I wouldn't know it. I'm not sure you even know where I went. Keene State. It would've been big enough for me to never see you. To just miss you in a building or to live on opposite sides of the campus. Until one day. Or that maybe I had friends who were friends with you, and it would come up. But you never showed up again, ever. No one even . . . I'm sorry, but no one even mentioned you at the reunion, and I kept wanting to ask. Because then, even though I kept thinking you'd show up at school, when I went to the reunion I *knew* you wouldn't be there. I thought, *He's probably a bartender somewhere.* I thought, I don't know, you'd be good at that."

He imagines Jack smiling and talking to regulars with unsolvable problems. He imagines Jack talking to new people, women smiling at him, and Jack's lightly freckled face smiling back. Maybe some days in the summer, Jack would be at an outside bar. On a patio with his shirt off. People would know him; he wouldn't feel like he needed to run anywhere. Todd could have walked in and ordered a drink and surprised him.

If he starts with the back teeth, maybe there will be one more day. It would be harder that way, but there would still be a face to talk to above the neck and torso and limbs all gone missing. In spots across Jack's body, blisters have welted up. Todd gets pliers and a bowl he's brought down. He's wearing one of the blue shirts, the shirts Elaine had bought. He sits down on the floor.

He traces his hand down to Jack's mouth and opens it. The tongue is dissolving, and a smell of damp garden soil rises out. He lets it fall closed again.

"We were different versions of each other," he says blankly. "Because you were thinking of me too. I must have been around the corner for you the whole time. Phantom pains. Brothers. Phantom brothers." Jack's jaw is somewhat askew, like he's grinding his teeth, like Todd does now.

He thinks about the parts he's cut off. Phantoms. Before they're smashed and cut up and pulverized, do they long for him?

He holds Jack's chin and reaches back with the pliers, grabbing a molar, near where the wisdom teeth had already been pulled by someone else. It comes away easily, no longer rooted by circulating blood. Todd drops it into the bowl, where it clatters and rests. Then he goes to the other side, not sure why the symmetry matters, but it does. Then to the top, till the molars are out, close to each other in a way they never were before, huddled in the bottom of the bowl.

Todd takes them to the worktable and hammers at them. The first one, he sees, doesn't split and splinter and break like the bones had. It shatters and flies, so he puts down a piece of paper beneath them and positions himself to make sure the shards won't go everywhere. He smashes one. And smashes the pieces. And then smashes those pieces. A shining white and dull yellow sand starts to form. Then he holds the edges of the paper to make a spout and pours the grains into a baggie, his hands starting to tremble.

"Is everyone . . ." he begins, and then starts trembling suddenly, lightly, then more. He walks over to Jack and sits on the floor, and the words come urgent and halting at the same time, trying to wrench themselves out of him. "Is everyone always suffering; everyone locked away; my parents, my ex-wife; my son; and this boy at my school, you *know* him, you *know him*, you threatened him in the parking lot the day we met; and now he's . . . he's struggling because I made him tell the class . . ."

He presses his palm flat against Jack's cheek and braces his shaking hand. He knows he can't do any more today.

"And what do I do now, Jack? What do I do? Elaine is coming here because of me, because she thinks that this will go somewhere; and the librarian at school, he's lonely, he's . . . Is everyone unhappy? Is everyone stuck? I think, Jack, I was happy sometimes; no, I *was*, I *was* before you, before you showed up; and you were happy when you got here, and Livia was happy before she met me, and Anthony was happy; and then, what? Everything is fine and then something shows up and you can't be happy after that; what is that? It's an *interloper* or . . . *usurper.* Why? Why?"

The shaking starts to calm. And he settles and waits for his lost breath to return.

"Why did you get to win?" he asks.

The question is precise and distant from him, like stars behind night clouds.

He closes the container and walks up the stairs, the bag of shattered teeth sparkling on the table as the light switches off.

SEVENTEEN

Then he wondered if things were normal.

Whatever you did long enough was normal, whatever you were told was okay was normal.

But he was cutting vegetables at the counter, broccoli and carrots. He was crushing tomatoes. He was putting garlic in the garlic press. There was arrabbiata sauce and an extra pan of plain tomato sauce that wouldn't be too spicy for Anthony.

Was this, even if it was framed by pain and phantoms, a life that others had?

Maybe life wasn't punctuated with pain, maybe it was the opposite. Pull the glove inside out: life was pain with moments of respite.

Elaine would be here in a half hour, and Livia would be here shortly after. He thought for a moment that he should have been quicker in his work belowground, but he knew that things were taking their own time. If he forced them to go faster, he'd stumble and not recover.

Anthony was drawing with crayons at the kitchen table. An animal, unidentifiable.

"Anthony, what was your favorite part of the summer?" he asked his son. He filled a pot with water.

"The beach," Anthony said.

"Will you draw the beach?" he said. He turned on the heat underneath the pot.

Anthony flipped his sheet of paper over and started to draw.

He's always liked drawing, Todd thought.

He used to draw when he was a kid too. Monsters, mostly. Right into high school, never showing anyone, skeletons with flames rising from them, vampires, werewolves gnawing on bones. His mom saw them on his desk once and had left a note: *Why does it all have to be so violent?*

He didn't stop drawing then, but he didn't draw monsters anymore.

His mother didn't like him to watch violent movies. She would sometimes take away the novels he was reading if they were horror novels. Right now she was probably on the sun porch with his dad. Were they watching a storm gather and smelling the air turn wet? He hadn't spoken with them in months. Normal.

Todd looked into the water, which was steaming. It had formed its first tiny, heated bubble. The bubble could appear anywhere on the bottom of the pot. It was random. But once it showed, the rest of the boiling would coalesce around it. One moment of freedom, of randomness, and then the rest was determined.

"Look, Daddy," Anthony said, and held up the drawing.

It was a line of beach drawn with black crayon and a line of blue crayon above. Standing on it, a man, a boy, and a woman.

No Jack.

"That's me, right?" he said, and pointed to the man.

"Yes."

"And that? Who's that?" Todd pointed to the woman.

"Ms. Paige," Anthony said.

"That," Todd said, "is the perfect picture."

Why had he started boiling the water so soon? The vegetables and pasta would only take a few minutes. He turned the front burner off, steam still thickening the air.

There was a knock at the door. It was early, too early for Livia, but it might be. She might show up to surprise him. Anthony jumped out of his seat.

"I'll get it," Todd said.

It was Elaine; it hadn't even occurred to him that she might be early. But she was happy and wearing a light dress, bright gold, which she immediately commented on.

"It's freezing," she said, "but I like it. I never get to wear it."

"You look great," he said, and ushered her in. As they entered the kitchen, Todd glanced at Anthony's beach drawing quickly. No change, he was on to other things.

"Hi, Ms. Paige," Anthony said. "I drew a beach and now I'm drawing a seahorse."

"Wow," she said, and leaned forward. "And what's this?" She pointed toward a little boxy drawing in the background of the beach.

"A dog," Anthony said.

"All alone on the hill?"

"So he doesn't bite me," Anthony said.

"Oh, I'm sure he'll be fine," she said. "Have you ever had a dog?"

"No," Todd said.

"But we're going to get one," Anthony said.

"Is that so?" Elaine asked, and looked to Todd, who, over his shoulder, smiling, shook his head.

"Have you ever had one?"

"Just once, sort of," he said, stirring. "In college I had an apartment off-campus and the guys had a dog. A little Jack Russell."

"Do you still keep in touch with anyone from school?"

"No," he said flatly. He thought about everyone shuffling around him in school, how he did make some friends, how he'd go out with them sometimes, but was always at a distance. He'd convinced himself he was a student focused on his studies. That was something people did in school if they wanted to withdraw from the clatter. The little fights and the drinking in dorms and the puking and the late nights. The point was to get to the other side so that the life you had before college was no longer your life.

"Me neither. Look, we have so much in common. Two people without friends." She laughed.

"I'm your friend," Anthony said. "And Daddy's."

"Aren't you the sweetest?" She regarded the stove and the ingredients. "How can I help?"

"You can't," he said. "I mean, just hang out. Talk."

This was normal, he thought. This would go on being normal until the next knock at the door felled it. He knew that knock was coming soon, and that now was just the rest between emergencies, a tide pool left to its own life until it was reclaimed by the rising water. He turned the burner back on again.

"I hope you're okay with spicy," Todd said. "It's arrabbiata. There's an extra pot of non-spicy sauce for Anthony if you want."

"No!" Anthony said suddenly. "That's mine!"

"There's enough for both of you," Todd said.

"No-oo," Anthony whined.

"Anthony, can I draw with you?" Elaine said; and then, to Todd, "Spicy is fine." She picked up a red crayon. "So, what do you want me to draw?"

"A hawk," he said.

Suddenly Todd yowled.

He'd sliced into his finger while cutting through a tomato. The acidic juice slid into his wound and blood poured onto the cutting board. Elaine went to him.

"Are you okay? Here, let me see your hand."

"No," he said. "No, it's nothing." He turned on the water and held his finger under it as his blood washed out and into the pipes. He sent Anthony upstairs to get the Band-Aids, and when he came down, let him wrap it around his finger for him.

When they'd finished dinner, Livia still hadn't arrived. He put Anthony on the couch and turned on the TV.

"I brought dessert wine," Elaine said. "I wasn't sure if there would be dessert or not."

"I was going to get ice cream, but I forgot," Todd said. It wasn't true; he hadn't even thought of dessert. She got two glasses from his cupboard and poured the wine slowly into them. It held to the edges of the glass, sweet, thick, and heavy.

"How's your hand?" she asked.

"Honestly, I'd forgotten until you brought it up," he said. Now he looked at his finger, holding the glass, wrapped in a cartoon-decorated Band-Aid.

"Oh, sorry. It looked bad."

"I've seen worse," he said.

"Oh, well, a combat veteran." She smiled.

"Nothing like that," he said.

"Actually, there are a lot our age, aren't there? The wars."

"We're not the same age," he said. "You're a bit younger than me, right?"

"Well, okay, but you must know some people who enlisted. A few of the boys I went to high school with went to Iraq. And"—she sighed—"that was it. Dead a few months later. It's so sad. What makes someone sign up for something like that? Men are so eager to go off to their doom, aren't they? It can't just be the money. The money can't be that much. Or worth it."

"Maybe it's to be around each other," Todd said. "Just to be with other boys, or men . . . Sorry, I'm rambling."

"No, keep talking," she said.

"I don't know, I think I've taught too many books about male bonding and camaraderie. *A Separate Peace, Catcher in the Rye, Of Mice and Men, Lord of the Flies,* on and on."

"When I was in school, I wanted to read books about girls," she said. "But we never did. We had to read the boys' books too. They weren't . . . bad. I liked them! But I don't think I understood them, really. Because I was never in them. It was like I didn't exist."

"That's how it feels to be a boy sometimes," Todd said. "I see it in my students too. When you're a boy, it's like no one else exists except the constant looming presence of other boys."

"I don't think that's the same," Elaine said.

"You're right." Todd nodded. "But it's something, anyway."

"So why would you want that? In the military?"

"I mean, I don't know. Maybe it's because you're not competing with each other. You're proving yourselves, I guess, but that's different? You're all in it together, under the same pressures and controls. And you're all allowed to feel real feelings. Because you might die. Death gives you some sort of permission. You could just be around other men. And no one's competing for women."

"Women are in the military too."

"Yeah, of course, of course. But everyone's separated out."

"Are they, still?"

"Honestly, I have no idea. I don't really know how anything works, don't listen to me." He was dimly aware that he was enjoying the conversation, or at least could be enjoying it if he weren't so focused on the fact that Livia hadn't shown up. He drank a gulp of the wine, too much honey and flowers, like a sacrifice.

"It seems like we should know," she said. "If people are going to die, we should know why they're willing to. Aside from religious ideals or whatever, the reasons *they* do it. What do you suppose they think of death, anyway? Or maybe I should ask you what you think about it." She laughed a little. "Is that, is that a third-date question? 'Do you want to get married and do you want kids and what happens when we die? Todd? Oh, I'm sorry, I'm moving too fast. Even a joke about marriage is still a mention of it. And now I'm mentioning it . . .'"

"Nothing happens when you die," Todd said.

There was a pause.

"Oblivion, then? That's a bit depressing," she said.

"No, I mean nothing changes. I mean—"

And there, then, was that knock at the door.

"Weird," he said, and stood up.

"It's almost nine o'clock," Elaine said.

Anthony was already at the door, the sound having pried him away from the movie he was watching; life was still more interesting at this point.

"Come here!" an aggressively delighted voice came echoing through the house. Livia held Anthony in an unreciprocated hug. Slowly, he embraced her back. "Aren't you happy to see me?"

"What are you doing here?" Todd said, storming into the room.

"I'm sorry I'm late, I—"

"Late? You're an hour late and about a week early."

Livia held on to Anthony and stepped back. "What? You said Tuesday?"

Anthony turned his head into her shoulder.

"Next Tuesday, I said, at eight if you could come at all. Jesus, have you lost your mind? Anthony, come here."

"Is David here?" Livia said. And then, to Anthony, "Where's Daddy's friend?"

"Elaine," Todd said, and Elaine came into the room and took it in.

"I told you," he said to Livia. "Elaine, this is Livia, my ex-wife—"

"Anthony's mother," Livia corrected. And then, "What about Daddy's friend?"

"There is no friend," Todd said. "Anthony, come here." But Anthony seemed frozen in her arms, unable to enact anything, except to just live, to keep breathing, to keep his heart beating.

"Livia, this is Elaine, my girlfriend."

Anthony raised his head from Livia's shoulder. "Ms. Paige is your girlfriend?"

"Well," Elaine said, taken aback.

"Anthony," Todd said again, and Anthony reached for him, but Livia held on. He squirmed in her arms and then started to cry.

"Let go of him," Elaine said, "you're hurting him."

"I'm sorry, who are you again?" Livia said.

"She's—"

"No, I mean who does she think she is?" Livia said angrily, and now Anthony was screaming. No words, only a high-pitched wail, his eyes swelling.

"Shhh, shhh, it's okay, Mommy has you," Livia said. But Todd reached forward and pulled Anthony away and he settled. "No, no, no!" Livia said. "Todd, give him back. Anthony, come back to me." All of Anthony's senses were awry, confused. He stopped crying but drew in short, quick, stifled breaths, barely exhaling between.

"You think you can just come in like this?"

"*You told me to come here*," Livia said, desperate.

"This is like when you came to the school," Elaine said. "We had you thrown out. You're lucky we didn't call the police. Should we call them now? I'm going to call them," Elaine said, and went back to the kitchen for her phone.

"No," Todd said. "No, that's . . . No. Not in front of him."

"The school?" Livia said, baffled.

"I'm Anthony's teacher," she said.

"I didn't tell you to come here," Todd said.

"You said I could meet the woman you were dating," Livia said. "You told me—"

"She's lying," Todd said quickly. "Sorry, do you really think I'd ask you here while I was on a date? Jesus, you really have lost your mind." Now Anthony started to struggle against Todd and started crying again.

"Daddy, stopppp," he pleaded. "Daddy, let me goooo."

"Don't hurt him!" Livia shouted, Anthony struggling until Todd put him down. He started to push on Todd's legs. "Leave her alone!"

It was a sudden change of heart, but not significant, Todd thought. This would be over soon.

"Let me spend some time with him," Livia pleaded.

"No," Todd said sternly.

"A minute, just a few minutes!"

"No," he said again.

"Todd," Elaine said. "We can stand right here."

"Anthony, stop pushing me!" Todd said.

"Please," Livia said, kneeling. Anthony turned to her.

"I love you," she said to him, and he quieted. Sniffling. "I miss you so much, and I'm going to find a way to spend time with you. Would you like that?" He nodded his head meekly.

"Okay," Todd said. "Anthony, go to your room."

Anthony lingered.

"He doesn't want to go," Livia said.

Again, Anthony began to sob. Screaming, almost. Like an echoing, slaughtered sound. Screaming, screaming, with barely any room for air.

"Take him up," Todd said to Elaine, and Elaine took Anthony's hand. He pulled it away from her instantly and petulantly, but still let himself be led away.

"You really think you could take care of him?" Todd snapped. "You're crazy. You start texting out of the blue, you accuse me of being with . . . a *guy*, you show up in town, you show up in school. You need fucking help, Livia. You were *an hour* late. An hour! Is that someone who wants to see her son? Do you understand how much you would fuck him up? You're like a whirl of chaos here."

"You said you didn't invite me, if you didn't invite me why would I be an hour late—"

"If you ever, *ever* come here again, there's going to be a restraining order, and then you're going to jail. And then I'll tell him that you're dead. You won't even exist anymore. You understand?" Then he laughed a little. "Come on, Livia, you think you know how to be a mother?"

There was an awful moment of silence. Then, meekly, she said, "I'll come back."

"No, you won't," he said.

She turned to the door, then turned back. "When did you become so horrible, Todd?"

"Maybe I've just been keeping it in." Behind him, the statuette stood still and cleaned and in constant struggle.

"You would never call the police," she said.

"Leave," he said. Now there was nothing for her to do other than run up the stairs to Anthony's room or turn around and go. She slammed the door behind her, and he heard the car start. He imagined Livia in her car, shouting at him, alone, from behind the wheel.

A fight. A fight could be normal, he felt.

Elaine was sitting at the top of the stairs.

"Sorry," he said, and he came upstairs to sit next to her. She shuffled over to make room. "I'm so sorry. We'll have a normal night soon enough, I promise."

"Do you want to know how he is?" she said flatly.

Todd stood again.

"No, no, don't go in, I think he's finally calmed down."

"It was a fight. A fight is normal. I mean, not like this. But he can see a fight from time to time," Todd said, looking down at her.

"Todd. It's his disappeared mother coming in and basically trying to *take* him from you." She paused. Then, with hesitation, "You said she was an hour late. If she wasn't supposed to come, how could she be late?"

"If she were coming," he said quickly. "I mean, on the day she was meant to show up. Which she thought was today. She would have been late." A slip. How many times had he slipped about other things but not known? Had he given himself away, somehow, to Sahir or his students, or to someone he hadn't thought of? A clerk at the grocery store? He had to be totally controlled up here, aboveground with everyone. He had to walk like everyone else. Talk like others. Be normal, or else.

"Oh," Elaine said. "And what's this about a *guy*?"

"Livia's crazy," he said. "She called the wrong number a few weeks ago and someone answered and kept running with it, pretending he knew me. She's been obsessed with it ever since."

"So . . . not Jack."

"What, my son's imaginary friend?" Todd gave an exhausted chuckle. "No. No, this guy's name was David, I think? Daniel? And he was *real*. Presumably. Who knows?"

Images ran about his head: Jack's wife, Linda, appearing on the news eventually. It would be a whole state away, so it probably wouldn't show up here. But what if it did, and Elaine heard about a wife looking for a Jack somewhere? She'd probably ignore it and not put two and two together. She wouldn't know that Todd had gone to school with Jack anyway. Or what if Linda were one of those wives—and she very well might be—who went from town to town up and down New England putting up flyers? Knocking on doors? Then at least someone from the boardwalk would have seen them, or wherever Jack went looking for a job. But she wouldn't. She wouldn't. If everyone who lost somebody did that, it would be nonstop. Even in the direst circumstances, people didn't want to have to put in effort for something. They weren't committed. Not like he was, every early morning.

"I think you're right, that she's crazy. But did you have to be so . . . I don't know. You were so forceful. She just wanted to see her son," Elaine said.

"Elaine, I think you'd better go," he said.

"Well, this was a terrible night," she said. "Terrible."

"Everything is on edge right now," Todd said quietly.

She sighed. "It wasn't all bad. Dinner, and talking. I liked that part." Todd remained silent.

"I just wonder if there's any room for me, with all this going on."

"I don't know," Todd said.

She stood and faced him in the narrow hallway. "Can we . . . should we see each other again?"

"Well, I guess we have to after school every day," he said.

She looked down.

"I'm sorry, I didn't mean it that way," he said. "I meant that I *will* see you. I'll even see you tomorrow. So maybe we can take a minute before planning the next date. If you still want one. I can't think straight right now."

"I'm sorry, Todd," she said.

"I'm going to go in and check on him, will you let yourself out?" he said. "And stop *apologizing*," he said.

"Sorry," she said reflexively, and walked down the stairs. "Not because I did anything wrong, I just . . . Sorry. That's all." Todd imagined that she was thinking of what else she could say, but she didn't say any of it. She just left.

Standing just outside of Anthony's door, he thought about how well everything had gone. Painful, but well. He slowed his breathing. Livia was out of the picture, with no suspicion that he'd had a man around the house anymore. He'd gotten Elaine to leave without any sort of fight. He did like her, he thought. The feelings were far from him, and he had no idea if they were anything other than plain amiability. But he was happy it hadn't escalated, in care or conflict. And Anthony had seen his mother be terrible, loud, disruptive. He was upset, but he would be okay, Todd was sure.

As he opened the door to Anthony's room, there was something wrong. There was Anthony facedown on the bed, floating like a dead body on the surface of a pool. And a grain, a shard of something, was in Todd's mouth. He fumbled around with it on his tongue as he approached the bed, and then reached in. A piece of tooth rested on his fingertip. He traced along his teeth with his tongue and discovered the back molar was jagged now at the edges, like rocks at the edge of an ocean. He stuck the shard in his pocket. There was no pain, but he'd have to go get it checked out. He thought back to when there was time for that sort of thing; for the doctor, the dentist, for things that other people did to take care of themselves.

He sat next to Anthony. "Hey, there. You okay?" He rubbed Anthony's back. Anthony didn't move. His body was still but flushed with warmth.

"Ms. Paige is gone. And that other woman is gone, too," Todd said. He waited, cautiously, for Anthony to protest this, but he didn't. "That was a little bit of a rough night, huh? Do you want me to go get some ice cream at the store?"

Anthony turned his head to the side.

"What flavor do you want?" Todd asked.

"I want Jack!" Anthony said, and it struck Todd with such force that inwardly he swayed. He closed his eyes and opened them again.

"You . . . you know Jack's not here," Todd fumbled. "He's not real."

"*Yes, he is,*" Anthony said. "*I want Jack!*"

"Stop," Todd said.

But Anthony shouted it again. "*I want Jack!*" And then again. "*I want Jack now!*" The sound bounced across the walls, shattering into each room.

"*Stop,*" Todd shouted back, and then pulled Anthony up so that he was sitting face-to-face with him.

"*I want—*" But this time Todd interrupted him with a hard smack across the face. Open-handed, big enough to connected with his entire head, rattling him into a stunned silence.

Anthony's eyes went wide.

Time stopped.

And then time reopened with screams of fear and pain. Tears glittered across Anthony's face, his left cheek flushed now.

Todd pulled him close and held him to his chest. Anthony tried to push away, but Todd held him tight as he cried and screamed. "*Let me go! Let me go!*"

Like a rabbit bitten on the neck by a fox or an eagle, he struggled and struggled. Until his body finally relented.

"Shhh," Todd said. "Shhh, it's okay, it's okay. I'm sorry, I didn't mean to do that. Daddy didn't mean to do that." He rocked back and forth and kissed Anthony's head. Back and forth, back and forth, until the crying stopped too. And turned to a whimper. Back and forth, a trance, like the waves, Todd rocked him past the whimpers and into exhausted sleep. Then he put him down on the bed and turned the light out and closed the door.

EIGHTEEN

Down the stairs. Into the kitchen. Down the stairs again.

At the bottom of the basement steps, Todd starts to talk out loud.

"Fuck you," he says, rifling through the tools. "Fuck you," he says, and he finds a hammer and walks to the container and opens it. "*Fuck you*," he says, and lifts the hammer up and brings it down on Jack's face and skull. A low crack at first. And Todd lets out a moan, a cry of his own pain that continues and untethers from itself and becomes something different.

This is not the sound he made the first time he struck Jack with the statuette.

This is a basement sound.

He smashes Jack's skull. It's a wailing-stuck-inside-a-throat sound.

Pieces of it fly up at him. The rounded right side of Jack's skull goes wayward like a bowl broken in half, but the skin still holds it together.

The wailing goes on, a shared sound. The nose caves in.

And the eye socket explodes and the jaw shatters and the brain flies apart and it's all coming apart now until Jack's face is pulverized, smashed, a nest of fragments and rubbery flesh and organ, and the broken spaces of Jack's face in front meet the broken jagged edges of his head in the back, and Todd has gone through, now, all the way through.

PART FOUR

He doesn't remember his dad hitting him in his bed the night before, *remember* is not the right word, because most of his memory has been swallowed; like an egg swallowed by a snake, the shape of it is becoming him; so it's more like: anger, a feeling where the image would be; more like: too many currents running through to sort it out; once he tied his shoelaces into a knot so tight that his dad had to cut them open with scissors, that's a memory; red shoelaces on a shoe off his foot, he had tied the laces again and again, but his dad wasn't proud that he could finally tie his shoes, then came the scissors, and the sky is thickening with dark clouds, there hasn't been a storm in a while, but there's a rumble from near the beach.

He plays hide-and-go-seek, but there's no one to hide from since there's no one to play with; but he imagines Jack, Uncle Jack, trying to seek him out, and there's not many places to hide in the backyard except up a tree he's still afraid to climb, or deeper in the woods where he doesn't want to go yet; he crouches behind the legs of the grill but he knows that's stupid, knows he could be found, except that he won't be, since there's no one to find him.

There's a memory like this, at the old house empty, the floors wide open, light filling it; Daddy, he said, Dad, Dad, let's play hide-and-go-seek; because he knew that with the broom closet cleaned and the rest of their world in stacks of boxes that he could shuffle into it and hide standing; so Daddy closed his eyes and said, One, two, and Anthony said, No peeking!, and Dad counted, three, four; and he ran past stacked boxes into the kitchen and opened the door slowly so it wouldn't creak the way it creaked when flung open, and got inside and was contained, so that he stood straight up with no way to move in total darkness, he could barely bend his arms; and from the world outside he heard, Ready or not, here I come!; he couldn't help himself, he laughed a little, because he would never be found in this dark thin place; there were footsteps, there was his dad's voice saying, I'm going to find you; saying, Are you under the table?; saying, Are you in the cupboards?; there was the sound of cupboards opening, but not the broom closet.

That is the memory: the dark place, with his father outside, and neither of them could see each other; he doesn't remember that his father couldn't find him, never thought to check the broom closet; he doesn't know that there was and would always be one black rectangle of negative space that never enters anyone's mind and that this time it was the broom closet in the empty house that he stood in; and there's no memory that he stood there for twenty minutes in pitch dark, unsure of what to do, until his father called out frantically, Anthony where are you, Anthony, come out right now, Anthony, Anthony; he doesn't remember being sure that he would be found and at the same time sure that he wouldn't be found; because memory isn't really like a snake swallowing an egg, it's like a leaf unraveling its surface to the sun for the first time.

Well, this place is different, way out in the open, covered only by the grill's thin legs and the fact that he is alone, because Uncle Jack was not his uncle, and the Woman Who Said She Was His Mom was his mommy or not his mommy; and also she was gone, like Uncle Jack is gone, he's not sure where, but it is unraveling in him; and his daddy is in the house, and he doesn't want to be around his daddy right now anyway.

He feels along the side of the grill leg to where the mud wasp had built its bubble, like a stone with its babies inside; he knew not to touch it because that was a lesson from nature: if you reach out, you might get stung or bitten or scratched; like the dog that lunged to bite him; he wouldn't remember that dog, only that dogs are angry; or Uncle Jack picking him up and Daddy getting mad about that; he wouldn't remember that, exactly; and where is Uncle Jack he wonders again and the answer moves like the sun is moving, behind the clouds, and some of the clouds are a heavy and troubled gray; so the leaves would be opening up to nothing now, and the sun is not really moving and the answer of where Uncle Jack is wasn't unraveling in him but opening; because memory isn't like a leaf unraveling its surface to the sun that's not there; memory is like awareness of death: a flower opening, and just as it unfolds, it is about to die itself.

Because at first he thought that it was the tooth fairy's worktable, because next to the bag of shining shattered pieces there was a full tooth, a big tooth; but he couldn't go down again because Daddy had put a lock on the door after that; but maybe if he put the bag somewhere very special, these shards that he wasn't sure were teeth but could maybe fool her, and the bag with the tooth in it now, then she would come at night and take the bag and leave him something enormous, who knows what; but after the first day when he checked it was still there, and after the second day when he checked it was still there, and he started to get a feeling that something was wrong with the bag and the tooth and the basement and the time when Jack was on the floor and his dad was standing there and rushed into the kitchen and held him by his shoulders and started to say frantic things, and it was a feeling like an opening of a flower, but no, no, because awareness of death is not like an opening of a flower, it's like a logic that sets its own course up to the sky and down to the center of things and out to each end of the earth; it's the growth of the entire plant; it's the flower and the root and the leaves and the stem; awareness of death is a logic that grows in all directions at once.

So he goes from the grill and decides to find a rock instead; because even if you can't play the hide part without a seeker, there are always things to seek out and find out and unearth and unbury; and this rock is long and uneven and there's another memory, a strange memory, a memory of a dream; that is, a memory of something that both did and did not happen; a dream of a horse's skull that looked like this stone; he doesn't remember ever seeing a horse's skull in person—he did, at a museum as a child—but there was one in his dream and he knew what it was; the way the teeth met in the front, and the hollowed cheeks and the giant eye sockets; and the skull was the size of this rock in front of him now, not the size of a real horse's skull, and it spoke to him, though he doesn't remember what it said because he was always dreaming of animals because children always dream of animals; so the memory is not of the dream exactly, but how the dream showed up for him later when his dad was reading a book to him; this was a book about Ice Age animals and all of them were giant versions of animals that are alive now; a giant lion, a giant and hairy elephant, a giant deer; all of them could step on you and smear you out across the ground or maybe if they were friendly you could ride them but he knew not to reach out, because maybe they would eat you and you'd become part of them, but they were all huge except these little horses on a certain page that ran in little herds; and they were called dawn horses like when the sun first shows up to fall on the unraveling leaves; dawn; and he saw them and said, That's like my horse, Daddy; but his father didn't understand, and said, We don't have a horse, and smiled a little; but because the dream became a part of him like a swallowed egg and because he didn't know that to articulate the dream would help his father understand, he did not know he could say, There was a little horse, a skull of a horse in my dream, and it was the same size as this one; so instead he felt a separation from his father; that is, he realized he was someone else and that would never change; that his dad was like a breath he could never breathe; so there was distance on distance and nothingness adding to itself like more space; this is something that flashes through him, contained in an image of a little horse's skull as he lifts the long rock that looks like a little horse's skull.

Under the new light that unravels and unfolds and swallows the darkness, the tiny bugs rush to hide; the gray ones that roll up into balls and the brown ones that curl up into spirals and smell when he picks them up and the rust-colored one that sidewinds beneath a dead leaf; pill bugs and millipedes and centipedes: he remembers their names, but like most names he forgets when and where he learned them; and there's a shiny black spider crouched into a nook, trying to make itself small, so he wonders how does the spider live under here with the rest of them because don't spiders eat other bugs, how do they live together under this long rock like a horse's skull with that constant threat, and how does the spider hold itself back; and nearby, under the dirt, there's a dull pink movement that he pushes with his pointer finger, and a stretch of worm, half underground, contracts and expands itself to dig deeper, down, away from his touch; so he pulls the worm up, like the robins do, and it resists like when he pulls the knot through in his shoelace, but then it's up and he's holding it, and a pointed end of it turns in the air, searching for the ground; he tries, and he tries, to feed it to the spider, but the spider only hunches more, maybe the worm is too big for it; so he reaches toward the center of the worm, where the thick band is, and he pulls at it, because he knows, but forgets how he knows, that worms grow back if pulled in half and that there will be two worms after this, so isn't it a kind favor to pull this animal in half; he pulls on it and at first the body resists, but then it gives way and there's a green mush the color of his snot at the broken ends and one side of the worm keeps turning slowly, and the other flips frantically in his hands and there, then, is an image of drowning.

No one has to tell you about drowning, no one has to tell you don't drown, you just don't drown, you just don't breathe in the water, you just hold your breath, so he held his breath underwater at the public pool; not in the deep end but not in the shallow end either, but in the middle, he held on to the stone edge, and his dad was a few feet away on a towel on the grass, among the other parents, where he could see him appear and disappear right at the edge as he ducked his head beneath the surface; beneath the surface, he said words to see what they sounded like underwater, he said Horse and said Flower and said Dog and said Hide-and-Go-Seek because it was a sort of hiding, down beneath the surface, that's what this reminded him of; so Todd was right there and so close watching him go under and come back up again, saying Hi! and Boo! and laughing, with the other boys and girls walking by, then going under while his fingers were on the edge in the middle between the shallow end and the deep end so that Daddy could've jumped in to save him if he saw anything wrong; but Daddy didn't see when another boy walked by, that that boy stepped on one of his fingers while he was under; so he'd let go, pulled his hand back in pain, slipped under, away from the surface, and thrashed his arms to grab the side again, but scraped his finger and pushed himself down farther till his feet were touching the bottom and he pushed himself back up, but he was too far from the wall now and there was nothing to grab on to and a panic seized him, and Daddy must have thought he was under saying words, just saying words, but he was under panicking because you just don't breathe underwater, but he had to breathe, and you just don't drown but he was drowning, not that he knew what drowning was; not that he thought about how his fingers were close to everyone's feet, that he knew but did not know he knew it, that his father knew but did not know he knew the danger there, that of course that was where you'd put your fingers if you wanted them stepped on, if you wanted to sink, if you wanted your body to panic like a pulled-apart worm, searching for something, some ground somewhere to hold on to, to pull you back to life; that we carry our deaths inside, because awareness of death is not like a logic that grows in all directions at once, but a condition that is always with us, waiting to float like a body to the surface.

He didn't drown, he pushed himself up, finally, and in the right direction, and grabbed the side and got out of the pool and ran to his dad and cried and neither he nor his dad knew why and they couldn't talk about it and there was a distance between them so he takes the two ends of the worm and instead of feeding it to the spider tries to put them back together, the slow one and the frantic one with its snot-green wound, and he holds those edges together, but they don't fuse and become one again, they keep moving at different paces and though it hasn't begun yet to rain, the smell of it is coming into the air, the clean smell before the thunder and lightning come; but the worm doesn't grow back into itself there's nothing to hold it together.

Not like the anger and the memories and the memories that are not memories; not like the parts of him he doesn't know and the time he wasn't found and the narrow dark and the dreams that won't go away and the Mom Who Is Not His Mom; not like the shattered teeth held in the bag and held between the mattress and the box spring; not like the spider that holds itself back and the lungs that stop breathing to save his life and the time his dad held him by the shoulder and said, Don't tell, don't tell; not like the storm clouds above now and Daddy dragging Uncle Jack into the basement and the pain that flushed in his face when Daddy hit him; not like any of that because it's all held together by him, all alive and writhing in him, all ready to live itself out through him; so he puts the worms that won't come together on the exposed side of the rock like a horse's skull and he picks up another stone, a smaller one, and raises it, and the raising reminds him of something and he's not sure what.

And the bringing it down reminds him, and he brings it down, and he smashes the slow half of the worm, it stops moving; and he brings it down again, it's just guts now, then he smashes the frantic half, which flips two more times, then gives up, and he pounds it into pulp.

And then it starts to rain, and then he goes inside, because death is like memory.

It's not like something that floats to the surface, and it doesn't grow in all directions, and it's not a flower, and it's not a leaf, and it's not a snake swallowing an egg.

Because death is like memory and memory is like love.

And they are all three like a snake swallowing its own tail.

Becoming itself to destroy itself.

PART FIVE

ONE

He was seven, like Anthony almost is. There was a cherry tree.

On the couch, falling into sleep then rising out of it again, Todd thought of the only time his father had hit him.

In the backyard of their first house in Pennsylvania. A tree Todd tried to climb for years; the absence of low branches preventing him, but that year he made it to the thick limb out of reach, jumping to it, wrapping his arms around it, pulling himself onto it. He thought of being a fruit-picker when he grew up, though he didn't know what that meant. He reached for the shiny red and yellow cherries and imagined he'd be like Johnny Appleseed as he spit the pits to the ground. If he could plant those, there'd be cherry tree after cherry tree lining the yard and he could move from one to another like a monkey. He could live there, maybe. He could sit on a huge branch and ask his mom to bring him peanut-butter-and-jelly sandwiches.

I live here now, he said.

He nuzzled his face against the pillow and thought of Jack doing the same. He opened his eyes and looked at the fabric; he could see the grooves of it in the dark light that was left in the room from the moon. He closed his eyes again.

The last summer at the house, the tree was shot across its trunk with an orange fungus, and he shouldn't climb it anymore, his dad said. The branches were getting weaker, and they'd have to cut the tree down if they weren't moving to a new house. But the cherries were still ripening and falling off, the leaves were still there, and it didn't seem dead.

The three of them were sitting in the backyard, drinking lemonade, and a citronella candle was burning.

"Plants take a long time to die," his mom said. "They don't just"—she snapped her fingers—"and that's it. It has to get into the plant over time."

"Fungus?" Todd said.

"Yes," she said. "Any kind of death."

Todd picked up a stick and walked over to the tree and swung at the fungus, which had grown so fast into bright, fire-colored planes that it seemed to have appeared overnight. When he struck it, a few chips of it flew away as he squinted his eyes.

"Go away!" he shouted. "Go away!"

"What are you doing, Toddy?" his dad asked.

"I'm saving the tree," he said.

"There's no saving it." And as Todd raised the stick again, he grabbed it from him. "And no climbing it either." He threw the stick to the far end of the yard and picked Todd up and away.

From the couch, he could hear the ocean. That was ridiculous, he knew. But he could. He could hear the ocean.

He climbed the tree, of course. As soon as his parents went in. Not to say goodbye, exactly, but to show the tree he cared about it, some-how. To pat the trunk, to snap a twig off and to keep it with him, so he'd remember the whole from its one small part.

And he fell.

Above the branch he stood on so often was another branch, a smaller branch, that he could swing on sometimes, when he was daring. He'd take a little hop and grab it and it would support him, dangling there. Letting go was the scariest part, because he figured if he didn't land the right way, he'd tumble off the rounded edge. So he jumped, and the branch was in his hands, and he hung there. He even closed his eyes. And then he opened them to a tickling, a little hello, of a yellow jacket crawling across his index finger, searching for sugar, for crushed cherry. Todd saw his hand let go and the yellow jacket hover away in incomplete circles. He saw his other hand let go, and then when he fell, the big branch hit his calves and he spun as he fell, all the way around so that he landed on his back, faceup; bouncing as he hit the ground. He couldn't breathe. For the first time, he'd had the wind knocked out of him. He was stunned, there was a blackness that filled everything.

The memory slipped into an image of a woman he'd never seen, the black stained sides of her pants, and she slipped, like the memory, away into nothing, her husband discovering and her son discovering her, like Anthony had discovered him and Jack. Was Jack's father still alive, and if he was, did he feel it when his son died? Was there a tremor when your son died? A shiver in Jack's father's spine, a tremble as Jack went into the gulls, into the ocean, into the sand, and into the fish.

No, it wasn't the ocean he was hearing, Todd realized. It was his own breath, lapping against the pillow, lulling him into the depths.

On the ground, he saw the little clover flowers beside him in the grass, he saw the sun above him. When he could breathe again, he wailed in fear. Mom ran outside, Dad ran outside. Dad ran toward him as he yowled, snot coming from his nose already, tears drying in lines of flight.

"Are you okay!" his Dad shouted, too loud for it to be concern alone. Too loud for it to not be anger too.

"I'm . . . I'm . . ." Todd stammered. But he *was* okay, he thought. Nothing hurt; he was just scared. His father ran his hand up and down

Todd's legs and arms to see if anything was broken. He saw Todd moving his head. "I'm here," his father said. "Here I am."

And Todd was drifting, then, in the backyard, black and bright white, not unlike how he was drifting now, in a sway, like Livia those last few weeks of their marriage. Drifting, till she was away in another country arranging for Todd to get money. She was beautiful, but always distant from him even as she swayed close. It was his fault, he realized, he never tried to reach her. He recognized for the first time that the money was a sort of kindness, the limited kindness she could grant. She couldn't hold her son then but she still gave the money; maybe she was broken now, on her way to the water in Positano, not like the water here which was dark, and covered itself with its own motion. The water in Positano was blue and clear like the sky above him that day when he was seven. You'd let that water take you alive.

Would she make another move against him, or would she finally go now, drifting back into her life before she punctuated it with this stupid act of violence and anger, coming here to reclaim someone she'd given up on so long ago? *I need you to feel things more*, she'd said to him once.

Maybe she was back in the walkways in Venice. She would have lost Anthony there, he was sure of it. The narrow corners, he'd disappear behind her or ahead of her. Even the water streets, even the sound, even the tallest and oldest buildings could be concealed by those narrow passages. "I'm here," she'd say when she found him, "here I am."

His father swore at him. "God*damn* it, *Todd*," he said, and pulled Todd close and hugged him, then pushed him away.

"It wasn't the branch . . ." Todd began, but it was too late. "I told you not to go up in the *goddamn tree!*" his father said. He pulled Todd's shorts down. Todd's legs were tangled in them, tangled at the ankles, he couldn't be free. His father spit in his hand and smacked Todd so hard that he screamed, and then again, and again, each time spitting in his hand first to make the hit bruise less and sting more; something his own father had taught him by example.

It wasn't fair, he'd thought then, it *wasn't fair*! It wasn't the branch that made him fall, but the yellow jacket, if only he could get his father to understand!

On the couch, he remembered the distance from his father, and the plea, and the single welt on him for days. He remembered the way, after that, though he never hit him again, his father would spit in his hand whenever he wanted to warn Todd. He remembered the sounds of the smacks of his father's rough hand against his smooth white legs and buttocks. He remembered the sound he made when he hit the ground.

And so, when the explosion came, the banging, loud and singular and final, he thought, at first, that it was a memory.

The world took a moment to come back, like light gathering in rubbed eyes.

Then it was there. The sound had come from the basement.

He stood, naked, and pulled his underwear—hanging off his foot—up around him. The house was dark and blended into itself. The living room was still. The kitchen was still. The padlock was still on the door.

He reached above the basement doorframe and got the key. When he unlocked the door, something rose to greet him.

A smell. A terrible, deep, but sharp, muddy smell. Like the flies had found something. Todd groaned and covered his nostrils and mouth with his hand and turned on the light. He descended slowly. It was the smell of shit and ferment, something turned inside out. At the bottom of the stairs his mind strained to understand the scene. The lid of Jack's container was up against the wall, the container open.

"J . . . Jack?" Todd said.

There was a moment when he expected a response.

But everything held until he saw the flecks of flesh. The pieces of

Jack's abdomen. The smears of brown and string-bean-colored fluids on the walls and the lid and the floor.

Jack had exploded.

The gases in his belly and abdomen had gathered and gathered as pressure until there was no room left in him. There was a hole now, black inside with ooze. There were folds of exploded skin, hanging off and bunched off like popped balloon flesh.

The smell rolled over Todd and pulled back; rolled over and pulled back. He would have to take care of this now, in the waves of it.

He got the bottle of white vinegar and the bottle of carpet cleaner. He got scented candles and room fresheners. He got towels from upstairs and paper towels from the kitchen. He couldn't do the rest of Jack's torso. Not his ribs or what was left of his heart and lungs and spine. But he'd have to do the whole gut tonight. He wrapped a blue shirt around the bottom of his face and got gloves.

Later, at the beach, his backpack was drooping down with the weight of fluids and flesh. Todd headed toward the water and stopped halfway and looked at the sand. This felt like the spot where Jack had shown up that first day. It was a stupid guess, he knew. There wasn't any trace of that spot, of course. Just the feeling. He set the bag down and knelt to touch the sand. Ran it past his fingers. Surely, now, there were bits of Jack's bones sifted through the beach. When it was warm again, people would stand on him, play on him, breathe him in.

The wind slipped around him, trying to get by, and the surf was loud as always, but as he knelt there, he thought he heard a small moan through it. He stood slowly and brought the bag back on his shoulders and tilted his head. There it was. And then another one, from behind him. His car was in the lot up the hill, but that was where the sounds were coming from. He could walk farther down the beach, he supposed, but he had to be sure that he wasn't seen. He couldn't leave the bag.

He went quietly to investigate, concealed in the wind, footsteps muffled by the shifting ground. As he closed in on the lot the sounds intensified. A man moaning. Two men, their breaths overlapping and outrunning each other, from around the shower and changing area. It was locked for the season; they must be on one side of it.

He walked along the exposed side and turned his head around one corner. There, standing, were two men, trousers down around the ankles. Both facing the stone wall, one was fucking the other. Todd's body seemed to pull in two directions, his eyes staying on them, his right foot stretching away from the scene, readying him to run. A belt buckle was jangling against the pavement. The one fucking had a beard, and his shirt was pulled up past his belly so that it was pressed against the other man's back. The other man was darker-skinned, his face was pressed fully against the wall, his palms up and against the wall too. His eyes were closed. Todd didn't recognize the first man. The man against the wall was Sahir.

"Fuck," the other man kept saying in a loud whisper. Each time he said it, it didn't keep pace with his thrusts, his body and voice out of step. "Fuck, fuck, fuck."

Sahir moaned again and then opened his eyes and saw Todd, who quickly ducked around the corner. "Fuck!" Sahir said, but in the other way.

Todd rushed back to his car and heard the pair shuffling. Had he seen Todd fully? Was it too dark for Sahir to have made him out? When he got to his car, he opened and closed the door as quietly as he could, then drove out of the lot with the lights off, down the road. He would come back in an hour; they'd probably have fled by then.

TWO

There wasn't much left now.

Rib bones and some spine. Back flesh. A soft heart. Todd could do all of that in an evening.

The day after seeing Sahir, Todd sat, mildly delirious, at the table with Anthony, and poured him some cereal, which his son only stared at. Anthony picked up his spoon and tapped the tip of it on the table, like he was trying to dig the wooden surface up from itself.

"What's wrong?" Todd said, but his son kept on swaying the spoon handle back and forth, trying to push the rounded edge deep.

"Anthony," Todd said again, and took Anthony's spoon away. His son looked up. "What's. Wrong?"

"The tooth fairy isn't real," he said.

"Sure she is. That kid at school is full of shit." Usually cursing in front of Anthony would get him to smile or laugh and playfully scold him. This time, nothing. Todd handed the spoon back. "Eat your cereal."

Anthony pushed the spoon onto the floor.

"No, she isn't, no, she isn't."

"Come on," Todd said. "Pick your spoon up."

He sat there.

"Just because one kid at school says she isn't real doesn't mean she isn't real," Todd said, and picked the spoon up and put it in the sink.

"She doesn't always come," he said.

Todd wasn't sure what Anthony was getting at. Had he missed a tooth?

"If she's not real, how did you get that money under your pillow?"

"You put it there," Anthony said.

"If I put it there, wouldn't I always come, though? I know every time you lose a tooth," he said, searching his thoughts for a tooth he might have missed. Maybe Anthony had swallowed one, like some children do; a baby tooth in the back. He was too tired to think straight. He got another spoon from the drawer.

"Besides, I'm sleeping at night. I don't wake up just to take . . ." He stopped himself and changed tactics. "You know she doesn't come for bad kids. She doesn't want their teeth. That's why that whatever-his-name-is says she's not real. She doesn't come to him."

For this, Anthony had no response.

"Eat," Todd said.

Without a sound, Anthony pushed his bowl off the table, the milk and the cereal and the porcelain cracking and splashing together on the floor.

"Congratulations!" Todd said angrily. "You're going to clean all of that up now."

"I don't want to clean it up, you clean it up," Anthony said, and ran from his chair to the front door.

At school, Todd tried to remain on automatic. Just say the words, just make the kids talk to each other, just walk through the halls and check the boxes in the attendance book. Before lunch, he saw two other boys he didn't recognize and Banner Bolland in the hall. The two boys were holding their phones up by Banner's face. On it was a dog, barking in a way that made it sound like it was saying, "I love you."

"Ri ruv roo!" one of the boys said in a mock-dog voice at Banner.

"Ri ruv roo too!" the other boy said, and they both cracked up.

"Fuck you!" Banner said, desperately.

"Ruck roo!" one of the boys said, and gave him a small push, then they walked away.

Todd wanted to say something, but Banner had slammed his locker and turned from the scene, so Todd walked to the library instead.

It was empty, except for a girl he recognized from his afternoon class. She waved at him. "Hi, Mr. Nasca," she said. And then, more quietly, in deference to the library, "Oh, sorry, hi, Mr. Nasca."

He was too tired to remember her name now, even though he knew he knew it. "Hi," he said back. "Is Sahir here?"

"Who?" she said.

"Mr. Azar," he said. "Never mind." Why was he asking her?

He walked to the librarian's office and knocked on the door and opened it slowly. Sahir was at his desk looking at his phone.

"There are no windows in here," Todd said. "How do you deal with that?"

"Can I help you, Todd?" Sahir said flatly.

What had he come here to say? *I'm sorry I saw you getting fucked while my backpack was full of blood?* The thought so absurd that a low and brief chuckle escaped him.

"What?" Sahir said. "What's funny?"

"Oh, nothing, I. Wanted to see. How you were. How you are."

"I'm busy," Sahir said.

"Okay, I wanted to say, it's okay."

Sahir didn't respond. Had he not been able to see that it was Todd after all?

"I didn't want you to think that I—"

"Todd," Sahir interrupted. "What are you talking about?"

The interruption was too quick; a barging in. Sahir was too flat, too forceful. He must have known that Todd knew.

"Seriously," Sahir said. "Sometimes you're too busy to talk to me? I'm too busy now."

"Never mind," Todd said. "It doesn't matter." He turned and left, and felt this was precisely true. It didn't matter. Not Anthony pushing his bowl off the table, not Banner Bolland, not Sahir, none of it mattered. Soon Jack would be all taken care of, his body cast to the world, and Todd would be done. And Todd would be free. He would be free.

THREE

At the bottom of the container, there was a shadow in the dark.

He touched the stain.

He was resting his hand on it, Jack's shattered ribs and heart in bags behind him. It wasn't an outline of a body, but more like a landscape, a gathered blotch of bruised woods, a rounded side and a pointed side, darkening in varying degrees, painted on over the weeks of discarding the corpse.

Hawk Mountain, he thought, and had the strange feeling that his whole life was contained in it. But he shook the thought away.

There would still be work to do, labors great and small. Like, would he throw the container away? That was a small one, but still a tangle of problems. He couldn't throw it in the ocean. He didn't want to chance throwing it in a dumpster; what if someone saw him; what if someone found it? He could cut it up and burn it, he supposed. Melt the plastic. But that would send fumes up that might alert the neighbors. Leave no trace, that was the idea. Like they say when you're hiking. Leave no trace, no suspicion that you'd been there. But what they meant was don't destroy anything, don't harm anything. He meant something different. Leave no trace.

And then he was thinking of Hawk Mountain again. The distance he felt from the other students. The way he fell, alone, to the ground. The way Jack blotted out the sun. Their hands touched. *Keep moving*, he thought against the memory.

He could wash it. But there was always a bit, wasn't there? He'd have to wash the whole basement, he realized in that moment—and maybe wash the living room again. Get a new carpet. He imagined the police scraping samples of everything in the house. Probably the best thing to do would be to put the holiday decorations back in the container, to fill it with its former guts. The police would open it, push through them, see nothing strange.

"The police aren't coming," he said out loud. "Because nobody knows."

The waiter at the diner. Maybe some of the diner patrons. Some people at the beach and boardwalk. The couple with the dog. Some other people Todd didn't know of, but nothing major. Those were the only people who had seen Jack; all fleetingly. So that was a smaller work, as well. They'd have to see a photo of him, remember him, and then remember he was with Todd, and know who Todd was or accurately describe him.

There's Anthony, Todd thought. All the while, he was still touching the stain. That was the great effort. Starting a new life with Anthony, who had seen what Todd had told him he had not seen. What Todd had said—that Jack wasn't real—that would have to become the truth for his son. So they would never really be together again; they'd be next to each other every day but would inhabit different worlds; Todd would know one truth, Anthony would know something else. The thought turned back on itself in him, like a confusing and dark road. It would be a familiar relationship; the kind that could turn on him at any moment.

Anthony was asleep in his bed, two floors up, closer to the sky than to his father.

Todd put the bags into his backpack. It had taken days to smash the ribs into brittle, tiny pieces. The bone had to not look like bone; had to be so small that if someone saw one piece next to another, they wouldn't think, *Bone*, much less, *Human bone*. Of course, no one would see; the bones would dissolve and sink. The directions he flung them in were too far apart, the waves were too hungry.

Then he put in the bag of heart and lung, cut and pulverized, not that it had needed much help, all softened and liquefying by now. The plastic bags hung heavy like a cut of beef from the butcher, the juices bulging.

That was Jack now, he thought. That was what remained.

He walked to the beach, and this early morning, no one, not even the sun, was out. No one was fucking. The air was colder than it had ever been since he'd started. Todd pushed into the waves.

First, the bones. He walked through the water like a person pushing through a hard future, taking effortful steps. Sometimes he cast the bones like seeds, and other times he'd take a handful and hold it under the surf and let the motion take it. He walked parallel to the shore for a half hour, clung to by his soaked clothing, dispersing bones.

Then the heart, the lungs. He could hear the gulls before he even opened the bag, their precise calls and wheezing above. Their white bodies began to show in the dark, and as he flung Jack's heart and lungs, they caught the flesh in midair. Then there were dozens hovering, as if they'd found a shoal of dead fish or a slaughtered whale. They swooped at him and swallowed what he gave. And for the bits they missed, they landed on the surface and tucked their heads beneath the skin of the ocean. They found every piece of this dead person, this disappeared person, this murdered person. They ate Jack's flesh. They drank Jack's blood.

Free!

Todd put the plastic bag into his backpack and zipped it up. He was free now.

He took his shirt off, soaking, it stuck to his skin. He pulled off his sweatpants. Free. Free! He held his clothes in one hand, and the backpack on his back, and he was naked as he went under. The sway of it held him, and back and forth with his eyes closed, naked; every part of him swayed and he would rise up free now, he said to himself in the slate-gray nowhere of the underwater world, rise from the skin of the water and be free!

And when he surfaced, as he took a deep breath of air, things had changed, because the sky had opened, and a rain was coming. He walked back to his shoes, trembling and shivering. He hoped it was like being born, and that so much had happened in those few moments he was under. He put on his shoes and walked as quickly as he could, naked and on the beach as the rain beat down, back to the car. Then he took off his shoes and put on new clothes.

He pressed the horn and it let out its one note. And then he pressed it again, longer, so that it carried the note longer, and louder, it seemed. No one was around to hear, but more importantly, it wouldn't matter if anyone heard him, now. The body was gone, and he was free! Free, free, and bound to the knowledge that nothing could come with him.

FOUR

Anthony was awake.

Just like the rain had stopped and the sun had started to come back, Anthony was sitting at the kitchen table. "Where were you, Daddy?" he said, as soon as Todd walked in. He was in his pajamas still.

"He-ey, what are you doing up?" Todd said.

Nothing.

"I was just outside," he said.

"I looked outside," Anthony said.

"Did you go outside?" Todd said.

"Yes," he said, and Todd saw that there was dirt and dead grass on his feet. His son had woken up and gone outside, and no one was there for him; the thought would have torn at Todd, but everything was different now. Todd was free and he couldn't feel for his son in the same way. Not until he knew it was safe.

"I was outside, but at the beach!" Todd said, with an upswing in his voice. "I wanted to go walk on the beach for a minute."

"It's too cold for the beach," Anthony said.

"You don't believe me?" Todd said. "Look!" He stamped his feet so that the sand shook off his sneakers. And from the edge of the right toe of his shoe a fleck of brown meat, dotted with grains of sand, flew off, too. Todd moved his foot quickly to cover it.

There was a quiet moment of them both staring at the floor where the sand was, and where his foot concealed the rotten flesh. The tiles shone dully.

"I don't like what you did, Daddy," Anthony said quietly.

"What did Daddy do?" he said quickly, and picked Anthony up, groaning a little as he hoisted him into the air.

Anthony put his face on Todd's shoulder.

"What did Daddy do? Is it because Daddy went to the beach without you? You want to go to the beach too?"

"I have school," he said into Todd's shirt.

There was a pause and then Todd acted animated. "So what! So what, let's go to the beach!" He moved up and down slightly, so he was vertically rocking his son. "I'll tell them we're both sick."

"But I'm not sick," Anthony said.

"I *know*," he said, frustrated at first. Then, calmer, "I know you're not sick, but you have to tell them that you were when they ask, okay?"

"Lie?" Anthony said.

"No, no, not lie, just . . . have a secret with Daddy, okay? You can even pretend, if it comes up. You can remember it that way."

"Daddy, you're confusing," Anthony said, and Todd laughed.

"Go get anything you want to take to the beach," he said, and set him down.

Anthony ran up the stairs, and Todd called the school.

"We both have a bug, I'm afraid," he said to the woman in the office, and then again to the man at the desk at Anthony's school. This was all right, wasn't it? To celebrate a new life with his son.

Anthony came down soon with *Wolf Story* and the toy dog and a robot action figure, and he seemed excited.

But when they got to the beach, empty and run-through with wind, Anthony said it was too cold.

"We took the day off so you could come play," Todd said. "So play, I'll be right here."

"It's too cold," he said, holding his dog and his robot.

Todd grabbed Anthony's toys from him and put them on the sand.

"*Be a kid!*" Todd said. "*Play!*"

FIVE

"Are you feeling better?" Elaine asked quietly. It was a Sunday afternoon, and they were at the Highfeld, the nicest restaurant in town, empty at the odd hour, except for the two of them and the staff.

"What?" Todd asked.

"Oh, sorry," Elaine said, and spoke up. "I feel like I have to whisper in here because it's so quiet. I asked if you were feeling better."

"No, I heard you, I . . ." He caught himself and laughed.

"You weren't sick, were you!"

"No," he said.

"Was Anthony?"

"Let's order first, and I'll tell you." He looked at the menu calmly, a little shaken by his slipup. But then, he reminded himself, he could relax a bit now. Taking the day off wasn't a crime, even lying to your job wasn't a crime. These deceptions would happen less and less, he felt, until they faded into a sort of softness in the past. He only had to keep one secret.

He'd hired a babysitter to watch Anthony for a few hours. He'd found her number on the bulletin board at the little grocery co-op. She seemed nice enough; skinny, tall, she smiled when he talked about Anthony. He wondered about the parents of other kids, and if the fathers hit on her, and if she therefore felt a sort of relief or contentment knowing he had no interest. She could feel safe at his house. He mulled over whether or not to mention Anthony's imaginary friend but reasoned that it was only a few hours. He told her, instead, "He's been through a lot this year, with starting school. So he can get a little emotional." She'd smiled and said no problem, she'd babysat nightmare kids and Anthony seemed perfect.

He would repress Jack as much as he could now.

They ordered salmon and lamb and Todd ordered a beer.

"It's early, but it's Sunday," he said when the beer came.

"You can do whatever you want," Elaine said. "Don't mind me. But, okay, tell me."

"Well, I wasn't sick, I just wanted to celebrate," Todd said.

"Celebrate what?"

"Nothing!" he said, laughing. "I know that sounds bizarre, but what I mean is nothing in particular. Anthony is having a hard time with his whole mom situation, and at school—"

"It's okay for you to say you're having a hard time with it too," she interrupted.

"Yes, okay. I was too. And school just started for both of us, and it's a whole new town, and we're really . . . I don't know, we need to celebrate making it through everything. If that makes sense."

"That's sweet. So what did you do?"

"I took him to the beach. It was freezing out, but he wanted to go."

"He must have loved it," she said.

Todd took a drink. They sat in silence for a bit.

"Ask me something about myself," she said finally. "I ask you questions all the time."

"I'm . . . sorry. I'm an asshole," he said, and smiled.

"Hey, stop talking about you. Don't worry, you'll get through it, you'll be okay," she said, and laughed.

He thought of Hannah at graduation and smiled.

"What are you smiling at?" she asked.

"Well, there was a girl I went to high school with and you reminded me of her just then when you said that."

"When I told you to ask me something about myself?"

"No, though she would have done that too. It'll sound weird, but she once told me I'd be okay in a moment when I was sort of . . . embarrassed. I didn't realize it, but she was really *seeing* me then, I guess. It's—it's too much to explain."

"Well," Elaine said slyly, "she sounds great. So I hope you're not still in touch with her."

"No, she's . . . dead." He cut her off at the pass, "And before you say you're sorry to hear it, I'd lost touch with her long before that."

There was a silent moment till she spoke again. "Well, I didn't want you to lose touch with her *that* way. At least, I don't think so." They both smiled.

"Okay, okay," he said, "a question." This was how people were supposed to talk with each other.

He closed his eyes for a minute and saw Hawk Mountain there. Jack's hand, holding his.

"When's the first time you were in love? I don't mean a relationship, unless they're the same. I mean, in love. Maybe you were a kid and looked up to someone, or maybe a crush, or you had a friend you were in love with."

"Wow, okay," she said. She picked up a piece of bread and pulled away a smaller piece from it. "It was a teacher, actually."

"Oh, well, I'm flattered," Todd said.

"Oh, you know what I mean, not you!" she scolded him playfully. "I was thirteen? I think. It was ninth grade, so no, I was fourteen. A substitute teacher, Mr. Duracinsky. He was so handsome, and he was only at the school a few times, but whenever I saw him, I felt *interested*, you know? Then one day he was subbing for my geography class, and one of the boys—Andy Botassi, I remember it so clearly—Andy Botassi flicked one of those triangle paper footballs at me, and the other boys laughed. So I turned to him, and I told him to fuck off. I actually said 'fuck off,' and Mr. Duracinsky heard me of course and said . . . Oh, this is so stupid, Todd."

"I'm listening," he said.

"He said, 'If you keep talking like that, I'm going to flick one of those at you myself.' And I was so embarrassed, and it was so *unfair*, I thought, but then the boys laughed. And when they laughed, he told them to shut up, and they all shut up. Even though he was a substitute, they all listened. After that, I'd write his name on my notebooks. I even found out his first name: Jim. On the back pages of my notebooks. Jim Duracinsky. Jim Duracinsky in a heart. Jim Duracinsky and I'd draw flowers and stars. So cheesy. That's the end of the story."

"I guess it would have to be," Todd said. "You obviously couldn't tell him your feelings. Do you know what happened to him?"

She shook her head. "But you have to wonder, don't you? What happens to you when you love someone, and you can't tell them? What does that do to you?"

Todd looked off for a moment, then, "Why do you think it was that moment that made you fall in love?"

"That's a good question. But I don't think you can know, can you?"

"Maybe," Todd said.

"Maybe I thought I wanted to be him, in a way. Not *him*, if you know what I mean. But he . . . I think he was doing what was right, or at least what he thought was right, but totally doing it. I wasn't spared, the boys weren't spared. Love, maybe, is seeing the person you want to be."

The waiter came and set their food down and talked with them for a minute.

"This looks great," Todd said, and they began to eat.

"So what about you?" she said. "When was the first time?"

Todd's phone vibrated in his pocket.

"Hold on," he said. "I just want to make sure it's not the babysitter." He pulled it half out of his pocket and looked at it.

> HI TODDY, THIS IS YOUR MOTHER. HAVEN'T HEARD FROM YOU IN A LONG TIME. ARE YOU ALIVE??? WE GOT A VERY ALARMING LETTER TODAY. YOUR FATHER IS OKAY.

"Is everything okay?" she asked.

"Hold on," he said again.

> At dinner, what letter?

he texted back.

"Is it the babysitter?" Elaine asked.

"*Hold on*," he said forcefully. He waited for a minute and another message popped up.

> I KNOW YOUR DAD WOULD LIKE TO HEAR FROM HIS ONLY SON, SO CALL US AND WE CAN TELL YOU ABOUT EVERYTHING AND THE LETTER TOO

"Fucking *come on*," he said out loud. He looked up, and Elaine had a disappointed, searching expression.

"I'm sorry, it's . . . my parents. I haven't talked to them in months, and then . . . this."

"What?"

"Just, they said . . . They're not exactly present in my life. They only text to, I don't know, make me feel bad."

"It's okay," she said.

"No, no, it's not. Or it *shouldn't* be, at least. It shouldn't be—"

"Let me make my own decisions," she said, irritated. "I can make up my own mind about if I want to be around you, or do you want to throw that into the mix too?"

"You're right, you're right," he said. "I'm sorry."

"Remember what you told me?" she asked.

"What?"

"Stop saying you're sorry."

"I'm . . ." and he stopped.

"See?" she said. "Not so easy."

They ate slowly and quietly.

"Do you not get along?" she said finally. "You and your parents."

"I don't know," he said.

"You don't know? That seems like something you'd know: whether or not you get along with someone."

"It does seem like something someone should know," he said. "But I don't."

SIX

When he got home that night, Anthony was sitting on the couch with the babysitter, watching a movie. He paid the sitter and asked how everything was, and she told him it was fine, but made a comment about how bossy he was. "He's going to be a good lawyer one day," she said. Anthony had told her he didn't have to go to school anymore, and that Todd didn't, couldn't, make him go.

When Anthony was in bed, Todd unlocked the basement. He was halfway down the stairs before realizing he didn't have to go there anymore. The work was done, but his body had its rhythm. He wavered on the step, and then followed it all the way down.

In the dim light, he looked over to the container, open, airing out, empty. He got a screwdriver and walked over to it and peered again into the stain, then put the lid on. He walked to the top of the stairs and opened and unscrewed the padlock frame, pulling it away from the doorframe. There were holes in the door now. Should he get a new door? Even if he did, there'd be holes in the frame too. That would be more expensive to replace. It was a perfectly good lock, but he threw it away. Forget about it.

He put a sweater on and walked out onto the porch. He could be asleep by now, he thought. He could be in bed sleeping, like the other teachers no doubt were, tending to their health and clearheadedness, making sure they'd be present for their students. A pang of desire filled him up, a longing to get a new house entirely. To get a new job, to be somewhere away from everything that had happened. But he didn't have the money to do that now. And anyway, where would he go? There was nowhere.

A scratching sounded from the ground, then. There was a movement, a noise, from below. And a thump. A hollow wooden knock that shivered through the porch. He didn't want to move, but he didn't want to sit still either.

"Hello?" he whispered.

Nothing, nothing, and then the sound of quick breaths and shuffling. Todd turned the light on his phone toward the spot, and two eyes glowed back at him, then four. A pair of raccoons, scrambling out from under the porch.

Those fucking raccoons, he thought, *how many times are they going to get under there?*

"Get out of here," he hissed at them, and they hesitated, and then ran, lumbering away in their fat bodies toward the dark.

A few minutes passed, then suddenly Todd sat up straight. A chill ran from his tailbone to his brain.

How many times were they going to get under there?

They'd never been under there before.

This was the first time he'd seen them.

Raccoons under the porch was a story he'd made up, to explain away the smell of Jack's rotting body.

SEVEN

Whether he'd said he wanted to go or not, Anthony went to school. Maybe his son had forgotten he was upset, had forgotten what he wanted and what he didn't want. Maybe he didn't remember that he could refuse anything at this point. That was what a child's memory was like; it always seemed to swallow itself.

Now that Jack was gone, the world reflected a new, dull light where everything was noticeable. The white drop-tile ceilings in the school, marked with divots from thrown pencils and pens. One pen still hung from the ceiling, like a tiny Sword of Damocles. The boxy lighting, mottled plastic and fluorescent white shining through the bodies of dead flies that no one was ever willing to clean out. The flat caramel color of the desks and the shining bore of steel legs. The small instance of graffiti on the wall behind his chair, the word CROWS in black marker, the size of his thumb. Where did all of this come from?

In one corner of the room there was a stand with a map on it. Blue water, multicolored countries. It was worthless in English class, but he'd left it there. He barely noticed it from day to day, large as it was. Had it gone unnoticed by everyone?

When the students sat down in his first class, he told them to close their eyes.

"What's in the corner of the room to my right?" he asked. No one said anything. They sat with their eyes closed, restless.

"No peeking," he said.

"Really? No one?" Todd asked. "Come on, what's standing up in the corner right next to my desk?"

"This is sort of creepy, Mr. Nasca," said one of the boys he had seen picking on Banner Bolland. They all laughed, of course.

"Okay, fine, open your eyes," and they did, and looked to his right. "No one remembers this map?"

"Did you bring that in here today?" a girl asked.

"Nope," he said. "It's been here the whole year."

"That's so weird." There was grumbling.

"What I want you to do is write down everything you see in this room. Everything."

"Just like in the room or people too?" a boy asked.

"Everything."

"So if it's like someone's eye, do I have to write left eye, right eye, one eyelash, two eyelashes, and then do that for everyone . . . ?"

"Use common sense, okay?" Todd said. The question was irritating, a reminder that in school they didn't want to get any meaning out of what was asked of them, they just wanted to get it right. "We're going to keep going. Just keep writing and writing. Any other questions?"

A hand went up and the handsomest boy, who was too ordered and mannered, asked, "Why?"

"What?" Todd said.

"Why are we doing this? Is this related to the upcoming book?"

Todd felt overheated for a moment. He couldn't remember what the next book was. He had no idea why he was asking them to do this.

"Yes," he said anyway. "I want you to see what's missing. The obvious things that you overlook. You'll see how it's related later."

The kids took a collective breath and started writing.

In the afternoon, he received a note from the main assistant to the principal; the principal, Mr. Murphy, wanted to see Todd in his office. A funny feeling, still, being pulled into the office as an adult. He flushed. Had Banner Bolland gone to him after all? He'd have to find Banner at some point, apologize to him. That would be possible now. Now that Jack was gone.

He walked the hall to the office, coming up with the best story he could. He just meant to have Banner read out loud? He was going to have all the students act out different characters but didn't have time? Yes, that would work. He leaned his head in through Mr. Murphy's doorway.

"Hi," he said.

"Oh, come in and sit down and close the door," Mr. Murphy said.

"Am I in trouble?" Todd said, and laughed as he sat down.

Mr. Murphy, white-haired and husky, didn't smile.

"Todd, this is sensitive."

"Okay," Todd said, and sat up straight.

"I'll get right to it. Tell me about Mr. Azar."

Todd froze inside for a second. He wasn't sure what direction to go in. His first thought was to say, *With all due respect, that is not getting right to it.*

"Sahir?" Todd said.

"Yes, go ahead."

"Well, he's a nice guy? We talk from time to time."

"Come on," Mr. Murphy said.

"What?"

"What have you *seen*, Todd."

"Oh . . ."

"Listen, I know you might feel like you need to protect him, honor among thieves and all?"

"Thieves?"

"Well, teachers. Teachers are the thieves in this case."

"I'm sorry, Paul. I don't understand."

"Well, let me put it this way. We're revising the sex education program here, and we can't have one of the faculty *demonstrating the new lessons in his car.*"

Todd stood abruptly, and then sat down again.

"Paul? You have to tell me what you're talking about."

The principal was quiet.

"It's okay, you can tell me. I genuinely have no idea what you mean."

"Mr. Azar was in his car a couple days ago, before school. He was . . . kissing someone. A man. One of the boys saw him and told us."

"Who?"

"We don't know who he was," Mr. Murphy said.

I meant who was the boy, Todd thought. But he let it go. He thought of Sahir's hands up against the stone wall of the changing area. How they saw each other. The man behind him with the beard.

"So the guy was in his car?"

"And then drove his car away after Mr. Azar got out. And the students saw him."

"So he was in his car and . . ."

"Kissing some man. And the students saw him."

"Listen, it sounds like nothing," he said, which made Mr. Murphy shift in his seat. He didn't know Mr. Murphy well, and so was unsure how to respond. He looked at his fat hands and saw a gold band. "If you came to school and your wife dropped you off and kissed you goodbye—"

"That's completely different, *completely different*, and you know it," Mr. Murphy said.

Neither of them said anything for a minute; they stared at each other across the desk.

"Not because he's . . . whatever," Mr. Murphy said. "He's already, you know, *marginalized*, because of . . . Well, he's already seen as an outsider here. Can you imagine how he'll feel if the kids start talking about that?"

"So it's about . . . him? So. You need to have some sort of tolerance or diversity education for the kids, then?" Todd offered.

"I need all the faculty to be in cooperation here," Mr. Murphy said. "I need you to keep your eyes open, to make sure if it happens again, that you tell me. Whoever it is, that's against the code of conduct. In the parking lot."

It was such a jumble of messages. Todd didn't know what to say. He could try to talk to Sahir again. Let him know.

"Can you let it go?" Todd said finally.

"That's not funny," Mr. Murphy said.

"Okay," he said. He stood up. *Jack is gone*, he thought. So before he left, he said, "Paul, it's none of my business."

"The students are your business."

"Not in this way," Todd said.

The principal sighed and his shoulders dropped. "Things are complicated, Todd," he said.

"Not like this," Todd said, and left.

None of it felt right. Even his resistance. He'd been emboldened by the thought that Jack was gone, like a rush of confidence. But something still felt off. A false boldness. Something missing.

What the fuck? he thought, as he walked down the hall.

And then, as if he'd manifested the words, he heard a boy's voice from around the corner say them.

"What the fuck!"

It was Banner Bolland, and two boys in front of him. Banner's books were on the floor and he knelt down to pick them up.

Todd watched. He thought of himself distantly, as another person. *He should help*, he thought, seeing his body do nothing.

One of the other boys kicked a notebook and it spun off down the hall.

"Go fetch," the boy said to him.

I should stop this, Todd thought, *I should help.*

But he didn't.

By the end of the day, he felt tense, like a wire had been pulled through him. Both incidents, with Sahir and Banner, would find their own footing and pass. All of them would become inconsequential. All of them would die into nothing. Jack was gone now; that was what mattered. That and Anthony. But the hum of the rest of the world wouldn't die away. In the last period, when the students were doing an assignment, he got up and went to the boys' bathroom.

He walked into the stall and undid his belt and tried to masturbate. He wanted to think of nothing. He tried not to think about anything, he didn't even want to jerk off, he thought, he just wanted to become physical, tense up in the right way until his shoulders let go and his brain was swimming in that cool wave of endorphins. But in the void where fantasies appear, the mountain rose up, briefly, like it often did. The sky a Rorschach test formed by the trees. He was on the ground, looking up, and then there was a hand holding his hand. And when he tried to banish it, other images stumbled through. Banner Bolland's notebook spinning on the linoleum. The basement door. Livia. Nothing was happening the way it should.

A door opened, and he heard someone come in and piss at the urinal. It was taking too long to get past all his images. He stopped and buttoned up and then went to the sink and splashed water on his face. His students would be talking by the time he got back. They'd be crazed and copying each other's work. They'd need him to be there to calm themselves.

EIGHT

By the next afternoon, he realized that the scattered conflicts of the previous day gave him comfort. The world was opening up in normal directions, now, wasn't it? Of course there were problems that weren't about him and Jack and everything that had consumed his life in the past weeks. *Has it only been weeks?*

New things could happen. Killing Jack, cutting him up, those things would pass. Smaller. Smaller. Gone. New conflicts meant there was hope.

He decided to call his parents.

Anthony was in the backyard by the grill, imagining something, Todd guessed. Todd was sitting on the little square of concrete outside the doorframe. He had them on speakerphone.

"Carl, it's Todd!" his mother shouted, her voice echoey, and Todd guessed he was on speakerphone too. He heard his father groan in the background and shuffle into the room with his mom.

"How are you, Dad?" Todd asked.

"No, how are you?" his mom said.

"I'm fine—" Todd began, but she cut him off.

"Actually, first, can we talk to Anthony?" his mother said. "We want to say hi to our grandson."

"Come here," Todd said. "Grandma and Grandpa want to talk to you." It felt strange calling them that.

"Hi, Anthony!" they both said.

"Oh, we should've used video call," his mom said.

"How's school?" his father said.

Anthony looked down at his feet.

"How's school, Anthony?" Todd said, prompting him.

"I hate it," Anthony said. Todd closed his eyes tightly and took a deep breath.

"Ah, you don't like your teacher?" his mom asked.

Anthony went quiet again.

"He's going through a rough patch," Todd said.

"That's okay," his dad said uselessly.

"Anthony, are you sad?" his mom said. "Listen, Anthony, we know you miss your mom and she loves you very much. Even if she's not around, that doesn't mean—"

Todd hung up on them. "Come *on*," he said out loud.

"Sorry," he said to Anthony. Anthony shrugged and walked back to the spot by the grill, and Todd's phone lit up again. He took it inside.

"What the *fuck* is your problem?" he said.

"Don't talk to your mother like that," his father said, though his voice still sounded slow.

"I was talking to both of you. Why would you bring Livia up? You know I've been trying to get him adjusted."

"We'd know more if you *called* us more often. Or stopped by, even."

"This kind of thing is why I don't!"

"You haven't even asked about your dad's health."

"I'm fine, I'm fine," his dad said.

"No, he's not fine, he's anemic."

"Why would you say that to Anthony? And when did you talk to her?" Todd demanded.

"We got a letter. An actual letter in the mail," his mom said. "From Livia."

Silence.

"Tell him what it said."

"Well, first of all, it said she missed us and that she was in Italy. But then it said . . . Well."

"Just read it to him," his father said.

She read:

I am mostly writing you to say hello, but also to say I think your son has been living a double life. I'm so sorry to be the one to share this with you. I called a few days ago and a man named David answered your son's phone and said they were dating. Todd told me I'd called the wrong number, but obviously I can see the numbers I call on my phone, and it was his. I've been trying to see my son, and Todd won't allow it, and I now know it's because he's hiding someone there. Maybe you knew about all of this?

Obviously, there is nothing wrong with being that way, but Anthony is growing up without a mother, and I was worried that it was all happening in secret. If he's not telling me, I feel he's not telling you. Shouldn't it be out in the open? Wouldn't it be healthier for everyone? Isn't that what everyone agrees on now? That we should be proud to be who we are? I hope this doesn't upset you too much, but since I can't get through to him

myself, I thought you'd have a better chance. Please tell Anthony
his mom loves him. As I'm sure you know, Madeline, there's no
replacement for a mother. (No offense, Carl, ha ha.)

"Then it's the end of the letter."

"Mom, I want you to listen to me," Todd said sternly. "Livia is not . . . right. She hasn't been since she left me and Anthony. She went to Anthony's school without me knowing . . ."

"That's her son, though," his mom said.

". . . and *then*," Todd continued, "she came here while I was on a date with my girlfriend."

"You have a girlfriend?" his father asked.

"Yes. Elaine. She's Anthony's . . . You know what? Why am I explaining this? Why are you excusing her? Why are you taking her side on this?"

"It's not about sides. Are you living with a man?"

"No! She's making it up, isn't it obvious?" Todd said, exasperated. "I don't even *know* any Davids, except for one of my students."

"It's . . . okay to tell us?" his mother said, trying a new angle.

"Maybe your student answered?" his dad said.

"What? Just *forget it!*" Todd snapped. "What *is* this? You don't call me. You don't visit or help. You've never been there, and now all the sudden you're concerned because Livia wrote you a *letter*? Oh, and *mostly* to 'say hi,' but then she goes on to pit you against me."

They talked, but he couldn't hear them. When Jack was tormenting him in high school, when his life with Livia was falling apart, it was all *right there*, inches away from their lives, but they didn't see it. They didn't see him. That was the start of this drifting, he knew. They made brief appearances to trouble the water. Not to be close to him or talk to him or to protect him. And now they were a blurred presence. Voices in the distance, mottled through walls and floorboards, like the sound of their fighting when he was a kid. He wondered why they didn't get divorced then. But they were calmer with each other now.

"I'm hanging up now," he said. And he did, then blocked their number. So what if Livia enlisted them again? He could get Elaine to vouch for him.

The door opened, and Anthony came in. The knees of his pants were covered in dirt.

"Do you want something?" Todd asked.

"Did they talk to Mommy?" he asked.

"No," Todd said. "Go play."

But Anthony only stood there, waiting for something to happen.

NINE

When would the feeling of a new life start?

Todd had spent the day in a fuzzy static, emerging from the drinks he'd had the night before. Maybe the trick was to act like other people, he'd thought. To drink at night in front of the TV and be normal. He wasn't really hungover, but everything seemed louder and he felt slower.

When would be the first day of his new life? he wondered.

Or was a new life just a process of elimination, one day gone, then the next, then the next? A Meister Eckhart line he'd learned in college was playing behind his consciousness.

Only the hand that erases can write the true thing.

Only the hand that cuts you up can write the true thing.
The hand that helps you up or pushes you down.
The hand that strikes you down.
The hand that closes into a fist and punches you in the stomach.

The hand that touches your face.

Strange to think that this was true.

A new start, that day, with his son, in front of the car and Elaine standing by. And it would be Anthony's small hand, offering something up.

"Don't you ever see other kids off to their parents?" Todd asked, smiling.

She didn't smile back, though.

"Todd, Anthony has . . . something."

"He's sick?"

"No," Anthony said.

"No," she said. "Well, I have it now. He pulled this out in show-and-tell."

She handed him a sealed plastic baggie, shining from its guts with tiny white shards. It was filled with the powder and fragments of Jack's crushed teeth. A wave of ice and shock went up him.

"It's—" Todd stammered.

"Teeth," Elaine said.

"No, it's—"

"Or, at least that's what he said. He said he had proof that the tooth fairy wasn't real. She wouldn't come for this."

"Whose. Whose?" Todd said. "Whose teeth?"

"Todd," Elaine said, "they aren't really teeth." She held up the bag. She opened it. She looked in. "Are they?"

"No," he said, trying to remain calm. "I meant, what did he say they were? They're shells. We collected. Can I have that, please? We collected them. And then he smashed them with a hammer. *We* smashed them with a hammer."

"No, they're not, I *found* them," Anthony protested. "There's a big tooth, too."

Todd knelt down, holding the bag. "Anthony. Get in the car."

"No!" he shouted.

"Anthony, listen to your dad," Elaine said.

"*I don't want to*," Anthony shouted, then stepped forward and swung a little fist at Todd's head. It was an unbalanced and imprecise blow, but jarring anyway.

Todd didn't say anything, he lunged for his son and restrained him, and Elaine opened the car door. The other parents looked his way.

"*Stop!*" Anthony shouted. "*Stop! Stop! Stop!*"

Todd pointed a finger right in his son's face. "If you don't stop scream-ing—" he began.

But a man had rushed over to the scene and was asking, "Is every-thing okay?" He was tall and athletic-looking and too concerned, Todd thought. Todd stood up out of the car and slammed the door.

"What's going on?" the man asked.

"It's okay, Bill," Elaine said.

Todd should know him, know some of the other parents.

"Is he hurt?" Bill said.

A few feet away, a girl, a little older than Anthony, started crying. She was alone on the sidewalk.

"Don't you think you should get back to Gracie?" Elaine said.

"Oh, sorry, yeah, I thought . . ."

"It's fine," Todd said.

The man glanced to his daughter and turned to walk away. Then pointed at the ground. "You dropped your . . . cocaine? What *is* that?"

Todd picked up the bag quickly. It had opened at one of the corners, a little wedge of space. He saw that inside was a piece of flattened mer-cury filling. And besides that, a whole tooth, round and dumb, buried in the surrounding white sand. Had she seen this? She couldn't have. He stuffed the bag in his jacket pocket.

"It's shells," Elaine said.

"Daddy!" the girl screamed.

"Well, okay," Bill said warily. "Elaine, I'll see you soon." He rushed back to his daughter.

"Todd," Elaine said, "it's really time to get him some help. Like, professional help."

"For bringing shells to school?"

"Are you really that *out of it*?" she asked. "No, not for bringing shells to school. For saying they're teeth! And for *punching* you. Kids can do that sometimes, but not like that. Not out of that kind of violent resistance. And I know you have a lot going on, but you really have to, Todd. If for no other reason than for the class, for *my* class."

Todd looked down. He had his hand in his pocket, and his index and middle fingers in the bag, he was wiggling them through Jack's teeth, feeling the grains shuffle across his fingertips. *No wonder I haven't felt my life start yet*, he thought. *Jack is still here.*

"He brought them in and said to Ethan, 'See? The tooth fairy isn't real. I told you.'"

"Ethan . . ."

"The boy he kicked for saying the tooth fairy *wasn't* real. Now Anthony is saying he knew it all along. To the boy he attacked."

"Attacked? Elaine . . . you know kids always want to be believed," Todd said. "Even if it's not the truth. That's what the truth *is* to a kid."

"I'm an elementary school teacher, I know that, remember? It means, though, that he's doing it because he has a grudge. Todd, he's so *angry.*"

"Okay, okay," Todd said. "I'll do something."

"Do you need a recommendation?"

"No," Todd said. "I'll figure it out."

TEN

"What else?"

From the backseat, Anthony didn't say anything.

Todd turned down a different road; one that didn't lead to the house.

He pulled over on a worn-down shoulder and unbuckled his seat belt and turned around.

"What else is there? Is there more of . . . Daddy's teeth? Kids aren't the only ones that lose their teeth." This was going to be the way of it, making up things as he went.

"Anthony," Todd said.

"I want ice cream," Anthony said.

"No, you've got to tell me, did you find anything . . . else?"

Anthony's arms were crossed. He was looking out the window as Todd looked at him. Some of the trees were skeletal above, now, branches like splayed, crooked bones pointed out in every direction. Many still had leaves, but those would go, and the sky would be exposed for fall, and then the bells of the last winter, promised by the poem in the book on the shelf that would not be read again. In the small frame of silence, Todd thought about saying, *When you hit Daddy it makes him sad. Is that what you want?* But the time for that sort of child-rearing was past. There had been a bend, somewhere, in his son's heart, and he was only seeing it now.

Anthony spoke.

"I'll tell you," he said to Todd, slowly, testing his new power, "if you get me ice cream."

The ice-cream stand was closed for the year, so they went to the supermarket. Todd got a pint of strawberry ice cream and Anthony handed him a box of ice-cream cones. He didn't ask, *Can we get ice-cream cones?* He just handed them to Todd with silent expectation.

A boy just shy of seven. But most kids his age hadn't experienced what he'd experienced. Todd didn't protest.

At home they sat at the table and Anthony ate his ice cream. He poked two holes in it with his finger and one with his tongue. It looked like a distressed face with its mouth wide open.

"Daddy, look," he said, and turned the top of the ice cream to him. His son seemed cheerful once again.

"Are you ready?"

"Yeah!" Anthony said.

"Okay, go ahead."

Anthony got up and walked to the back door and held out his cone, which had a bite out of it now. Pink melted ice cream was streaking down its side. Todd took it from him and he opened the door.

"Is it . . . out there?" Todd asked.

"Daddy, close your eyes," he said.

"Anthony . . ."

"Close your eyes, close your eyes, close your eyes," he whined.

Todd closed his eyes and felt the ice cream melting down across the top of his hand.

"Okay!" a small distant shout came. When Todd opened his eyes, Anthony was gone.

"Anthony, we're not playing right now," Todd said into the yard. There weren't many places to hide, he could find him easily. Behind the grill, behind the one tree, on the side of the deck steps. That was it. "Come out," Todd said sternly.

Time froze; nothing moved. There was a rustling and a blue jay screaming.

Then Anthony came from behind the tree.

"No, Daddy, I want to play hide-and-go-seek."

"It's not playtime, you said if I got you ice cream—"

"Play, Daddy," Anthony interrupted. "Play!"

Todd closed his eyes again. "Okay, go hide."

He heard Anthony run back into the house.

When Anthony was hiding, Todd looked around his son's bedroom. There was some tooth dust between the mattress and the frame. And when an email from Livia's lawyer came through, he sat on the edge of the little bed and read it.

It has become clear to my client that you've been hiding a relationship. As you know, my client seeks partial custody, and we intend to pursue it to the full extent, etc., etc.

He thought, for the first time, about giving Anthony to her. But the thought went quickly from him. There was no way to do that now. And besides, Anthony wasn't *hers*, he was barely her son. A psychologist was also out of the question, of course. Anthony couldn't be in the room alone, unburdening himself to someone.

"Daddy, come find me!" he heard Anthony shout from the other room.

The world doesn't stop, he thought.

It comes for you and it
comes for you and it
comes for you.

Todd waited until Anthony finally gave up and left his hiding place, wherever it was, and when he did, he commanded Todd to read *Wolf Story* to him.

Todd read nearly half the book to him, then they watched a bad cartoon movie together. Anthony fell asleep next to him on the couch and Todd carried him upstairs.

Todd went back down and opened a bottle of whiskey kept in a high cupboard. He drank from it, then set it on the kitchen table and wandered back down to the basement, which felt uneventful now, but still occupied. He hadn't yet filled the container. He opened it and saw in the dimness that the stain held itself in place.

"What do I do?" he said. "Tell me what to do. *Please.*"

But there was no one and no body to talk to, much less to answer.

The baggie was still in his coat pocket. Emptying that would bring clarity, maybe. But not at the beach this time, there was no point. It was powder, and a filling, and one tooth. His head swarmed with thoughts in alcohol; he hated the sloshing feeling, but not as much, tonight, as not having it. He made his way back to his coat; his heart raced as he checked an empty pocket first, but the baggie was in the other one. He went upstairs into the bathroom and sat on the floor next to the toilet.

He sifted around for the shiny filling, and when he found it, he threw it into the wastebasket. Jack must have gotten that when he was younger, no one he knew got metal fillings anymore, they were all tooth-colored. Did his father take him to the dentist? Todd couldn't imagine that. Maybe when his mother was still alive. He'd never know. There might not be anyone who knew except the dentist who did it. So much of a person's life, Todd thought, was invented to be forgotten.

He took out the whole tooth and put it on the side of the sink, emptied the powder and pieces into the toilet, where some sank, some of it floated. Break down anything small enough, even bone, and it leaves the realm of gravity. He flushed the toilet and watched the powder disappear. Then he picked up the tooth and, eyeing himself in the mirror, swallowed it. He felt Jack trace his way down into him.

He walked to his son's room and opened the door. The night-light was on, and this boy, who had given him so much happiness, but now, also, so much trouble, was fast asleep. His head was so small on the pillow.

It would be easy to smother him with it.

The thought came on its own, like most thoughts do, rising from a dark cloud. But it grew as a distant panic in him. He shut the door and went back downstairs and picked up the bottle and drank more in a huge gulp and then another, and then he looked for his phone.

He fumbled with the letters and texted Sahir

the principl is afte rtryou

and then

I saw your and it s ok toadmit it I dont care

Then he got his keys.

The road was confusing in the dark, the whiskey in the passenger seat next to him. He thought about getting pulled over, but he knew he wouldn't be. *Just follow the lines on the road, try to keep pace with them, try to keep the same distance between your car and them.*

"Z Y X W V U T S R Q P O N M L K J I H G F E D C B A," he said out loud, testing himself. No problem. As he was driving, he stretched out his arm and index finger, and then brought his finger toward his nose, then a shadowed animal jogged across the road.

He swerved to miss it. His car rumbled onto the shoulder and side-winded back and forth, clouds of illuminated dust rising around him. Finally, he regained control and came to a full stop.

"Fuck," he said, rolling down the window. In the cold air, two raccoons ambled across the road, just behind the one he'd barely missed. He looked back farther down the road, past his skid marks; no police, no other cars around. He put his elbows on the wheel and his face in his hands, recycling his own breaths for a few minutes, as his heart beat fast with the slow alcohol in his veins.

Then he drove to Elaine's. The lights were off when he got there. Up the porch stairs. It was a little house in a development of houses that looked exactly the same, inches from each other. He had a thought that it might scare her to hear banging at night, unexpected, on the door. But he banged on the door. A light in a house across the way went on. He banged again and almost laughed at the thought of cinematically shouting her name. But then she answered, backlit, in sweatshirt and matching sweatpants.

"Come in," she said hastily, "before you wake anyone else up."

"I need help," he said, before he was even in. "I need help, I need help, I need help."

"How long has this been going on?" she said, and helped him sit. The room was carpeted and the chair he sat in was thick and puffy. She switched a lamp on.

"You. Know?" he realized this couldn't be true. "No, you don't."

"I don't know from my own experience," she said. "But my uncle was an alcoholic, and he turned off a highway once. The wrong way. He hit the guardrail and flipped over. He struggled his whole life with it, but never actually asked for help."

"No," Todd said. "I don't drink."

"Todd, you're drunk right now."

"I know, I mean—"

"You know you could get fired for this! You have to be careful or you'll do something you can't take back."

"I'm going to," he said. "I need help."

"You can't drive home," she said. "But you can't stay upstairs either. That chair actually folds back into a single bed. Here." She leaned over him and felt along the bottom of the fold-out chair for a lever. It flattened out and he fell back with it.

"Let me get you some blankets. She went to the stairwell, a few feet away in the same room. Then she stopped on the first step. "Todd. Where's Anthony?"

"Asleep."

"*Alone?*" she asked.

"No, he . . . has a babysitter."

"An overnight sitter?" she asked.

He stood up and wobbled toward her. "Elaine," he said. He approached her.

Then he got up on the first step with her. He kissed her. At first, she leaned into it. She closed her eyes. She felt his weight leaning clumsily into her, backing her into the wall. Then she pulled back and turned her head. "God, Todd, you taste like a bottle of it."

He stayed on the step and let his head hang with his eyes closed.

"Listen, it's not that I don't want that. Or that I didn't used to want it, anyway. But never like this. I mean, come *on*, Todd. Just. Just stay here."

She walked up the steps to get him his blankets and pillows and he stumbled back to the chair. By the time she came back with everything, he was out.

ELEVEN

He woke disoriented, in the dark.

Her face was inches from his; holding a stern look.

"It's five-thirty, you better get going," she said.

The memory gathered, and he realized he was at her place, that he'd come to her last night to flee his thoughts. Had he told her anything? Panic washed over him.

"I . . . I didn't mean to do this," he said. "Did I say anything last night—"

"No," she said, "but you have to get up because I have to get going soon. And you're going to be late if you don't get back, and I'm guessing your sitter will want to leave soon too."

He almost said, *What babysitter?* but caught himself, and realized what a disaster that would have been. "Fuck," he said instead.

She put her hand out to help him up, but he didn't take it, and stood uncertainly.

His clothes were on, even his shoes. He could smell whiskey coming through in his sweat.

"Elaine—"

"Listen to me," she said. "I'm not here for this. This is what my aunt said to my uncle before he died: 'I'm not here to make cameos in the drama of your life.' And I'm not. Men always think we've got the supporting roles. But I've got my own life, Todd. If you can't get your shit together enough to make room for me—"

"I've got it, Elaine. You're right."

He walked to the door. "Where are my keys?"

"Hold on," she said. She walked into the kitchen and he heard cupboards open and close. The room was small but warm. A comfortable place he couldn't imagine ever being in again. She came back into the room with the keys on her finger.

"I didn't want you to drive away."

"Thank you. You're right," he said.

The day hadn't started yet, and he traced his way back on the roads he'd driven to Elaine's. When he drove past the black ribbons of his tire marks, he cursed himself quietly. And less than a mile from those, a dead raccoon was turned over in the other lane. It must have been killed last night, since its red guts were smeared in a fast line across the street. Was it one of the raccoons he'd lost control avoiding? He thought that maybe, yes, it was. A feeling of inevitability was growing in him, as sure as the endlessness of waves. Everything that was going to happen had already happened, every place was set.

He pulled into his driveway, and when he got out, before he got into the house, he could hear his son crying through the walls. It was almost six.

The door opened, and a backdraft of wailing hit him.

He ran to him.

Anthony was standing in his pajamas in the middle of the kitchen, screaming. Clear snot was bubbling from a nostril; he was bereft, beside himself.

When he saw his father, instead of saying, *Where were you?* or reaching for a hug, Anthony instead shouted, "I'm going to tell! I'm going to tell! I'm going to tell!" He screamed it as Todd picked him up. *"I'M GOING TO TELL!"* Coughing between breaths.

He's a child, Todd thought. Then, *Yes, but children grow up.*

"Tell what?" Todd said. *"Tell what?"*

Anthony leaned back so that he was bent away from Todd's embrace, still crying. Todd carried him this way up the stairs.

"Get dressed," Todd said, setting his son on his bed, and walked out and into his own bedroom.

His phone buzzed.

A message, from Elaine:

> I'm going to have Anthony stand with Mrs. Campanelli for
> pickup and drop off for a while. She knows we were dating.
> I won't say anything to her about last night, but she'll
> understand. Please give me space. And take care of yourself.

He typed back

> Fuck you

then deleted it.

Then another popped up from her.

> If you don't, I will have to say something.

He typed

Be careful how you talk to me.

He stared at it for a long time. There was no reason to drag her into the picture any more than she already was. Finally, he deleted that message too.

Okay

he typed, and sent it. It was still angry. Curt and without warmth. But it was the best he could do. She couldn't help him. It was stupid to think that she should.

TWELVE

Anthony and the rushing water.

His son sat naked in the tub, and Todd's wrist was under the spigot. Warmer than flesh. There were dumb blunt toys floating next to Anthony. A shirtless, muscled action figure, a plastic shark from a boardwalk stand, and the toy dog stood on the edge of the tub.

The day had been outwardly uneventful, except that Sahir had nodded at Todd in the hall, and then sent him a message back. It read, *Thank you.* Todd had forgotten he'd sent the messages at all.

Todd looked at his son. His smooth pink body, pushing out from the center toward the edges, displacing his youth, growing into adulthood, turning him into something else. His body would rush over with hair, his hair would get darker, his face would deepen.

"I want Juff," Anthony said. It was the name of the penguin on the cartoon he liked; he had a rubbery plastic version of him.

"Where is he?" Todd said.

"Get him, Daddy," Anthony said.

"Is he in your room?"

"I don't know."

"Is he downstairs? Is he by the sink?"

"Oh yeah," Anthony said. "He's by the sink."

Todd stood. His shirt had dark circles on it from where the water had splashed. He went downstairs for the penguin and, when he got there, stood on his toes to retrieve the whiskey from the shelf above the fridge. He unscrewed it and drank a gulp, reaching for the penguin, which was, indeed, by the sink. He stuck the penguin in his pocket and rescrewed the bottle. When he set it back in its place, he peered through the kitchen doorway into the living room.

Something was wrong. Off, somehow.

There was a hint of an object, looking back at him from the floor. He walked in and turned the light on.

Still paralyzed in its conflict, the statuette was lying on its side, alone in the middle of the floor. Right where Jack had collapsed.

Todd walked toward it slowly.

He stood above it. The room was dark, but still he saw the lion's expression of pain. He saw Heracles's blank expression of valor. It was clean, but he remembered the rivulets of blood in its crevices; the strings of wounded flesh in its muscles.

He turned his head slightly from side to side, scanning the darkness.

"Hello?"

Nothing.

He knelt down.

"J . . . Jack?" he said quietly.

He touched the statue. A scream came.

From upstairs, Anthony was calling.

"The water! The water!"

Todd picked the statuette up and put in back on the stand.

"You're not here," he mumbled. Then went back up the stairs.

The water had risen too high and was glugging in the second drain beneath the spout. Todd turned the knobs off. He dropped the penguin in the water, and it bobbed at the surface.

How had the statuette gotten there? He thought of asking Anthony but didn't. He thought of Jack instead, and then thought of Hawk Mountain. The ground, the light. Jack's hand.

"I don't want to go to school tomorrow," Anthony said.

"Let's put the shampoo in."

Todd squeezed a glob of clear shampoo into his hand and ran it through his son's hair. Anthony closed his eyes.

"Daddy, can you make it a bubble bath?" Anthony said.

"All the water's in already," Todd said.

"Jack would've made it a bubble bath," Anthony said.

"It's time to go scuba diving," Todd said. "Ready?"

"Hold on," Anthony said. His eyes still closed, he took a little wrinkled hand out of the water, shook it off, and then pinched his nose with it.

Todd held both sides of Anthony's head and pushed him under.

He looked at his son beneath the surface. Eyes tightly shut. Fingers closing his nostrils. Lather floating away from his hair and clouding the image.

He held him there.

He held him there.

Then he brought him back up. And Anthony took a deep quick inhale.

"Go again," Todd said.

And as Anthony went to squeeze his nose again, Todd pushed him beneath the water.

The bathroom was quiet.

The house was quiet.

Even the surface of the water was still.

Then the silence and surface were both broken by trouble.

Anthony came back up and breathed deeply and rubbed his eyes and wiped the water from his face.

He looked at his father.

"Daddy, why are you crying?" he asked. "Daddy. Daddy."

THIRTEEN

That morning, he'd dropped his son off clumsily. His little backpack was still at home, he realized, and when Miss Campanelli asked where it was, Todd said Anthony had forgotten it.

"Go back home and get it," Anthony said.

"Okay," Todd said. But he didn't.

Now a student was showing another student a video on her phone shortly after noon. Todd saw them gathered around, all trying to get a look. "Just look up 'fox door New Granard,'" she said to them, but they wouldn't disperse. Class was supposed to be starting.

"What are you looking at?" Todd asked, and peered into the congregation. He was dazed.

In the video, there was a fox, pawing at a sliding glass door, which made it appear as if the fox wanted to get in.

"Why didn't you let him in?" a boy said.

The girl, whose name was Kim, said she was afraid it would bite her or tear up the place. Another girl cooed.

"It has four hundred and fifty views," Kim said hopefully. "And I just took it this morning."

The fox shuffled away, not wanted.

Todd felt momentarily hopeful. They were looking at animals, and that could mean something. He wasn't sure what. He'd lost touch with them already. A bad thing, this early in the year. Or maybe he'd just lost touch with himself. They were a group of people he was meant to guide. Perhaps he could reset it somehow, to resurrect the possibility.

"You probably did all those views yourself," one of the boys said.

"Why would I watch my own video four hundred and fifty times?" Kim said. "It's just a stupid fox."

"Next time let him in, and more people will watch," another girl offered.

When they sat down, he started to talk about *Walden*, which they'd been reading. He had them write a short essay about it; it was veiled training for the essay-writing component of the state's mandatory standardized testing. They groaned when he told them this news.

He could tell them to write and they would write. He could tell them to be quiet and they would be quiet. He could tell them to answer questions and they'd answer.

A knock on the door. The principal's assistant again, opening the door as she knocked on it. "Mr. Murphy needs to see you," she said.

He looked across the rows and to Banner Bolland's empty seat. He hadn't been in class now for a few days.

"It has to be now, Mr. Nasca," she said. Then, "Are they taking a test? I'll stay here with them."

"Yes," he said unthinkingly.

"No, we're not," a girl said.

"Shhh," the assistant said with some authority.

"No, she's right," Todd said. "But they *are* writing an essay. I'll be back soon." At this the assistant shook her head no.

He wondered maybe if it was about Sahir, but again, on the way to Mr. Murphy's office, he prepared himself to talk about Banner Bolland, humiliated by Todd and, before that, Jack.

But the truth was, no one at this school cared about any of that. This was about Anthony.

"Todd, I know you've been having a hard time," Mr. Murphy said. "I know, for instance that your ex-wife is seeking custody of your son. I understand there was an incident?"

"Which one?" Todd said.

"Oh, she came to the elementary school more than once?"

"No. Forget it. What's going on, Paul?"

"Is there something you need to tell us about?" Mr. Murphy asked.

"With due respect, Paul, it's really none of your business."

"There's that phrase again," the principal said. "This school, I hope, is more like a family than a business. If one of our family members—"

"So you're kicking Sahir out of the house for being gay?" Todd grumbled.

"Mr. Azar is a separate thing," the principal said. "This is about you."

There was a pause.

"Okay, so . . . what is it?"

"Your son ran away from school today," Mr. Murphy said.

FOURTEEN

In the guidance counselor's office, there was a dolphin puppet sitting on a box with a picture of a dolphin on it, and Anthony sat in a small chair. Todd sat next to him in a normal one. Elaine, Mr. Foster the guidance counselor, and Ed Williams sat around him. The room was cramped. There was a poster that said IS IT A GOOD TOUCH OR A BAD TOUCH and a row of white-spined books called Value Tales on a shelf. Everything was aimed at fixing children somehow.

"Anthony isn't talking right now," Mr. Foster said. "He's working through it. Isn't that right, Anthony?"

"If he's not talking, he's not going to answer!" Principal Williams said, and Mr. Foster gave him a puzzled look.

"Elaine, will you tell him what happened?" the principal said gruffly.

Todd put his hand on Anthony, but his son squirmed away with a whine.

"He prefers to not be touched right now," Mr. Foster said.

"I was hanging up pictures of vegetables on the Velcro board next to their names. It's . . . I pretend I have a market—"

"Let's go, Elaine," Ed Williams said.

"I heard the door open and close behind me, and then Anthony was gone. And . . . well, it's not as easy as just running after him, because all of the other children. I can't leave them. And I've never had anything like this happen before. So I called Mr. Burker to come stay with the class while I looked for Anthony, and Ed and I went around the school looking for him."

"I was busy," Mr. Foster said.

"We went all over the place. We thought of course he'd hidden. But at a certain point—"

"It was only about five, ten minutes," Ed said. "Then we walked out and started looking for him."

There was an uncertain silence then, till Mr. Foster said, "Anthony, do you want to tell them what happened next?"

He shook his head. He'd been crying before Todd got there and was still sniffling.

"Does he have to be here for this?" Todd asked.

"It's good for him to sit with the process and to know his actions affect people," Mr. Foster said.

The whole meeting felt like an illusion to Todd. "Okay, so then what?"

"We went out into the field next door, past the parking lot, and we walked through to the trees. And, I don't know how you did it, but you saw him," Ed said.

"Yes. Up in one of the trees, sitting on a branch, bunched up against the tree trunk."

"Let me just say," Ed Williams added quickly, "that there was nothing we could do, nothing she could do about this. Anthony ran out! And he wasn't harmed. We'll look into disciplinary procedures for Elaine if we need to. But that's not what's at hand now."

Todd felt somewhere in him the urge to defend Elaine. She hadn't done anything wrong, except to get close to him and the wounds he'd tried to cover. He felt protective, but the feeling dissolved. The will to carry it into action wasn't there. What was the point?

"I'll take him home," Todd said. "I'll talk with him."

"It's past that a bit," Ed said.

"Past it?"

"When he came down, what was he saying?" Mr. Foster asked.

"Oh, he was saying you hurt someone," Elaine said.

"I . . . I . . ." Todd stammered.

"That's not atypical," Mr. Foster interrupted. "For a child to project a fantasy like that when he's upset about something else. But what is the something else?"

"I told you," Elaine said. "His mother."

"*I don't want to go home!*" Anthony shouted suddenly.

He ran for the door, but Ed Williams was up and put his hand against it, leaving Anthony pulling desperately on the doorknob.

Todd knelt down next to him, but Anthony shouted, "*I don't want to go home! I hate you! I want Jack!*"

The words shuddered through Todd. They made his teeth ache, his hand ache, his stomach grab at itself. Anthony pulled futilely at the door and finally Ed Williams shouted:

"Anthony! Let go and Sit! Down!"

The energy went out of him and he started to whimper.

Todd thought, *Don't yell at my son*, but couldn't. Everything was sealed now; sealed in, sealed out.

"I left his . . . backpack . . ." Todd said.

"This is about his backpack?" the principal asked.

"Who's Jack?" Mr. Foster asked. "Is that the person your dad hurt?"

Anthony nodded breathlessly.

"It's his imaginary friend," Elaine said. "Todd . . . Todd and I have been trying to get him past it."

"Well, it's hard to say goodbye to a friend, isn't it?" Mr. Foster picked up the dolphin puppet and started to put it on his hand.

"For God's sake, Barry, stop it," Ed said. "No puppets. This kid has got to go to a real therapist, and that's a condition of him coming back here."

Todd closed his eyes and listened to Elaine defend him, to Mr. Foster defend himself, to Ed Williams berate all of them, to his son crying. *Why* wouldn't *he run?* Todd thought. *Who wouldn't want to run from this place?*

"Jack's *real*," Anthony said quietly.

"Sometimes things are real to us but not to everyone else. They can seem *huge!*" Mr. Foster said. "As big as that tree you climbed up! But when they get that big and no one else can see it, sometimes you have to cut that tree down."

Everyone seemed to agree.

FIFTEEN

When Anthony was born, Todd held him while Livia lay in the hospital bed, despondent. She'd had grand plans for a midwife and home birth, but at some point gave up on the idea.

Holding his son's tiny body, he stared into his eyes and tried to inhabit him. He tried to think into him. *I'm here for you*, he thought, and wanted the thought to appear in Anthony's head. *I'm here for you*, and tried to radiate caring, so that his son would feel it. His son blinked deliberate blinks with huge eyes. He stared back at Todd in wonder, or in comprehension, or in confusion, or in stupefaction.

Before that moment, holding his son, he'd thought, no one was good. Not that everyone was bad, but that all people harbored horrible thoughts, and did horrible things. He would try to fill his son with something else.

Can you hear me? he thought. And Anthony blinked again. *I'll always be here for you.*

And they were together.

But now Anthony was in the car while Todd was at the register in the diner. He'd called in to his school and Anthony's and said they wouldn't be in today. Both principals sounded relieved. He'd called ahead and ordered food for them both, then he left his phone at home and got Anthony and Anthony's toys and a book in the car. But now, as he crossed the parking lot back to his car, he saw someone lingering nearby.

Sitting on the hood of a nearby car, Banner Bolland was smoking a cigarette.

"Banner?" Todd asked, as he approached. Banner reflexively threw his cigarette away.

"Why aren't you in school?" Todd asked.

"Why aren't you?" Banner responded sharply.

"I'm taking my son . . . You know, it doesn't matter. You haven't been around for days. Have you been skipping this whole time? And coming here? Why?"

This was the lot where Jack had threatened Banner, Todd remembered.

"I don't know, where else am I supposed to go? I can't skip school and stay home. I know you're going to tell on me, but I don't even care anymore," Banner said.

"I won't. I won't tell on you," Todd said quietly.

"Oh, well, good," Banner said, and pulled out another cigarette.

"I shouldn't have done that," Todd said. "I shouldn't have done that to you." He moved to hug Banner, put his arms around him. "I shouldn't—"

"What the *fuck*?" Banner said. "Jesus Christ, *get off of me, you faggot!*" He shivered as if the embrace were still clinging to him. "You have *no idea* what you did when you made me say that. You don't know what it's like now, people kicking my books down the hall and pushing me and my friends won't talk to me."

Todd stood silent, frozen.

"Oh what, you've never been called a name before? Anyway, you know what? We're not in school, so you can't do anything anyway." He started to light his cigarette, but then realized it was broken on the end now, smashed by the momentary hug. "You're right, I don't know why I came here. Last time I was here some guy said he would break my neck; this time my fucking pedophile teacher is trying to hug me." He threw the broken, unlit cigarette at Todd and walked away. *"Fuck this place,"* he said loudly.

Todd watched him go. And when he thought he was alone in the lot, a horn went off, and he jumped. Anthony had crawled into the front seat and pressed on it. Then again the harsh note punctured the air. Through the windshield, Todd could see his son was laughing at this, like it was the most hilarious thing.

SIXTEEN

At Hawk Mountain, there was no one to greet you anymore. There were no other cars; there was a wooden box to put money in for parking and admission. Above the box, there was a sign that read WILDLIFE CENTER CLOSED FOR REPAIRS. After they ate in the car in the parking lot, they made their way to the mountain.

Just as the land started to angle upward, Todd understood that there would be no sign of the place where he fell to the ground all those years ago, when Jack had reached out his hand. When he realized this, he stopped walking, and Anthony said, "Daddy, put me on your shoulders."

He knelt, and his son climbed him. And when he stood, Anthony was balancing, like a flower on a stem.

They made their way. Birds moved ahead of them, calling out. A cardinal moved from the ground up to a branch, a drop of blood falling upward. The canopy was coming apart in places, holding in others, leaves fluttering down to disintegrate in the litter. The light wind sounded different through each set of trees.

"Why did we come here?" Anthony said from above, as Todd trekked his way up.

"Don't you like it?"

Anthony didn't say anything.

"Daddy came here when he was a boy."

"When you were seven?"

"No, I was older than that."

"I want to go to the beach," Anthony said.

"Look," Todd said, and pointed to a tree with orange fungus growing up the side.

"What is it?"

"It's fungus," he said. "It means the tree is almost dead."

"Can we save it?" Anthony asked.

"There was a little house farther up," Todd said. "I think it's still there."

"Does somebody live there?"

"No," Todd said.

"I want to go to the beach," Anthony said again.

Todd bent toward the ground and encouraged Anthony off his shoulders. "Look," he said. And a little way ahead was the Wildlife Center. Anthony ran toward it; Todd came after him slowly.

There had been no repairs. The building was cabin-like, and the door lock was broken. Someone had spray-painted something illegible on the side, but whoever had done it, or had broken the door, only had a soft courage, because the insides remained intact. Anthony walked through the dark open doorway. When Todd followed, he found his son standing in front of a black bear. It was frozen in taxidermy, standing on its hind legs in a glass case. Its mouth was open, its tongue made out of plastic, its teeth bared. Anthony's form looked hopeless in front of it.

"Is it alive?" he asked, though he knew it was not. There was no placard explaining what happened or where the bear came from.

"Someone killed it," Todd said.

Anthony knocked on the glass. "It looks alive, though." Then he turned to see that they were in a hall of dead animals. A golden eagle, posed with its wings out; a red-tailed hawk, perched on a severed branch; both in glass cases. And here were animals not behind glass; a rabbit, a groundhog, a poorly recomposed fox.

"What about these?" Anthony asked.

Todd led his son toward the fox. He took Anthony's hand and put it on the coarse orange fur. "They're all dead, because that way you can touch them," he said, but Anthony pulled his hand away.

"I don't want to," he said.

"Go ahead, it's okay. You'd never be able to do this if it were alive." Todd petted the fox, demonstrating, but Anthony wouldn't do it. So Todd picked him up and held him inches away from the glass and the eagle's beak. His son stared at the eagle, and the eagle didn't stare back.

"Can we go back now?" Anthony asked.

"Not until we go to the overlook," Todd said.

"Overlook?"

"It's a spot up top where you can see the whole wide world."

"I want to go back."

"No, we're not going back," Todd said, exiting the Wildlife Center.

And they walked past an oak with a hole halfway up the trunk, a void made for things to live in. And they walked past another tree with a squirrel rushing up it to escape them. And they walked over branches, and the air smelled like cinnamon bark and clay. And when they came to a fallen tree, up the incline, wet and decomposing, Anthony balanced his way across it and stood, a little taller, now, than his father.

"I'm Jack!" he shouted. Todd didn't wince; there was no one to hear.

"Why?" Todd asked.

"Because I'm bigger than you now," Anthony said. "I'm Jack and you're Todd!" Then he laughed and hopped off the limb and ran up the hill and disappeared. Todd followed, he went up, up, and heard his son shout, "Daddy!" and it echoed, like the mountain had stuttered. Daddy, Daddy.

When he caught up, his son was at the overlook. The world was vast before them; everything could be seen from this cliff with no guardrail; a sheer drop down, hundreds of feet. An expanse of trees and hills; green pine and fir and spruce, flourishes of yellow and orange leaves between them, like the green was holding small fires. Turkey vultures hovered far from them, like motes in the sky's vision, holding over hidden dead deer below.

The sky was clear. A clear breath of vast emptiness above the trees.

Anthony faced the unguarded expanse, and, with his back to his father, exclaimed, "It's the whole wide world, Daddy!"

Todd took a step toward him.

And then another.

And then when he was close enough, Anthony turned to the side and shouted, "Look!"

Up in a tree, there was a hawk, clutching a rabbit. It buried its head into the carcass, steaming, then came back up, blood spattered on its face, swallowing.

The hawk peered back at them cautiously, pausing to take them in.

Todd covered his face with his hand and saw Jack's face in the nowhere space he hid himself in. The furrow of Jack's brow the first time he saw Todd in class; and Todd's own eyes mocked the expression, pulled into that shape. He heard a distant school bell. And then he saw the light behind Jack's head, the canopy, his outstretched hand.

He opened his eyes and picked up his son and held him close to his chest and walked closer to the overlook.

He wanted to say something. He held Anthony away from his body and looked at him. A boy in stark relief against the rest of the world.

SEVENTEEN

The light in the basement was on.

The container was open, its lid leaning against the wall.

The workbench was still, the tools were all washed again, hung up again.

Everything was quiet underground.

Then a door opened above, letting the noise back in.

Someone entering the house, and then the sound of another door, the basement door, opening above.

There were footsteps, one set of footsteps, finding their way slowly on stairs, and Todd's obscured form made its way down into the light.

He crossed the gravel floor to the container, and upstairs his phone buzzed; these were messages from Elaine, who wanted to know, *Are you okay?*

Todd knelt on the floor and touched the lip of the container and looked in at the stain, which no longer looked like a mountain, but a formless shadow where Jack used to be.

And above him, still unheard, his phone buzzed again, and these were messages from Livia, who said she was coming to see Anthony again and that she was bringing her lawyer this time.

Then Todd crawled in.

In the container, and in the belly of the earth, he pulled his knees up so he could fit, in the pose of a half-born child.

And he covered his face, and he thought of all of it, every moment.

That night, snow would come.

"I'm sorry," he said, crying.

"I'm sorry. I'm sorry. I'm sorry."

PART SIX

The sign says HAWK MOUNTAIN WILDLIFE PRESERVE and Mr. Appel confirms the reservation at the booth at the foot of the mountain.

He tells the students about timber rattlesnakes and to watch out while crossing over logs and big stones, because that's where they like to hide. Justin Geiger asks if there will be any bears and Mr. Appel says no, although it's possible. But no. Just don't get separated. And Hannah Grace asks, if they see one, should they run, and Jack makes a joke that no one has to outrun a bear, they only have to outrun Rick Barnes, and even Mr. Appel laughs. Todd is standing behind the group. He's looking at the trees, which are showing leaves again. Coming back to life. The bite from Jack's dog is almost healed.

The kids go up the mountain together.

Todd can hear the other boys and the girls walking ahead with the teacher. There are yelps and laughing, but he's stayed behind.

It's the end of school now, and he tells himself he wants to be away from them, even as he knows he has no choice but to be alone. After all those years together, they aren't his friends anymore; it's like everything has been erased.

And the clothes they're wearing today are different—they're all permitted to wear plain clothes on the field trip—and that's conspired to erase their connection too. Rick Barnes, who is up with the rest of them now, has a shirt with a giant rooster on it, and has told everyone it's his big cock shirt, but Todd only heard that from afar. He's not allowed to be in on the jokes.

It's quiet behind everyone. It's better to be alone. It's calm.

Then a tree root raised from the ground meets his foot, as if the world itself wants to trip him. He falls and knocks his shin painfully, as the voices go deeper into the woods and sound smaller and smaller. The distance between him and the rest of them is growing even now. The front of his pants leg is torn, and his exposed leg is scraped and bleeding, covered in forest dirt. He knows, as the pain soaks into his leg, that when the rest of the students see this, they'll make fun of him.

He brushes the dirt off his leg, and then, though there's no noise, nothing to alert him to the fact that someone is there, he turns and sees Jack, a few feet away. Jack, who must have stayed behind too. But why?

Jack gets closer, closer, till he's standing above him, looking down at him, scraped and vulnerable on the ground, with no one else around.

He reaches out his hand, but Todd doesn't take it.

"It's okay, it's fine," he says, and stretches his arm out a little more.

Todd reaches up with his unbitten hand and Jack holds it and pulls him up. They both feel the flush of life in their hands. Their life lines are touching.

Jack brushes off Todd's shoulder. There's dirt there, and leaves.

They look at each other.

"Why?" Todd says finally.

Jack doesn't say anything.

"Why did you help me up?"

"I'm sorry," Jack says suddenly. "I shouldn't have punched you. In the library. I shouldn't have done a lot of things."

There's laughter up the mountain again. Farther away, but not too far to catch up to now. And Todd starts to cry, silently. He turns his head, as if this will stop Jack from seeing his tears.

"Todd," Jack says. And Todd looks at him fiercely.

Jack leans forward and kisses Todd. Their lips are warm in the cold air. Todd gives in and they find each other. He can taste Jack and feel Jack's breath going into him. And when he pulls back, their foreheads are still touching. He puts his hand on Jack's face.

"Why?" he says again. He's still crying.

Jack looks into him with his sea-glass eyes. Todd can feel him then, inhabiting him, like that first day in class. But it's different now; it understands itself. Jack reaches up softly and Todd flinches, but then calms as Jack wipes his tears from his cheeks.

"Todd, I . . ."

But Mr. Appel's voice ricochets down the mountain to them.

"Todd! Jack! Are you down there? Jack! Todd!"

There's a breath, and a heartbeat.

I love you, he wants to say.

But then Jack turns and goes up the mountain to join the rest of them.

The words don't come.

And they never will.

Conner Habib is host of the popular podcast *Against Everyone with Conner Habib* which covers topics as broad as sexuality, spirituality, punk rock, occultism and poetry. His non-fiction has appeared in dozens of print and online publications. This is his first novel. He lives in Ireland.